ACK

Before I began, I have to show respect and give all praises to The Most High, The creator of the universe for protecting me from the dangers of this world and for allowing me to make a difference in people lives.

To my loving wife Mikeyta, who supported and believed in me, during my darkest moments. Words can't explain how much you mean to me. To my children, Emon'ey Tremaine, Mecca, Trio Zakiyah and Eli, you are the reason that I grind so hard. To my Mother and brother Darrell, I love you both for instilling the principles and ethics that has molded me into the man that I am today. My brothers and sisters, Brandon, Tammy, Renee, Reggie and Chaka, I love you all unconditionally.

To the entire Chapman family, thank you for accepting me for my faults and investing the time and money into me as if I was one of your own.

To my cousin C.C. and the C-Ray auto sales family, Rick, R1 and Mc Duffy auto, thank you for putting me up on game. Cal and Ru, I will always have love for you because you both are some stand up guys. We overcame some obstacles that most people would have folded under (Salute.)

To all of my comrades Uptown, representing that Bailey Block, love is love, no matter what city or state that I'm in, I will never forget where I'm from or what we've been though... 62ce for life.

Tie Kimble, you are the realest person that I know. In the 20 years that you have been locked up, I've never heard you complain once. You are the definition of a warrior! Brian Brown continue to go FULL THROTTLE without letting up.

AK Reed and the PURE family, thank you for believing and seeing the vision, we're about to make history. Fonz Carter, who rhymes harder, you have truly been a blessing to me and I am honored to call you my friend.

Ant Clark, Abdul Raheem, Dee Jay, Pow Wow, Live, Jamal, DQ, Toyln, Asha, Jetaun, Angie Smith, Mario, Marty(Fat Bob), Amir Williams, Calperta, my barber Troy, My man Curt up in Cleveland, Titus (RIP Jeremy) D Wilson, D. Levy, Damon, Dorian, Dre B, Ern Ski, Fuji, G-Lewis, Pooh, Heavy Solo, Dusty, Jay Scott, Jermaine, Lavon, Malik Campbell, ManZ, Rome, Mizz, Born, Macky, Lonette, Nathyia, Shams, Kydale, Anthony, Buck, Twan, Bobo and Baby G, I want to Salute you all for the Support.

R.I.P. to my Pops, Tre, Money Ern, Dirty Nate, and Boogie Brown, you will always breathe through me. Last but not least, to all of the soldiers locked up behind the wall. Continue to think big because dreams do come true, I'm living proof. BUFFALO STAND UP! If I forgot anyone, charge it to my mind not my heart!

CHAPTER 1

It was a cold November morning and the streets were notably vacant. The snow covering the pavement enhanced the winter chill invading the ghetto as a full moon hung above the city. Halfway up the block, Jihad and his cousin Jamal were watching a particular house from behind the tinted windows of a construction van. On the surface, Jihad seemed to be cool and relaxed but his adrenalin was pumping 100mph, anticipating their next move. If everything went as planned there would be no turning back and life would never be the same. Jihad and his crew had been doing their homework for the past three months and the moment they've been calculating had finally arrived.

"Where is this mutha fucka at?" Jamal broke the silence. "He should've been here by now."

The clock on the dashboard read 5:17Am.

"Give him a couple more minutes." Jihad replied. "He probably stopped to get something to eat after he left the club."

Before he could complete the sentence, a grey BMW turned onto the street. A soft thump escaped the stereo system as it eased up the block.

Jihad pulled out his IPhone and spoke into the receiver. "Get ready. Here he come."

"I see him." A voice echoed back.

Across the street, their partner Stone was already positioned in the bushes next door to the intended target. As the Beamer pulled into the driveway and parked, he sprang into action once the engine was shut off. Jihad and Jamal followed suit, pulling their ski mask over their face as they exited the van, leaving nothing but their eyes exposed. By the time the occupant got out of the vehicle, he was staring down the barrel of Stones Mac-11.

"Don't move mutha fucka!" Stone grabbed the man by the collar.

"Ahhhh!" A female screamed from inside of the car, realizing what was happening.

Jamal quickly maneuvered towards the passenger door and snatched the woman from her seat.

"Bitch shut the fuck up before I blow your head off!" He threatened with a 357 revolver to her chin.

"I'm sorry... I'm sorry... Please don't kill me." She pleaded. "I got a little boy at home."

Gamble stood there stunned. Too intoxicated to put up a struggle, he cooperated with the masked gunmen. Stone searched him for a weapon, discovering a 9mm placed against the small of his back.

"Now open the door!" He demanded.

After fumbling with the keys for a moment, Gamble unlocked the door and dis-activated the alarm system. Along with his female companion, he was shoved into the house and instructed to lie face down on the carpet. Immediately, Jihad bound their wrist and ankles with duct tape then sat them up on the couch.

"Where that paper at?" He spoke calmly, placing a desert eagle to Gamble's temple.

Gamble looked at him with confusion and said, "Do you know who you fuckin wit? When Blue hears about this all hell is going to break loose. If I was you, I'd walk away while I still had a chance."

Gamble was a lieutenant in an organization led by a notorious gangster by the name of Blue. Raised in a family of players, hoes and thieves, Gamble was the epitome of what a hustler should be. His velvet style of hustling caught the attention of Blue when one of the neighborhoods that the gangster controlled ceased to meet its weekly revenue. After surveying Gambles activities, Blue sent one of his soldiers at him with an offer difficult to refuse.

"Work for Blue and keep getting money or lose your life." The Soldier proposed.

Being the businessman that he was, Gamble didn't take the proposition as a form of disrespect but as an opportunity to expand his hustle. Without giving it a second thought, he had agreed to work for Blue and now here he was with a pistol to his head being robbed.

Jihad cocked the hammer back. "Don't turn this into a homicide playboy. You're not in a position to make threats. Now if I was you, I would tell me where that paper is at before shit get ugly in here. Quit worrying about Blue and start thinking about what you need to do to stay alive."

Gamble weighed his options. On one hand, he knew that Blue would blame him for allowing these nigga's to get the drop on him and there would be consequences to face. On the other hand if he didn't give these crooks what they wanted there was a chance that they might kill him. Defeated, he decided to go with his better judgment and live to see another day.

"The safe is in the back room behind the painting of Bob Marley."

"What's the combination?" Jihad questioned.

"Three, sixteen, thirty." Gamble confirmed.

"Keep an eye on this nigga while I check it out."

The master bedroom was elaborately furnished with an apple desktop computer, 45inch flat screen and a surround sound stereo system inside of a glass entertainment center. When Jihad entered the bedroom his eyes zeroed in on the picture of the famous Jamaican singer, hanging center of the wall above the canopy style bed. Quickly moving towards the bed, he removed the painting off the wall and found what he was looking for. Jihad punched in the code to the digital safe and pulled it open. A smile spread across his face as he stared at the contents inside.

"That's what I'm talking about." He thought to himself.

Quickly emptying the money and merchandise into a duffle bag, Jihad left the room.

Meanwhile, Jamal was up front peeping through the blinds making sure the coast was clear as Stone paced the floor with the Mac-11, shooting evil glares at Gamble.

Gamble couldn't believe what was taking place as muffled sobs escaped the lips of the woman sitting next to him.

"Stop crying Vanessa. Everything is going to be alright." He assured her.

"Shut the fuck up nigga!" Stone snapped. "Didn't nobody tell you that you could talk."

"C'mon dawg can't you see that my girl is scared? I'm giving ya'll niggas what you want so why don't you just chill out." Gamble replied with anger in his voice.

Stone walked over to where Gamble was restrained and smacked him viciously across the face with the machine gun.

"Arrgghh." Gamble screamed in agony.

"Who the fuck do you think you talking to? I'll kill you and this punk bitch if you keep runnin your mouth." Stone pointed the Mac in his face.

At that moment, Jihad appeared from the back carrying the duffle bag across his shoulder.

"Be easy fam!" He interjected. "We got what we came for."

"Fuck that! This nigga is about to die!" Stone declared. "He think that this shit is sweet. He think it can't happen."

"That's not what we came here for family. Let's stick to the script.

Stone gripped his weapon with murder on his mind, staring at Gamble with menacing eyes. With blood leaking from the open gash on his face, Gamble returned a threatening gaze of his own. There was something familiar about the masked men but he couldn't put his finger on it.

Please let me shoot this bitch ass nigga." Stone stressed through clinched teeth.

Jihad unzipped the bag to reveal their new found wealth, watching as both Stone and Jamal eyes grew with wide excitement.

"Are you willing to take the chance of someone hearing the gunshots?" Jihad compromised. "If you kill him then we got to kill her.

Jamal nodded in agreement ready for whatever decision was decided. Listening to reason, Stone lowered the weapon and whispered into Gambles ear.

"Today's your lucky day Scarface. If it wasn't for my man right here, I was going to rock ya ass to sleep without the lullaby. But since you were kind enough to give up that bread, I guess I'll give you a pass for now but I'll see you again. Plus, I think ya girl Vanessa here is kind of cute."

Vanessa pulled away, trying to avoid from being touched as Stone rubbed her cheek.

As they prepared to leave, Stone struck Gamble again with the Mac-11, leaving him unconscious. "Bitch ass nigga!" He spat as they exited the house.

CHAPTER 2

Angela awoke during the early hours of the morning to find an empty space in her bed. Her chocolate temple was yearning to be explored by the young man that she considered to be the love of her life. She grabbed the cordless off of the nightstand and dialed Jihad cell phone number only to receive the voicemail. Her suspicions grew as she thought about the awkward hours that Jihad had been keeping lately. If he wasn't staying out all night, he was creeping into the house after she'd falling asleep. She couldn't even recall the last time they'd slept in the same room together let alone the same bed. Angela was madly in love with Jihad, he was her everything. They had been together since their freshman year of high school and he was the only person that she'd been with physically. Since the moment she laid eyes on him, Angela had a thing for the young thug. There was something calm and serene behind his rough exterior. Jihad always seemed to be in control regardless of the situation. Mature beyond his years, he took on the responsibility of being the head of his household after his father was murdered during a corrupt drug deal in the early nineties. Eventually, he would follow in his late father's footsteps, resulting to the same streets as a means of survival. His life revolved around his family and the methods that he chose to provide for his mother and younger sister only enhanced the feelings that Angela harbored inside. She was intrigued at the fact that a kid so young had so much authority. By the time Jihad was seventeen, him and his crew of young gunslingers had made a name for themselves throughout the city of Buffalo. Now at the age of twenty three he had become somewhat of a legend uptown with the aspirations of a true gangster.

Tears welled up in Angela's eyes as she rubbed her pregnant belly. Images of Jihad lying next to another female danced around in her mind as she cried herself to sleep.

*****

Somewhere across town, Stone, Jamal and Jihad were at their honeycomb hideout, counting the money from the robbery. The honeycomb was a small apartment on the Westside that no one but the three of them knew about. This is where they felt safe master minding their schemes and stashing their drugs.

At the round table there were bundles of cash and bricks of uncut cocaine spread out in front of them. Get Rich or Die Tryin by 50 cent pumped softly through the speakers as a red nose pit bull roamed the premises gingerly on alert. On the wall above the three of them hung a black and white poster of the famous Harlem gangster, Bumpy Johnson.

Stone lit up a blunt of sour diesel. "What's the count?" He asked, releasing a ring of smoke.

"We got a hundred and eighty two thousand and seven bricks of coke." Jihad confirmed.

"What about the jewelry?" Jamal held up an iced out Franck Muller. "How much do you think its worth?

"I don't know but I'm going and holler at my man at the pawn shop."

"Are you talking about that Jewish cat up on Broadway? Stone questioned.

Jihad nodded. "Yeah, he got some people up top that'll take this shit off of our hands for half of whatever it's worth. We should at least get another fifty stacks."

"I'm going to keep this watch for my personal." Jamal said.

"We getting rid of all this shit." Jihad told him. "We don't need any extra attention that could link us back to the robbery."

"Ain't nobody go find out that we was behind the lick if I keep the watch. I'm only going to rock it when I go O.T."

"I'm not tryna hear that cousin." Jihad said. "Once that nigga Blue find out that Gamble got robbed, his ears is going to be glued to the streets trying to figure out who had the balls to rob one of his lieutenants and that watch could be the difference whether we win or lose. Plus we got enough money to get our own Jewels but we need to stay quiet until the time is right."

Stone blew out another stream of smoke before passing the blunt to Jamal. "If you would've let me rock that nigga to sleep, we wouldn't have to worry about shit coming back on us.'

A smile spread across Jihad's face as he looked up at his trigger happy friend. "Why every time we hit a lick, you want to kill everybody?"

"Because that's how I get down.' Stone emphasized. "If the nigga is dead then I don't have to worry about him coming back to rock me."

"Trust me bra, you'll get your chance to lay your pistol game down but right now I need you to play it cool."

Stone and Jihad had been best friends since the sand box. The two of them were like night and day; you couldn't have one without the other. Where Jihad was cool and strategic, Stone was wild and impulsive. He'd committed his first murder at the age of fourteen and has been bloodthirsty ever since. One evening, Stone arrived home from school to find his mother being brutally beaten by her live in boyfriend. Without hesitation, he reached into his book bag and pulled out a snub nose 38 and shot dude in back of the head, killing him instantly. Stone was only a juvenile so his charges were reduced from murder to manslaughter and he was sentenced to 18 months in a detention center for boys.

Every month until he was released, Jihad sent Stone money and pictures, signifying a loyalty that would last a lifetime.

Jamal was Jihad's younger cousin originally from Niagara Falls, New York. Due to his miscreant behavior, his mother sent him to Buffalo to live with his father, hoping that the presence of a man would have a positive influence on him. Jamal was naturally talented with a basketball and had the potential to take his game to the next level but like the old saying goes, you can take a nigga out of the hood but you can't take the hood out of a nigga. By the time he was a junior, Jamal had traded in the basketball for a pistol and began running with Jihad and his crew of young bandits, robbing and hustling crack on the street corner. Although he lived a dangerous life, Jamal was something close to a pretty boy. His curly hair was cut into taper fade, complimenting his almond complexion and his wardrobe was impeccable. There were a variety of women at his disposal captivated by his charisma. Jihad often joked, saying that Jamal was the flyest gangster in the city.

"Here's the deal." Jihad said. "We're going to keep the same routine that we've been keeping. We don't want Blue to suspect that we were behind the robbery."

"Fuck Blue!" Stone barked. "That nigga bleed just like everybody else."

"He also got the town on lock. He got niggas from here to Chiraq that'll kill for him at the snap of his finger not to mention the police and judges that he got on his payroll."

Stone took a minute to consider what Jihad was saying. "I'll be cool."

"Just until we get ourselves in position. It's about time that the town seen some new blood and if everything go as plan we'll be millionaires by this time next year."

"I know that we got a bunch of young guns on the squad ready to put their work in but Blue is not going to lay down that easy." Jamal reminded them. "Robbing him is one thing but taking over the town is another."

"That's why we keep our friends close and our enemies closer." Jihad told them.

"What?"

"The best way to destroy an empire is not from the outside but from within."

"Huh?" Stone and Jamal were still confused.

"When Blue finds out that somebody robbed Gamble, he's going to want their head on a chopping block." Jihad explained. "He'll be mad about the money that was taken but he's going to be extremely upset that somebody had the balls to try somebody in his organization and that's where we come in."

"Where we come in?" Jamal questioned.

"Yeah, because more than likely, Blue is going to think that it was an inside job so he's not going to trust anyone who he suspects knew anything about Gamble's spot."

"I still don't see where we come in at?"

Stone turned to Jihad and smiled. He knew his partner long enough to know when he was up to something. "You're a smart mutha fucka. Crazy as hell but smart."

Jamal still didn't understand so Stone enlightened him. "We're going to work for Blue."

"Exactly!" Jihad nodded. "The money that we took is the same money that we're going to spend with him and Moe to put us in position to take over."

"And what makes you think that Blue is going to put us in position?" Jamal asked.

"Like I said it's time for some new blood. All you gotta do is trust me."

Jamal looked at Jihad with uncertainty in his eyes then focused on Stone. "Fuck it; we don't have shit to lose." He finally said.

"Alright then." Jihad spoke. "We're going to take five grand a piece to keep the lint out of our pocket, pay some bills and do something nice with your lady but don't draw any attention to yourselves. The rest of the money we're going to put in the stash."

"What about the work?" Stone inquired.

"Set two of the brick aside for phase two of my plan which I'll explain to y'all once I work out the details. The rest of the coke, we're going to cook up and break down into twenties and fifties like we've been doing until they present us with an opportunity."

"And how can you be so sure that the opportunity will present itself?" Jamal asked.

"This is not something that I just threw together in one day; I've been working on this for a minute so you're going to have to trust my instincts."

"I trust you cousin but how do you expect everything to fall in place. What if something goes wrong?"

"That's the chance that I'm willing to take but I know this shit is going to work as long as we stick to the script." Jihad said. "They've been monitoring our moves for a couple of months and they don't consider us a threat and that's how I want to keep it."

Stone nodded his approval. "I'm wit you homie. As long as you think this shit will work, I'm wit you."

"Good because I'm counting on ya'll boys when it's crunch time."

The sun had begun to rise, causing the daylight to peak through the darkness. Jihad checked his messages on his voicemail and listened to Angela question his whereabouts. He closed the phone and thought about how he'd been ignoring her lately. She was a good girl and Jihad feelings ran deep for her. Everything he did in the streets was for their future but at times Angela couldn't understand his dedication.

Stone noticed the distracted expression on Jihad's face and asked him, "What's the matter with you?"

"It's Angie." Jihad answered. "She worried about a nigga. Since we been laying on this lick, I haven't been spending much time with her and she's starting to feel a certain type of way."

"Go ahead and get to the house before Ang flip out and kill yo ass. You know that she's crazy as hell."

"I know you didn't make it this far to let ya girl knock you off." Jamal joked. "I can see the headlines now. Gangster gets murdered by pregnant girlfriend."

"Ya'll niggas silly as hell." Jihad laughed.

"Nah, but on the real, I feel you." Stone admitted. "Wifey been on some bullshit wit me too lately"

"Alright, I'll holla at ya'll boy's on the A.M." He grabbed a small portion of the money off the table before he bounced.

After Jihad left the house, Stone and Jamal counted out five thousand for themselves before stashing the remainder of the cash along with the coke and jewelry inside of an iron safe hidden in the basement. A blunt and a half later, they we're watching Straight Outta Compton on the 42 inch plasma attached to the wall when Jamal asked, "You think that we can really take over the city?"

"What?" Stone was high and half way asleep.

"All that shit that Jihad was talking about taking over the city and becoming millionaires. Do you really think that it can happen?"

"Let me tell you something about your cousin." Stone yawned and rubbed his eyes. "He's a real ambidextrous type of dude."

"Ambidextrous?" Jamal wrinkled his brow. "What the hell are you talking about?"

"That means that he's real clever in difficult situations. Jihads the type of nigga that could have been a C.E.O., running some fortune 500 company or some shit but he chose the streets. Or maybe the streets chose him, I don't know! But whatever the case may be, I know that he is a sharp nigga who has never let me down."

Seeing that he had Jamal's attention, Stone continued. "Yeah, I believe that we can take over the town but I also believe that it's going to be a lot of bloodshed in the process. The question is are you prepared to die for what you believe?"

Jamal thought about that last statement for a moment. "Yeah, I'll die for what I believe in." He said indecisively.

"I hope so because the time may come when you might have to make that decision between life and death."

CHAPTER 3

Jihad awoke later that afternoon to the sound of running water coming from the bathroom. Angela wasn't anywhere in sight so he assumed that she was taking a shower and making preparations for the day. He rolled over on the king size mattress to grab his cell phone off of the charger, sitting on the nightstand. There were three missed calls flashing across the screen. He recognized Stone's number but couldn't identify the other two. Jihad pressed the send button and listen as the phone began to ring.

"Who is this?" He asked as a female answered the other line.

"Who is this?" She snapped. "Nigga, you called my house!"

"Did somebody call Jihad from this number?"

"Oh, what's going on Jihad? This is Roxy."

"What's up baby girl? Did you take care of that business that I needed you to handle?"

"I'm still working on it."

"Well I'm going to need you to work a little bit harder baby because I'm depending on you to make this happen for me."

"Have I ever let you down?" Roxy asked.

"Nah, you been on point so far but these ain't ya average niggas." Jihad warned. "This shit could blow up in our face if we fuck this up and I can't afford for you to get hurt behind my bullshit."

"Aww, Jihad worried about me. Ain't that sweet."

"I'm serious Rox. Don't fuck this up!" Jihad told her.

"I got this boo. Quit worrying and just trust me. Remember when you were worried about how you were going to get them Jamaicans from New York City? I got that done for you, didn't I?

"Yeah, you pulled that thing off for me!"

"Okay then, relax. How many niggas do you know that can resist this pussy?"

"Not many!" Jihad breathed heavily. "As a matter fact when are you going to quit playing and let me sample that thang?"

"Sorry boo but you know that I don't mix business with pleasure."

"So what are you saying, I got to play to play?"

"Roxy laughed. "No smart ass. What I'm saying is that if I fucked you, it would complicate our relationship."

"You don't seem like the emotional type."

"Oh, it's not me that I'm worried about getting emotional." She stated. "And I don't have time for the baby mama drama."

Jihad smiled at her sarcasm. "I was just fucking wit you ma. You know I got to check and see where your head's at. Make sure that you're still a professional."

"Nigga, you know that I keep it G all the way around the board.

"True that!" Jihad said.

"And as far as that situation goes, it's all good. I supposed to start working at one of the restaurants where the big man conducts most of his business so I'll be able to keep an eye open and play up under the nigga."

"That's why I fuck with you."

"Whatever Jihad! Just make sure that you got that bread for me when I get back from Philly because a bitch got bills."

"When you coming back?"

"Tomorrow night at 9:30"

"Alright, I got you. Call me when you touch down." Jihad told her once he heard the shower stop.

"Okay, I'll talk to you later."

When he hung up with Roxy, Jihad dialed the other missed call. Once the person answered the phone, he recognized the voice.

"What up Fam; where you at?" The person asked.

"What's good Remy?" Jihad replied. "I'm at the building; what's up?"

"The block is bleeding right now and nigga's don't have any band aids to patch it up." Remy spoke in code.

Remy was one of the young guns from the neighborhood who hustled for Jihad. He was eighteen years old, standing 5'11 and weighing approximately 175lb. The dreadlocks hanging shoulder length gave Remy a grim appearance. Built to win but born to lose he entered the world at a disadvantage. Conceived by a woman who was addicted to crack his father could have been any of the many men that she tricked off with to support her habit. When He was thirteen, Remy began hustling the same poison that was destroying his mother. Jihad took a liking to the young kid and put him under his wing, schooling him about life in the streets.

"Give me a minute." Jihad told him. "I'll be through there when I get up and out of the house."

"That's what's up." Remy said before hanging up.

Just as Jihad ended the call, Angela appeared in the bedroom with a towel wrapped around her torso. Beads of water rolled down the nap of her neck as she made her way over to where Jihad was sprawled across the bed.

"Are you still taking me to my doctor's appointment?" She sat beside him.

"Damn boo; I forgot that your appointment was today." Jihad checked his watch. "What time do you have to be there?"

"At two o'clock and it's already a quarter to one."

Jihad hopped up out of the bed. "Yeah, I'm going to take you. Give me a minute to take a shower and get myself together."

As the hot water drenched his muscular physique, Jihad allowed his mind to drift back to the conversation that he held with his comrades the night before. He knew that his plan was complicated but he was up for the challenge; he just hoped that his crew was prepared for what was about to transpire. At the thought of his boy's, Jihad reminded himself to return Stone's call. As he stepped out of the tub steamed filled the air. He walked over to the sink and wiped the mist away from the mirror, checking his reflection.

"I need a haircut." He rubbed his wavy hair.

Angela was dressed in a smoke grey cashmere sweater with matching slacks when Jihad stepped back into the room. Her hair was pulled into a bun as she applied mac gloss to her luscious lips. He stood in the doorway admiring her angelic features. It seemed as if the pregnancy had enhanced her beauty.

At that moment, he realized how much he appreciated her. The encrusted diamonds in her ear lobes illuminated her smooth chocolate skin and her dimpled smile caught the attention of anyone that came into her presence but it was the touch of innocence that kept them captivated. As she finished preparing for her appointment, Angela noticed Jihad staring at her through the vanity mirror.

"What are you doing?" She spun around. "Why are you standing there staring at me?"

Jihad strolled up behind her and wrapped his arms around Angela's waist. He placed his hands on her stomach and kissed the back of her neck.

"I love you." He declared. "I was just admiring how beautiful you are."

"Hmp! You love me huh?" She questioned with a hint of sarcasm.

"You know that you're my world."

"You haven't been acting like I'm your world and I sure as hell haven't felt like I've been being loved lately."

Jihad loosened his grip and stepped back. "What is that supposed to mean?"

"Where were you at last night Jihad?" She stared at him with an attitude.

"Where was I at last night?" He repeated.

"You heard what I said Jihad don't play stupid. Now answer the question."

Irritation spread across Jihad's face as he turned around and stepped towards the closet.

"I was working. He barked.

"Don't walk away from me." She grabbed him. "You think that I'm stupid or something? I know that you were laid up with one of them little hoe's that you be fucking with. I swear Jihad if you bring me…."

"Whoa, hold up Ang!" Jihad cut her off. "First of all, I don't have time to be fuckin wit these bitches and if I did, I'm not about to lay up with a hoe when I got a queen at the kingdom."

"Well why didn't you answer your phone when I called you last night? And I know that you got the messages that I left on your voicemail so don't try and lie."

Jihad sighed deeply, thinking of a way to make her understand his dilemma. "Listen baby." He looked her straight in the eyes. "I got something real big that I'm working on right now. I know that I haven't been spending much time with you lately or giving you the attention that you deserve but I'm out there in them streets tryna make something happen."

"I understand that you're out in streets trying to provide for your family but that's not a reason for you not to answer your phone."

Jihad smiled at her, revealing all thirty two teeth. "You're absolutely right, I can't argue with you about that but I need you to understand that when I'm in the trenches that's where my mind needs to be. Niggas is hungry and if I'm not on point then I start to look like lunch meat."

"I still don't understand what that has to do with you answering your phone?" There was still a trace of anger in her voice. "You could have at least called me back and let me know that you're alright. I be worried about you. What am I supposed to think when you run in and out of the house at all hours of the night without talking to me? A relationship is about communication."

"I feel where you're coming from baby but I have never exposed you to my lifestyle and don't intend to start now."

"Just because you don't expose me to your lifestyle doesn't mean that I don't know what's going on. I'm not stupid Jihad and I know that these scandalous hoes come along with the world you're involved in."

"I think this pregnancy got your emotions running wild." Jihad remarked. "I'm not thinking about them bitches so that should be the last thing on your mind. If it's not about money, I don't have any talk for them."

"That's what your mouth says."

"C'mere." He pulled her close and stared into her eyes. "You're the only woman that I want. Everything that I'm out there doing is for us. I'm about to go hard with my hustle and once I stack enough money, we're going down south to start all over. I just need you to have faith and believe in me."

"I do believe in you but I don't want to wake up one day lonely." Angela said. "I don't know what I would do without you.'

"Don't worry about that baby; I'm always going to be here for you."

Angela smiled. I hope so because I'll hate to have to kill you and your little girlfriend."

They both laughed as she fell into Jihad's arms. He kissed her passionately in the mouth and moved towards the bed.

"Uh uh Jihad." Angela pulled away quickly. "I got to get to my appointment."

"C'mon boo just let me taste it."

"No! I'm going to be late for my checkup."

"You can re-schedule." He pressed while sucking on her earlobe.

"Come on and get dressed before you start something that you can't finish."

In the heat of the moment his phone vibrated. With Angela straddled on top of him, Jihad reached over and answered it.

"What's good?" He spoke into the mouth piece.

"Did you get my message?" Stone shot back.

"I see that I missed your call but I didn't get a chance to check my voice mail. I was about to hit you back in a minute. What's up?"

Suddenly Angela removed the towel from around his waist and started fondling his dick.

What time are you coming through the hood? Stone questioned.

"I don't know. I got to take wifey to the doctor's office at two." Jihad replied a bit distracted. "But I need you to go through there and holler at the youngin. He called and said that the block was bleeding but they didn't have any more band aids."

"I'm about to go and pull up on them now and see what they talking about."

Angela placed all eight and a half inches of Jihad's swollen penis into her mouth and started bobbing her head up and down slowly. She added a slight twist as he ran his fingers through her hair.

"Go ahead and take care of that and I'll get at you in a minute." He laid back, allowing her to do her thing.

"Alright. One."

"One."

Angela stopped and got up when he ended the call.

"What are you doing?" He whined. "Why did you stop?"

"Because it's time to go." She wiped the spit from her mouth.

"Oh that's how you go do your boy?"

"If my boy brought his ass home at night, he would get it whenever and however he wanted it." She teased before disappearing into the bathroom, leaving Jihad lying on the bed with an erection.

"That's fucked up." He shouted out to her. "That's fucked up."

CHAPTER 4

After leaving the doctor's office, Jihad and Angela were traveling east on the 33 expressway, excited about the news they'd just received. DR. Middlebrooks had informed them that Angela was pregnant with a girl. Although Jihad was looking forward to son, thoughts of having a little princess running around, calling him daddy overwhelmed him with joy. Angela could care less about the gender; her only concern was giving birth to a healthy child.

"I know that you want to run over to your mom's house and tell her the good news so drop me off on the block." Jihad instructed.

"I thought that we were going to spend some time together." Angela responded.

"I got something that I need to check on right quick. I'll be home in a couple hours."

He pulled the black Expedition up on the block and parked. There were a group of teenagers across the street loitering on the porch of an abandon building. They were bundled up in leather jackets with matching skull caps. An assortment of Timberland boots laced their feet as they took turns running up the block to serve the crack fiends.

"Okay boo, I'll see you in a minute." Jihad got out of the truck.

Angela slid over to the driver seat and rolled down the window. "Will you be home before I fall asleep?"

"Only if you finish what you started earlier."

"That's not a problem." She licked her lips seductively. "But don't have me waiting for your ass all night. You know how you do!"

"I'm not worth waiting for?" Jihad gripped the crotch of his jeans.

Angela smiled. "You're so nasty."

Jihad peeled two c-notes off of a bankroll and walked back over to the vehicle.

"Fill the truck up then run and get some groceries for the house." He handed it to her. "I'll be home by seven o'clock so have me some turkey wings and rice ready by the time I get there."

Alright baby, I'll see you when you get home."

As he turned to walk away, Jihad zipped up his coat and covered his head with an oversized hood.

"What up?" He approached the youngsters on the porch.

An assortment of greeting was shouted back as he stepped up the stairs and gave the three young men some dap. "Stone been through here to holler at you boy's?"

"Yeah, he came through about an hour ago and straitened us out." Zae nodded. "He said that he'd be back later on."

"What's up Chris?" Jihad nudged the kid sitting next to Zae. "I heard you showed out in the championship game last Saturday. How many touchdowns did you have?"

"I threw for three and ran for one." Crhis confirmed. "And I had over three hundred in all-purpose yards."

Chris was an all-western New York athlete in both football and basketball. Although he wasn't cut out for the streets, everyone in the hood had love for him. Jihad allowed Chris to hang around but forbade him to hustle or participate in anything illegal. Instead, he encouraged him to pursue his dream, paying him fifty dollars for every touchdown he scored.

"I guess I owe you about a deuce huh?" Jihad declared.

A small grin spread across Chris's face. "Something like that."

"This nigga think he's a young Mike Vick or some shit." Said Lil P. "But I'm not going to front on the homie, he did his thing."

"I heard!" Jihad peeled Chris off two hundred dollars.

Lil P was another one of Jihad's young soldiers. He was the youngest out of the group but without a doubt the most dangerous. Quick tempered and always prepared to bust his gun, Lil P reminded Jihad of Stone when they were shorty's coming up.

A brown Cutlass pulled to the curb in front of the house and parked. The passenger side window rolled down and a scruffy looking guy poked his head out and asked were they working.

Zae hopped from the porch and motioned for the man to follow him across the street into a backyard.

"What's up Jack? How much money you got?"

"Do something nice for this fifty dollars nephew." Jack passed Zae the money.

Zae retrieved his stash and handed Jack seven baggies filled with crack. Satisfied, Jack tossed the packs into his mouth and hurried back to the car.

When the cutlass pulled away from the curb, Jihad turned to Lil P and asked, "Where is Remy? I thought that he was out here with y'all?"

"He'll be back in a minute." Lil P replied. "He had the fiend broad Lena run him to the weed spot."

10 minutes later Lena drove up and dropped Remy off. She was a woman in her early thirties who laced her cigarettes with crack from time to time. Although Lena got high, she managed to keep her appearance up to par. A light complexioned bombshell, she astonished niggas in the neighborhood on her worst day. Lena was known for sucking a dick to support her addiction so when Remy hopped out of the car smiling like Chester the cheetah, Jihad knew what was up.

"What's the deal Jihad?" Remy eased up the driveway.

"You tell me." Jihad shot back. "I see you're fraternizing on company time."

The porch broke out in laughter.

"Man go ahead with that shit. I went to get something to smoke." Remy defended.

"Niggas quit fronting." Lil P said. "We know that you dipped off and let Lena hit your head."

Guilt spread across Remy's face. "Fuck ya'll niggas! Yeah, I let the bitch suck my dick; so what, ya'll would've too."

"I ain't gon front." Zae spoke up. "I have let Lena break me off plenty of times. That bitch is a true freak and her neck game is serious."

Lil P and Remy both nodded in agreement.

"Ya'll lil niggas is going to get enough of letting these crackhead bitches suck on ya'll dick." Jihad responded. "That hoe has been around here fucking and gobbling dicks since I was a shorty. Don't let her good looks fool you and fuck around and catch something that you can't get rid of."

Suddenly Jihad's cell phone rang and he flipped it open.

"What's poppin?"

"Where are you at cousin?" Jamal replied.

"I'm out here on the block. When you get a chance come through here and snatch me up."

"I'll be through there in a minute."

"One!"

Jihad hung up and focused back on his young soldiers.

"A bitch will try to throw you off your game if you're not careful." He explained. "Bitches like Lena have ruined plenty of niggas out here in the game. Right now she's sucking ya'll boy's off for a your crack pieces here and there but somewhere down the line, she'll be tryna trick ya'll into getting high with her."

"I'm not about to get high with that hoe!" Remy barked.

"Word up, you buggin now fam." Lil P protested. "How did you jump from getting some brain to smoking crack? You trippin."

"Do you think that these crack head niggas just woke up one day and decided that they wanted to smoke crack?" Jihad questioned them. "Hell nah! The majority of them was freakin off with some broad who turned them out."

"God aint created a bitch that can turn the kid out." Zae gave Lil p some dap. "Your boy mind is too strong for that shit."

"Don't never think that you're exempt from falling victim to the allure of a woman. I've seen the smoothest hustlers and all type of gangsters fall weak to a hoe. Trust me, it can happen. All I'm tryna do is keep ya'll boy's on point."

Chris got up to leave once Jihad finished speaking.

"I'll get with ya'll boy's tomorrow." He said. "Aye, Jihad good looking out on that paper, I really appreciate it."

"It's nothing my nigga. Keep doing what you've been doing and I'ma make sure that you keep some paper in your pocket. Don't be like these knuckle head ass niggas right here."

"No doubt. I'll holler at ya'll boy's later."

Jihad watched Chris as he walked down the street. He really took a liking to the young kid. He had a bright future ahead of himself if he stayed focused. Too many prominent athletes had gotten caught up with the temptation of the streets, including Jamal but it was something about Chris that was different. He was going to make it, Jihad was sure of it.

For the next hour, Remy, Lil p and Zae were freestyling rhymes as they took turns serving the fiends that strolled through the block. For it to be the end of the month, the flow was pretty steady. Jihad observed his squadron with a diligent eye. Although he was the general of this small army, he played the trenches with his troops to keep his edge. He believed in the old theory which stated that a man shouldn't demand something of others that they wouldn't do themselves so he often stood front line, leading by example.

"Yo Jihad let me hold something until I get my check." Tony slid up on the porch.

Tony was a tall slender man in his mid-forties. He used to be somewhat of a ladies man before he allowed his addiction to drugs to take control of him. Jihad had known the old school player since he was a kid running up and down the avenue hustling him for quarters to buy penny candy. He remembered when Tony was at the top of his game because he had admired the smooth talking guy behind the wheel of latest Cadillac.

"When do you get your check Tone?" Jihad asked him.

"Next week." He replied.

Jihad nodded to Remy, giving him the okay to credit Tony until he received his check.

"Tone remember when I was shorty, running around here harassing you for change to get something from the corner store?"

"Yeah, I remember that shit." He admitted. "How can I forget? You and that crazy mutha fucka Stone was always into some shit. You two lil niggas were hell. I knew that ya'll was going to be hustlers back then because ya'll were always swindling and running game on somebody."

"Did you ever imagine that life would be like this?"

"Like what? Out here chasing a dollar to get high?" Tony inquired.

"Yeah because I remember when you were on top of the world. From the outside looking in, it seemed as if you had everything that a man desired. Pocket full money, cars and women so I was wondering how you lost your way and start using drugs."

Tone collected his memory as he stared off into space.

"I'll never forget the day; it was my birthday." He remembered. "My partner Nick had some freaks from California down here for the weekend and we partied nonstop around the clock. Cherry! Cherry Cunningham was her name. This bitch was built like a stallion and had the face of a goddess. Back then, I use to drink like a fish and smoke a little weed but besides that, I had never experienced with any other drugs so when Cherry pulled out a sack of china white, I was a little bit hesitant. She kept stressing how it would keep my dick hard all night and some other bullshit about how it intensified the orgasm so I tried it. Next thing I know, it was three days later and I was a couple grand short, the rest is history."

"So you let a bitch from Cali tricked you on the dope? Jihad quizzed.

"Unfortunately!"

Jihad's eyes shifted towards Zae and Lil P to see if they were paying attention then he focused back on Tony.

"My life hasn't been right since." Tony continued. "It was like the forbidden fruit that Adam took from Eve.

Remy emerged from the yard and handed Tony two dimes.

"I appreciate that young blood. I'll pay you back next Tuesday."

"Hold up Tone!" Jihad stopped him as he was leaving. "You said that Cherry gave you some China white? That's heroine! How did you start smoking crack?"

"At the time I didn't know that it was heroine, I thought that it was cocaine. That's just how green I was. I kept my fronts up for a while but after that night I sort of lost my way and started fucking with anything that would get me high."

Suddenly a cream Escalade bent the corner and came to a stop in front of the house. Jamal climbed out the passenger seat sporting a Louis Vuitton leather with chocolate Timberlands to match. The cuff of his jeans dragged in the snow as he mounted the steps of the abandon building.

"You ready fam?" He dapped up Jihad.

Jihad glanced over at the truck. There was a Puerto Rican chick behind the wheel, nodding her head to the music.

"Who is that?" He nodded towards the vehicle.

"That's this girl name Paula that I bagged up in Niagara Falls two weeks ago." Jamal replied.

"Paula must got some good pussy if you letting her push the Lac after two weeks."

Jamal let out a whistle. "Mami is off the chain with it." He confessed.

"I wanted you to run me to the crib but I don't want your shorty to know where I lay my head at."

"I can drop her off at the Telly. I need to chop it up with you about something anyway so c'mon and take a ride with me."

"Ya'll boy's hold the fort down while I'm gone." He spoke to his soldiers. "Tone stay up my nigga."

As Jihad stepped towards the Escalade with Jamal, he noticed a black Mercedes Benz creeping down the block. He inched his hand under his coat preparing for the unexpected as the car came to a stop.

CHAPTER 5

Seated behind cherry oak desk, Blue puffed on a cigar imported directly from Cuba. He tried his best to remain calm as Gamble explained the details of the robbery from the night before. Blue was the city's most notorious gangster. His rise to power began in the 80s, during the crack epidemic. Determined to escape the confinements of poverty, Blue resulted to extorting local hustlers and small businessmen. After serving a five year stint in prison, he returned to the streets with a diabolical and cold heart. He loved nothing but money and drugs, torture and murder was the way he obtained it.

Gamble felt uneasy the moment he stepped foot in the large man's office. He didn't know what to expect. On many occasions he'd witnessed his boss inflict pain upon men for minor mistakes so he knew that his life was in jeopardy.

Blue released a cloud of smoke. "So let me get this straight." He spoke in a raspy voice. "Three mutha fucka's walked you into your house and handcuffed you and some bitch that you brought home from the club then left with seven keys and a hundred and eighty thousand dollars of my money? Is that what you're trying to tell me?"

"Um ye…yeah!" Gamble stuttered in a low tone.

"What the fuck did you say?" Blue snapped. "Speak up, I can't hear you."

"Boss these niggas was…."

Blue silenced him with a wave of the hand.

"This shit is hard for me to believe since you're standing here in front of me instead of somewhere trying to find the niggas that took my shit."

Gamble's stomach twisted into a knot as beads of sweat trickled down his forehead.

"You come in here with a couple stitches in your head and expect me to believe this shit that you're telling me?" Blue snarled. "Who the fuck do you think you're dealing with; some chump? For all I know you and that bitch got my money."

"Blue, you know that I would never do nothing like that." Gamble said.

Blue raised up from his desk and said, "I don't know what you would do nigga. All I know is that my money is missing and until I get it back everyone's a suspect."

Gamble glared across the office at Moe, Blue's right hand man. He hadn't said a word since he entered the room.

"I'ma find out who did this. The town aint but so big and somebody is bound to slip up and say something." Gamble said.

While Gamble was talking, Moe slipped behind him and restrained him in a full nelson.

Still puffing his cigar, Blue walked from behind the desk. "The only reason that you're not floating in Lake Erie right now is because dead men can't pay debts." He growled, blowing smoke into Gamble's face. "I want my fuckin money and I don't give a fuck how you get it. Robb, kill or steal. I don't care if yo momma got to sell her pussy on the strip to get me mine; make it happen."

"I'm going to get you your money." Gamble responded with fear in his voice.

"You got two weeks to get my money and to find out who's behind this shit."

"I'm on top of it boss."

Blue took another pull from his cigar then crushed the burning end onto Gamble's eyelid.

Moe released him as he screamed in agony, falling to the floor.

Suddenly the office doors swung open and two of Blue's henchmen hurried in with their weapon drawn.

"Is everything cool boss?" The shorter of the two questioned.

Standing in the middle of the floor over the squirming body beneath him, Blue looked up with fire in his eyes.

"Does it look like everything is cool?" He kicked Gamble in the stomach. "Get this piece of shit out of my sight before I kill him."

The two men snatched the injured man to his feet. Holding his face, Gamble panted in pain as they dragged him from the room. Blue un-loosened his tie and took a seat in the leather swivel chair behind his desk.

Moe made his way over to the mini bar and poured them both a shot of Remy Martin. Stepping back across the room, he set the glass on top of the desk and sat down opposite of Blue.

Moe and Blue had been partners for the last two decades. Their relationship began in Attica State Prison when they were cellmates back in 95. They often shared war stories about the treacherous acts they'd committed when they were in the streets and many nights they discussed their plans to pick up where they had left off once they were released from prison. Being that they were from the same city they agreed to watch out for one another and their loyalty carried over into the free-world. Blue was already a certified gangster but Moe help solidify his rise to the top. Moe had come up the hard way. Raised in the Jefferson projects, he quickly learned what it took to survive in the streets. Cunningly dangerous, he wasn't a stranger to gun play and using violence to persuade his victims.

"You think Gamble is telling the truth about the robbery." Moe sipped his drink.

"Gamble doesn't have the heart to cross me but keep an eye on him; you can never be too sure what a nigga will do now a day." Blue replied.

"I'm trying to figure out why they didn't kill him."

"I don't know but I want the name of every stick up kid around the city that you think might have the heart to do something like that."

"What about the girl."

"Put somebody on her as soon as possible." Blue instructed. "She might've set this whole thing up. Find out if she has a brother, boyfriend or baby father; and I want the name of every nigga she's fucked within the last year."

Moe finished his drink in one gulp and stood up to leave.

"Aye Moe!" Blue called out to him. "Get to the bottom of this shit but do it quietly; I don't need any extra heat from the Feds."

"Don't worry, I got it under control. I'm going to put my nephew and his crew on top of it."

"Alright, but make sure they handle it properly."

Moe rode through the city searching for answers. Sitting in the passenger seat of the Benz, he stared out the window on looking the ghetto. A moment of nostalgia took him back to a place that he remembered all too well as he drove past the abandoned store fronts and run down tenements buildings that he once considered home. Moe recalled when the neighborhood flourished with black owned businesses and prominent people who carried themselves with pride. Now everywhere he looked there was desolation, despair and drug addicts traveling throughout the streets without hope in search for a hit. It seemed like every black male growing up in the hood wanted to be a player or a hustler, scheming on a dollar without understanding the consequences of the game.

Moe lit up a cigarette and cracked the window, allowing a winter chill to circulate through the car. Roscoe scanned the radio station for something to listen to.

"Do you want to get something to eat Moe?" Roscoe asked.

"Nah, I'm not hungry." Moe replied. "Run me uptown so I can check on something real quick."

Roscoe turned on to Bailey Ave and kept the car at a steady pace. They drove up and down a couple of side streets until Moe recognized a Escalade parked in front of a group of young men standing outside.

"Pull behind that truck." He pointed to the S.U.V.

As the Mercedes came to a halt, Moe observed Jihad walking towards the Escalade with his hand under his coat.

"Whoa nephew!" He announced, easing the window down. "Put your gun on safety cowboy, I come in peace."

A smile emerged on to Jihad's face once he seen that it was Moe.

"What's good unck?" He placed the pistol back on his hip. "What brings you to this side of town?"

"Get in and take a ride with me, I need to rap with you about some things."

Jihad looked over at Roscoe, trying to read his vibe.

"What good Roscoe?"

"Chillin!" He returned with a slight nod. "What's good with you?"

"I'm out here trying to get it in so I can catch up to ya'll rich niggas." Jihad said.

"That's what's up."

Jihad turned around and gave Jamal some dap. "I'ma call you in a minute cousin. Let me see what unck talking about."

"Handle your business." Jamal replied.

When Jihad climbed into the back of the Benz, Moe increased the volume on the radio in case the car was bugged.

"When are you going to quit nickel and diming and come and get you some real money?" Moe remarked.

"At the end of the day those nickel and dimes add up pimp." Jihad responded. "Everybody don't have the luxury to ride around in Benzes collecting money. Some of us got to get out here and get our fingernails dirty.

Moe chuckled knowing that Jihad was serious. He'd been watching the young man with a close eye ever since he had begun hustling. As a matter of fact, he was the one who had given Jihad his first package of cocaine. Moe wasn't actually his biological uncle but took on the role after Jihad's father Zeak was murdered. Zeak and Moe were like brothers when they were growing up in the projects. They lived on the fifth floor of the same rat infested building downtown and shared many of the same pitfalls of life. They were both born into poverty and destitution and the government assistance that their mothers received was barely enough to keep food on the table so they resulted to the streets for a means of survival. They started out doing burglaries and stealing anything that was considered valuable. Gradually they began doing stick ups around the city, earning a reputation for busting their guns if anyone refused to pay. When Moe was sent to prison for an attempted murder, Zeak decided to fall back from the stick up game and started hustling heroin. Being that he was thorough and ruthless, he exceeded quickly through the ranks of the dope game. By the time Moe was released from Attica State Prison, his partner in crime had gotten rich in the streets of Buffalo.

Moe glanced over at Jihad and recognized the same hunger that lingered in the eyes of Zeak. The similarities between the two were unbelievable. Jihad was like his father reincarnated. He still played the game by the old school rules which were uncommon in today's drug game. Majority of these new age hustlers were caught up with living an extravagant lifestyle of bling bling, popping bottles in the nightclubs and tricking big faces on every chicken head who smiled at them. Jihad was a throwback. He kept a low profile, and never flaunted his wealth. He didn't get high and only drank alcohol on occasions. Moe had seen the potential in him when he was just an adolescent selling nickel bags of weed in the park. He not only had heart but he was also smart and all the other kids in the neighborhood respected him.

"Since you like getting your fingernails dirty, I got a problem that I need you to look into for me." Moe said.

"Talk to me." Jihad replied.

"Do you know the boy Gamble from the eastside?"

"The funny looking nigga from Gibson Street?"

"That's him." Moe confirmed.

"What about him?"

"Somebody hit him for a nice piece of change the other night and I need you to find out who did it."

"How much did he get hit for?"

"Seven bricks and a bill eighty."

Jihad let out a long whistle. "Are you serious? I didn't know that home boy was eating like that."

"That's why it's important for you to get to the bottom of this for me." Moe handed him an envelope.

Jihad opened the envelope and took out the photograph that was attached to a piece of paper with an address written on it.

"Who is this?" He held up picture.

"That's the broad that was with him last night when he got robbed." Moe informed. "She might've set this shit up so check her out and see what you can come up with."

"I'll look into it and get back with you by the end of the week."

Moe leaned back against the leather upholstery and lit up another cigarette.

"If you prove that you can handle this for me, I'm going to make sure that you eat real well. Do you think that you're ready because once you're in, there's no turning back."

"I've been ready!" Jihad expressed with enthusiasm. "Just put me in the huddle and I'm going to perform."

"I'm not only going to put you in the game but I'm going to let you quarterback the offense so don't make me look bad."

After Moe finished giving him the rundown on what he expected, Jihad fell back into his seat with a smile curled up on his face. His plan was coming together slowly and once everything was in order, he'd be a force to be reckoned with.

Moe was right about one thing. Jihad thought to himself. *There was no turning back.*

CHAPTER 6

Later that evening Jihad entered the house to the aroma of turkey wings, rice and cabbage. He kicked his boots off at the door and hung his coat up in the closet.

In the kitchen, Angela was stirring jiffy mix cornbread inside of a bowl while gossiping on the phone.

"Girl, I saw Rachel in the mall the other day lookin a hot mess." She told the person on the other end.

Jihad shook his head at the idle chatter as he crept into the kitchen. He slid behind her and wrapped his arms around Angela, kissing her on the cheek.

"Is the food ready?" He peeked into the pot. "I'm hungry as hell."

Angela held the phone away from her ear as she turned around. "It'll be ready in twenty minutes. I ran you some bath water so go ahead and relax in the tub and I'll call you when it's ready."

"You know how to make a nigga feel like a king when he comes home."

"Your highness would get the royal treatment more often if he came into the castle at a decent hour." Angela sneered.

Playfully slapping her on the ass, Jihad headed for the bathroom. "

"Don't worry baby, I'm going to make it up to you." He shouted back.

"Yeah because you already know that you have a lot of making up to do."

As Jihad soaked in the hot water, he thought back to the conversation that he and Moe had earlier that day. This was the opportunity that he'd been anticipating. Over the years, Jihad had gotten extremely close with the old fellow that he claimed as his uncle but never pledged allegiance to the organization that he formulated. Despite the fact that Moe was the one who put him on, Jihad remained independent. Now that the stakes were being raised, he would have to humble himself and play his position for his plan to be effective.

His thoughts were disturbed by the sound of his phone ringing. He ignored the call, allowing it to go to the voicemail. Moments later, the phone echoed for a second time throughout the bathroom, causing him to reach over and answer it.

"Speak on it."

"Where you at cousin?" Jamal inquired.

"I'm at the building." Jihad responded. "Why? What's up?"

""I'm up here at Oak room and it's mad bitches up in the spot. Throw something on and shoot down here and have a drink with your boy."

"Nah, I'm going to fall back and cool out with wifey tonight. I'll get up with you in the morning."

"Angie got that ass on locked down tonight, huh."

From the slur in his speech, Jihad could tell that Jamal had already been drinking.

"Yeah, I'm going to put some time in with the home front tonight but I'ma link with you first thing tomorrow and let you know the science on that situation from earlier."

Jamal read between the lines of what Jihad was saying. "That's what's up; I'll check you on the A.M."

"Peace!"

After saturating in the tub for a half hour, Jihad made his way back into living room where Angela was still running her mouth on the telephone.

"Tell whoever it is that you're talking to that it's time for you to hang up." He spoke out loud. "You've spent more than enough time talking about other people business today; save some of that shit for tomorrow."

"Mia told me to tell you to shut up, Jihad." Angela said.

"Tell Mia that I said to quit running her dick sucker and get a life."

"I'm not telling her that." Angela screwed her face into a scowl.

"Then don't tell me what her raggedy ass said."

"Mia I'll talk to you tomorrow; my boo needs some attention." Angela ended the call.

She faced Jihad and asked, "Why are you so rude to my friend?"

"Because she's a bad influence on you."

"You don't associate with nothing but crooks so I know that you're not talking." She pressed against him.

He grabbed her by the waist while staring into her eyes. "You know that I love you right?"

"Tell me the reason that you love me."

"Oh, I need a reason to love you now?"

"Yep."

"I love you because you're different." Jihad said. "You're not like the rest of these trifling ass hoes out there in the streets. When I first met you, I knew that you were special. You're the only thing that I have in this life that still hasn't been corrupted and I love you for that."

"Aww baby, I love you too." She kissed him on the lips. "I rented some movies from the Red Box so go ahead and put one of them on while I go in here and fix you a plate."

"What would I do without you?"

"You're a smart person, I'm pretty sure you'd figure it out." Angela smirked as she walked into the kitchen.

After completing their meal, Jihad and Angela cuddled up on the sectional sofa and watch the movie Hoodlum starring Laurence Fishburne. Hoodlum was Jihad's favorite gangster flick. He was captivated by the fact that a nigga who came from the bottom went to war with New York's most treacherous crime figure and came out on top. After the movie, Jihad began nibbling on Angela's ear. She smiled and allowed his hands to explore underneath her Victoria secret nightgown. His masculine touch sent electricity through her body. Sprawled across the couch, they continued kissing and fondling one another. Angela felt the stiffness beneath his boxers as Jihad tightened his embrace. She was aroused, panting softly with every kiss as he removed the sheer garment from over her head exposing her nakedness. With every passing second their lust grew more intense. Angela practically lost control once Jihad buried his face between her legs, tickling the clitoris with the tip of his tongue. In the present moment nothing mattered except the pleasure that she was experiencing. Jihad removed his underpants and slowly slipped inside of her. Angela closed her eyes in ecstasy as he thrust her in a deep circular motion.

"Damn this pussy wet!" Jihad moaned in a low voice.

It had been well over a week since he had felt the warmth of Angela's silky vagina. He flipped her over into a doggystyle position and started fucking her from the back. Their rhythm increased with every stroke as Jihad's pelvis slapped against her voluptuous ass.

Just as he was about to bust, Angela spun round and took him into her mouth. She sucked her juices off his dick until he exploded. Palming the back of her head, Jihad released every drop of semen down Angela's throat.

"Damn, you a beast girl!"

Angela nodded in agreement, kissing the head of his limp penis.

"I missed my little friend." She smiled mischievously.

"I see!" Jihad replied. "If you keep performing like that, I might not never leave the house."

Angela sneered. "That's what you're mouth say but as soon as that phone get to ringing, you'll find some reason to get up out of here. Talking about baby, I got some business that I need to go and handle, I'll be back later." She mocked his vernacular.

They shared a laugh.

"Okay, you got jokes." Jihad said. "I'll give you that lil bit. Now go in the bathroom and brush that dick off your breath."

"Shut up!" She mushed him. "You need to be following me so you can wash my pussy off of your face."

When she returned from the bathroom, Jihad was deep in thought. Over the years that they had been together, Angela had seen that expression on many of occasions. The look on his face was confirmation that he was about to do something crazy.

Jihad had never brought the streets into their home but Angela had heard stories about the atrocities that he was capable of.

"What are you thinking about?"

"Jihad snapped out of his heavy contemplation and faced her.

"Baby we need to talk."

"What are you about to do?" Angela questioned. "I know when you got that look in your eyes that you're about to do something crazy. I don't have time for your..."

"Would you shut up and listen to me for a minute." Jihad raised his voice. "This shit is important so sit down and chill out."

She sat on the edge of the bed and asked, "What's wrong?"

Before answering, Jihad let out a deep breath."

"After the baby is born, I want you to move down to Virginia with your sister for a while." He looked her in the eyes.

Angela stared back at him with confusion.

"What are you talking about Jihad?"

"Listen to me Angel face. Something major is about to pop off and I don't want you or the baby to get hurt behind my negligence."

"I'm not going anywhere without you and I'm definitely not about to go to Virginia with my sister and her bullshit."

"Please do this for me Angie." He rubbed the side of her face. "I'm about to raise the stakes out here in the streets and I can't afford for you to get caught up in the crossfire. Niggas are going to try their best to get at me even if they have to harm my family to do it and I'm not going to allow that to happen."

Tears welled up in Angela's eyes.

"C'mon Ang don't do that to me." Jihad wiped away her tears with his thumb. "Don't break down on me now; I need you to be strong."

"What if something happens to you Jihad? What am I supposed to do then huh? Raise our child by myself."

"Quit thinking like. Ain't nothing going to happen to me."

"How can you be so sure? Can you promise me that my daughter is going to have a father? How do you know that you won't get killed or have to kill somebody and wind up spending the rest of your life in prison. Huh Jihad answer me that!"

There was an awkward silence in the air.

"Exactly!" Angela said. "You can't promise me that because anything is bound to happen when you're standing on dangerous grounds."

"I guess that you're just going to have to trust me."

"Baby, I do trust you but the odds are not always going to be in your favor. There's going to come a time when you're going to have to put the streets behind you, willingly or unwillingly. Were about to start a family and I'm afraid that I may lose you. Why can't we just leave together?"

"I'm not going to be able to do that right now; I gotta get this money first. Plus there's some unfinished business that I need to handle before I pick up and leave."

"You are so selfish. I can't believe that you are willing to risk everything that we have."

Jihad pulled her close to his chest and stared into her lovely eyes.

"Give me another year to grid my paper up and I promise that I'm going to fall back." He told her sincerely.

"You promise?"

"Cross my heart and hope to die, stick a needle in my eye." He raised his right hand while holding his left across his chest.

"You so damn silly boy." She tried not to laugh. "You make me sick."

"Sickly in love." He pulled her back on top of him. "Now c'mere and give me a kiss."

After another round of hot sex, they discussed their plans for the future until the early hour of the morning then dozed off to sleep.

*****

By twelve o'clock midnight, The Oak Room was filled to the capacity. Men and women alike had come out to unwind and enjoy themselves, forgetting about the struggles of everyday life. The Oak Room was a small bar that attracted many of the ghetto celebrities as well as young professional athletes. Hood rats in disguise wore their best costume with hopes of catching a baller by the end of the night. Dozens of people congregated around the bar, trying to get the bartender's attention for a drink. Others were off to the side talking and laughing amongst one another. When the song Energy by Drake came on, half of the women rushed the dance floor and started shaking their ass.

Ducked off in the corner, Jamal was sitting at a table, conversing with a nigga name Dog. He was nursing a double shot of Hennessey while his partner attended to a plate of hot wings and fries. Even though they were in the cut, the two men were far from inconspicuous. Their reputation exceeded them and majority of the club knew who they were and what they were capable of so wandering eyes continuously shifted in their direction.

The stones in Jamal ears brightened the natural glow of his brown complexion as he sipped his drink.

"Is Jihad and Stone coming up here tonight?" Dog asked between bites of his food.

"Nah, family said that he was going to fall back and chill wit wifey but Stone supposed to meet me up here." Jamal replied.

"True."

Dog was six feet and two inches of all muscle due to the short stints he spent at the Erie county correctional facility. A dark skinned brother with a low fade, he reminded people of slender version of Beanie Sigel. He was the serious type nigga who didn't smile much. Unlike Jamal, Dog was a heartless killer that ran with pack of wolves responsible for over a dozen homicides throughout the city.

Glancing across the dance floor, Dog noticed two females peeping at him and Jamal through the mirror as they gyrated to the music.

"You know them hoes over there?" He nudged Jamal with an elbow, nodding towards the dance floor.

"Where?" Jamal scanned the room.

"Them two bitches over there next to the mirror. They've been watching us all night."

After seeing who Dog was talking about Jamal shook his head.

"Nah, I don't know them hoes but I wouldn't mind getting to know them."

"Those bitches are ready to shake something." Dog professed. "Every time I look up they're in our grill. I'm about to go and see what's up."

"Go ahead and see what they're talking about." Jamal urged.

Demanding their attention, Dog gestured them over with a wave of the hand. Without breaking eye contact, the women sashayed through the crowd to where the gangsters were seated. The mocha complexion female looked familiar to Jamal the closer she got but he couldn't remember where he seen her before. Her body was banging. The Prada dress that she had on hugged every curve on her physical form, leaving little room for the imagination.

"What's up Jamal?" She spoke in the sweetest little voice. "I was wondering if you were going to holler at me before the end of the night."

"What's good ma; how have you been?" Jamal replied. "Your face looks familiar but I can't place where I know you from. Refresh my memory."

"My girls and I hung out with you and your crew in Toronto at the Caribana last year.

"Damn Trina, what's good?" A light went off in Jamal's head as he stood to give her a hug. Your hair was cut shorter back then and that's what threw me off. How have you been? I see that you're still looking good."

"I can't complain; life has been good." Trina smiled, revealing a set of dimples in her cheek.

"That's what's up!" he looked over at the woman beside her. "Are you going to introduce me to your friend?"

"Oh I'm sorry." Trina apologized. "Jamal this is my friend Chanel; Chanel this is the famous Mr. Jamal."

"I wouldn't say all that." Jamal shook Chanel's hand.

Calling Chanel pretty would be an understatement; the girl was drop dead gorgeous. Her smooth butter skin didn't have a blemish or pimple in sight. She had the face of an angel and the body of goddess. The leather skirt, gripping her ass revealed a set of shaven legs which stood erect in a pair of Jimmy Choo stiletto pumps, adding another three inches to her frame.

"This is my partner Dog." Jamal introduced his friend to the ladies,

They all exchanged greetings as the women took a seat.

"What are you girls drinking?" Dog asked, flagging the waitress over to their table.

"Order me a apple martini." Trina said.

"And I'll have a Hennessey and coke." Chanel added.

The waitress looked over at Dog to complete the order.

"Bring my man another double shot of Hennessey and bring me a double shot of Don Julio.

The waitress cleared the empty glasses from the table and carried them off to the back. While Dog engaged in a conversation with Chanel, Jamal focused on Trina.

"The last time that we saw each other, you were drunk as hell getting loose." Jamal laughed at the memory.

"I had so much fun with you and your boy's that weekend." Trina admitted. "I slept for two whole days after partying with y'all."

"Yeah we did do it big that weekend." Jamal confirmed. "The parade was off the chain and although it was raining, we still got it poppin."

"Especially when your friend stole that case of Champagne from out of the liquor store."

"Oh shit, I forgot Stone and em had run in the spot on Young Street and started snatching shit."

"Mmm hmm, I remember everything that went down on that trip."

"I bet you do."

"What is that supposed to mean?"

"You know what I'm talking about."

"Don't even start." She smiled. "What about your other boy Jiheed?"

"You're talking about Jihad."

"Yeah, Jihad! What has he been up to; he was cool as hell. My girl Nicky still be talking about him. She was really in to dude."

"He's been alright." Jamal told her.

The waitress appeared with their drinks and set them on to the table. Dog paid the bill, adding a healthy tip while instructing her to bring him a Heineken.

Jamal wet his throat with a sip of his drink.

"What about you?" He turned back to Trina. "What have you been up to lately?"

"Between work and school, I don't have time for anything else besides my kids."

"What about that nigga that you had in your life." Jamal probed. "Do you still have that problem?"

"Pst, that nigga ain't shit." Trina rolled her eyes with disgust. "I had to get rid of his ass. If it weren't for my kids, I wouldn't even speak to that bastard."

"Damn, it's like that?"

"You know how it is when ya'll niggas get out of jail and start getting a little bit of money? Ya'll start walking around here like ya'll shit don't stink; acting all brand new. Y'all forget about the ones that was there for you when you didn't have a pot to piss in or a window to throw it out of."

"So the nigga flipped the script on you once he got his paper up?"

"You know how ya'll niggas do." Trina said. "But I'm not going to talk bad about him because I still got love for him despite our differences and he is the father or my child."

"I respect that." Jamal said. "So where am I going to fit into your life?

"Where do you want to fit in at?"

"Hopefully I can be the rainbow after the storm and there's always a pot of gold at the end of every rainbow."

Trina smiled and tasted her Martini.

"Save all that game for them chicken heads who don't know any better. If you want to fuck just tell me that you want to fuck. You don't have to beat around the bush; I already know what time it is with niggas like you."

Caught off guard by her last statement, Jamal was at lost for words but quickly recovered.

"You don't hold any punches do you? He smirked. "I like a woman that's not afraid to say what's on her mind."

"Life is too short to be playing games." She told him. "If it's just going to be a fuck thing then we need to get that understood from the gate. I don't need you to fill my head up with a bunch of bullshit then shit on a bitch after you get the pussy. You never know, I might just want to catch me a nut without any strings attached."

"Oh yeah, I like you." Jamal nodded.

"Three Martinis and a shot of Vodka later, Trina had a nice buzz and was ready to leave. Her son was at her mother's for the weekend so she agreed to spend the night with Jamal at a hotel. She looked over at Chanel and Dog as they engaged in what seemed to be a deep conversation. They seemed to have a positive chemistry and from the look in Chanel's eyes, Trina could tell that she was feeling him.

"Excuse me Miss Thang!" She interrupted them. "I don't mean to intervene on your conversation but I gotta pee so can you come to the ladies room with me?"

"I'll be right back." She told Dog. "I'm going to run to the restroom with her right quick."

"Why do all females go to the bathroom together?" Dog questioned. "Do ya'll wipe each other's ass or something?"

"It's a girl thing honey, you wouldn't understand."

Trina led the way across the bar with Chanel on her heels. When they entered the ladies room, there was a woman occupying one of the stalls. She didn't pay them any mind as she powdered her nose with some Peruvian flakes.

Chanel was astonished when she realized what the woman was doing.

"Don't sweat it girl." Trina noticed the expression on her face. "That's how they get down in here."

At the sound of Trina's voice, the woman looked up from the package of poison. She walked over to the mirror and wiped the crystal fragments from around her nostrils.

"Do you girls toot?" She held out the bag of powder.

"Nah sweetie, I don't get down." Chanel declined.

Still clenching the bag of dust between her fingers, she turned to Trina for a response. Chanel stared at her friend in disbelief as she accepted the bag.

"Trina!"

"What!"

"Uh uh, I know that you're not about to do that?" Chanel barked.

"Don't trip!" Trina replied. "Every once in a while I fuck around but I'm not strung out or nothing. I just like to have a good time when I'm partying so don't spoil the mood."

Perplexed at what she was witnessing, Chanel watched Trina dip her pinky nail into the package and fill her nose with death. Allowing the drug to take its effect, Trina closed her eyes.

"That's some good shit." She opened her eyes.

"I'm Vanessa." The woman introduced herself.

Trina shook her hand and said, "My name is Trina and this is my friend Chanel." She pointed to the woman who was obviously vexed.

"I'm sorry, I didn't mean any disrespect." Vanessa apologized to Chanel. I just thought that you lady's might've wanted to have a little fun. I hope that I didn't offend you."

"You didn't offend me." Chanel tried to hide her irritation. "Do you! Who am I to stop you from doing what it is you do?"

The women made small talk for several minutes before exiting the restroom. When they stepped back into the party, Vanessa dispersed into the crowd as Chanel and Trina made their way back to the table.

Jamal looked up and caught a glimpse of Vanessa disappear amongst the large group of people in the room.

It hasn't been twenty four hour since she was duct taped and gagged and here she is back in the club getting her freak on. Dumb bitch!"

He brushed off the thought as his company returned to their seats. There was an awkward silence between the ladies and Dog and Jamal could feel the negative energy.

"Is everything good?" Dog spoke up.

"Everything is cool but I'm about to get ready to go." Chanel yawned. "I have to get up early and go to work tomorrow morning."

"I thought that we were going to kick it and get a bite to eat?" Dog sounded disappointed.

"I would love to go and get something to eat with you tonight but I can't afford to be late for work tomorrow; I have a meeting with the V.P. of our corporation and he can be an asshole at times."

"What type of work do you do?"

"I'm a financial consultant for a company called M&J Associates."

"Interesting!"

"Not really. It gets to be a headache sometimes."

"So when am I going to see you again?"

Chanel handed Dog her cell phone.

"Put your number in my phone and I'll call you tomorrow when I get off."

"At least let me walk you to your car."

"Are you ready to go?" She asked Trina.

I'm going to catch a ride with Jamal." Trina confirmed. "I'll call you tomorrow."

We all might as well bounce then." Jamal finished the rest of his drink.

They stepped outside and headed towards the parking lot. A gentle wind cut through the air as they made their way to their vehicles. While crossing the lot, a dark blue dodge intrepid blew the horn and flashed its lights to get their attention.

"Who is that?" Dog asked unable to see inside the car.

"I don't know." Jamal responded and kept it moving.

Suddenly someone emerged from the car and yelled, "Jamal!"

Upon hearing his name, he spun around and stopped. Stone was walking towards them smoking a blunt.

"What's up my nigga?" He passed Jamal the blunt. "I've been blowing you up all night; why you aint answer the horn."

Jamal took out his cellular and looked at the screen. There were several missed calls.

"I didn't hear it ring." He inhaled the smoke. "The music was loud as hell in there. I was wondering what happened to you."

"I've been out here parking lot pimpin for about an hour. I didn't feel like being bothered with the same broke bitches that be up in there every week."

"They were definitely up in there." Dog added.

"I already know." Stone said, looking at the two women standing beside them. "What ya'll about to go and do?"

"We was about to call it a night."

"Let's go and get something to eat."

"Let me walk her to the car and then we can do whatever."

Dog stepped off with Chanel, leaving Jamal and Stone to talk.

"Do you remember Trina?" Jamal pointed to her.

Stone stepped back and examined her from head to toe.

"Yeah, I remember Trina. She was up at the Caribana with us last year with her girlfriends. How you doin ma? Long time no see."

Trina smiled. "I'm doing good. How have you been?"

"It's the same fight but a different round and don't nothing move out here but the money."

"I know that's right." She replied then turned to Jamal. "Where are you parked at? I can wait for you in the car while you talk to Stone."

Jamal pressed the automatic starter button on his key ring, causing the Escalade to come to life 10 yards away.

"The CDs are on the floor." He handed her the keys.

She took the keys and said, "It was nice seeing you again Stone."

"It was nice seeing you too.

Stone and Jamal watch her ass jiggle over to the car.

Where did you find her at?" Stone inquired.

"She was up in the spot with her girlfriend eye fucking a nigga from the dance floor." Jamal responded. "I didn't even recognize her at first."

"What you bout to go and do; slide through the telly and dig her back out?"

"You already know that I'm about to go and smash that something proper."

"No doubt!" Stone gave him dap.

"Make sure that you hit me up on the A.M. so we can link with cousin and put the wheels in motion on that situation."

"That's a fact!"

CHAPTER 7

"Oh shit, I'm about to cum!" Trina moaned as she came to a climax

"Jamal tugged at her hair while fucking her from the back. Her head slammed against the wall with every stroke, screams echoing throughout the room. They had been at it well into the morning and Trina was working on her second orgasm. This had been some of the best sex she'd experienced in her twenty five years. Jamal had her wide open as he plunged into her canal. She took it like champ and Jamal was surprised when she didn't shy away but instead met him thrust for thrust. Switching positions, he laid back, allowing Trina to mount him. She stared him in the face and eased down slowly as she began rotating her hips. While entangled into one another her juices oozed down onto the sheets.

"Damn!" Jamal clenched her ass. "You like this dick don't you?"

"I love this dick!" She nodded, speeding up the pace.

The sensation sent chills up her spine. Without warning, Jamal flipped her over and pushed deep inside of her, causing Trina to squirm to the top of the bed. Hanging halfway off the mattress, she felt a mixture of pain and pleasure as Jamal beat the pussy with force. With every pump the pressure increased. He then grabbed her by the throat and began choking her lightly. She begged for more, gasping for air. This excited Jamal and he could feel himself about to explode.

"I'm about to bust." He warned, "Where do you want it at?"

"Wherever you want to put it." Trina exhaled as he released her throat.

Jamal pulled out and ejaculated on to her face. She opened her mouth, attempting to intercept drops of his semen. Jamal let out long grunt and collapsed on the bed. Exhausted, he laid back and closed his eyes but Trina was far from finished. Slowly crawling across the mattress, she placed it back into her mouth and started performing oral sex on him.

"Oh shit girl!" Jamal huffed. "What are you tryna do to me?"

Trina didn't respond as she stroked him with both hands, bobbing her head up and down. Her fingers were lubricated with spit, permitting slob to run down his balls. In a state of rapturous delight, Jamal slipped his thumb up her ass as he put two fingers in her vagina.

"Mmm." Trina moaned, continuing to please him.

She sucked his shaft with so much intensity that it rose back to the occasion within a matter of minutes. Grabbing a fist full of her hair, Jamal shoved himself back and forth down her throat. Oral sex was a talent that Trina had perfected when she was fifteen so she devoured the dick without gagging or scraping her teeth. Once he was fully erect, she pulled him on top of her and allowed him to go to work. With her legs on his shoulders, He hurled himself into her. Their bodies slapped together for twenty minutes and Trina was to the point where she'd had enough. She shook uncontrollably as Jamal released a glob of sperm into her before pulling out. Intertwined between the sheets, they laid there sweating and breathing heavily before passing out.

The next morning, Jamal awoke to the sound of housekeeping knocking at the door.

"Hold up!" He yelled out. "We're about to check out."

He rolled over and checked the time on his cell phone. It was a quarter past eleven. Trina was still asleep, snoring softly.

"Get up and get yourself together." Jamal shook her awake. "It's time to go."

Wiping the crust out of her eyes, she sat up and yawned. "What time is it?"

"It's time to go."

"Can I get another taste before we leave?" Trina licked her lips, reaching for his manhood.

"Bitch quit playing and get dress!" Jamal pushed her hand away. "I got some business I need to handle and I'm already late so stop fuckin off and come on."

"Oh now I'm a bitch?" She questioned flabbergasted. "Fuck you Jamal, I already knew what it was with you before we had sex so I'm not surprised and I'm not about to trip."

Trina got out of the bed and started gathering her clothing off of the floor. Jamal watched her rant and rave as she headed for the bathroom.

"I expected your trifling ass to pull some bullshit like this." He cursed him. "But you don't have to worry about me fucking with your ass ever again."

As she closed the door, she noticed Jamal rushing towards her. He pushed his way up in the bathroom and threw her against the wall.

"Who in the fuck do you think you're talking too?" He wrapped his hand around her neck. "I'm not one of these sucka's that you be out here fucking with so you better watch your mouth."

"Get the fuck off of me!" She struggled to get free.

Jamal subdued Trina with force and bent her over the sink and entered her from behind.

"Is this what you want bitch?" He rammed himself in and out of her. "Is this what you want?"

She stopped resisting and allowed him to have his way. Trina was aroused by the way that he was manhandling her so she slammed her ass back at him with every thrust he took. A sinister smiled curled up on Jamal's lips as he stared at the episode through the mirror. He could see that he had Trina where he wanted her by her facial expressions. He pulled out of the pussy and squirted cum on her back, marking his territory.

"Now quit playing with me and get your ass in the shower." He slapped her on the behind.

Trina sucked her teeth but complied with his instructions. She got in the shower and washed the scent of sex off of her body. Her pussy was sensitive from the pounding it had received. Gently scrubbing her tenderness, Trina thought about the incident that had just occurred. The way that Jamal Had forced himself on to her had actually turned her on. A man had never dominated her the way that he'd done and she couldn't deny the emotions swelling up inside of her. She was sprung!

A light draft went through her as Jamal pulled the shower curtain back and stepped in. Admiring his chiseled frame, Trina began to soap him up. As he rinsed off, she could see the tension melt away as the stemming water beat down on his body.

After getting out of the shower, they quickly dressed. While Jamal was busy talking on the phone, Trina examined herself in the mirror. Her hair was a mess. It had been sweated out and a small amount of sperm had dried up into her weave.

She walked over to where Jamal was finishing up his conversation and said, "Look at what you did."

"What are you talking about?" He closed his phone.

"You got it in my hair." Trina pointed to the nut stain.

Jamal laughed as he reached into his pocket and pulled out his money.

"I got something important that I need to go and take care of so you're going to have to catch a cab home." He handed her two hundred dollars. "After you get yourself together, I want you to go down to Salon Soar on Bailey Ave and ask for my home girl Candy. Tell her that I sent you and to call me if that is not enough money to get your hair done the way you want it."

"Thank you." Trina smiled.

"That's nothing ma! It get better than that as long as you're willing to play your position without letting emotions get in the way."

"I'm not going to let my emotions get the best of me but I'm not going to sit up here and let you disrespect me by calling me all types of bitches either."

"I didn't mean any disrespect when I called you a bitch that's just the way that I talk." Jamal explained.

Trina stepped up in Jamal's face and pressed her body against his.

"You keep fucking me the way you did this morning and you can call me anything you want as long as you call me. She grabbed the crotch of his pants.

"You don't gotta worry about that because as soon as I'm done handling my business I'll be calling to double back on some of that good throat that you got."

*****

By the time Jamal pulled up to the honeycomb hideout, it was almost one o'clock in the afternoon. When he stepped into the house, he was greeted by the fumes of cocaine in the air. Clad in a Brand New Life T-shirt, Red Robin jeans and Timberland boots, Jihad was in the kitchen hovered over the stove. He worked his magic as he mixed the contents inside of the Pyrex pot. Jihad had a serious whip game when it came to cooking powder. For every nine ounces cooked, he was able to bring back an extra four ounces of crack without losing its potency.

Stone was playing Madden on the PS4, smoking a blunt of Kush when Jamal came into the front room. He blew out a stream of smoke and passed him the weed as he continued playing the game.

"Shawty must've had some good pussy if you're just now getting your day started." He stated without looking up from the television screen.

"Shorty was like burger king." Jamal gripped his testicles. "I had it my way, anyway and in every way. I thought that the hoe was going to suck the skin off of my dick the way she was eating it up."

"She looks like she's an undercover freak."

Jamal hit the blunt and said, "Freak isn't the word to describe her. Ol girl is a real nymphomaniac and I plan to have some fun with her nasty ass."

"Don't fuck around and fall in love." Stone paused the game. "A bitch like that will throw a nigga off his square."

"Don't you ever disrespect my gangster like that nigga! You know that I don't give a fuck about a bitch. I don't need em. All I do is fuck em and leave em for the man to feed em."

Jamal gave Stone some dap as they burst out laughing. He hit the Cush a few more times then headed into the kitchen.

With his cell phone pressed between his shoulder and ear, Jihad removed the Pyrex from the stove and set it down in a sink full of ice. He acknowledged Jamal with a nod as he ran cold water into the pot, containing the drugs. Using a butter knife, he wedged a thick slab of crack from the bottom of the pot and put it on the countertop to dry. Jamal gave him some dap and looked at all of the paraphernalia lying around the kitchen. Next to the digital scale there was a box of arm and hammer baking soda along with two boxes of sandwich bags spread across the table. From the looks of it, it appeared that Jihad had cooked up three of the five bricks they had stashed in the basement.

"How long have you been at it?" Jamal questioned.

Jihad hung up the phone and replied, "I been here since nine o'clock this morning tryna get this shit together."

Jamal sensed the agitation in his voice. They were supposed to meet early that morning but he had allowed a piece of pussy to distract him.

"My fault fam, I got caught up with this little breezy that I bagged at The Oak Room last night and I fucked around and over slept."

"C'mon cousin that's unacceptable." Jihad shook his head. "We got a lot riding on this thing of ours so I need you to walk with me every step of the way."

Jamal understood where Jihad was coming from so he didn't contest his case. It would only lead to a dispute which he was trying to avoid. His head was already throbbing from the amount of alcohol that he had consumed the night before and arguing would only add to its annoyance.

"So what's the move?" He quickly changed the subject.

Jihad placed 250 grams of coke on the scale.

"Remember when Moe rolled up on me yesterday?"

"Yeah, I remember." Jamal responded with a raised brow. "What was he talking about?"

"He wants me to find out who ran up in Gamble's spot and took they shit." Jihad smirked, placing the Pyrex back on the stove.

Jamal laughed. "What did you say?"

Jihad shot him a look that said, *what the fuck do you think I told him?*

"I told him that I would look into it and get back with him by the end of the week."

Pouring baking soda into the pot, Jihad stirred it into the water until it began to fizz. Once it started to sputter, he added the 250 grams of powder into the combination and mixed the compound together. Jamal watched as the chemicals dissolved into a liquid form.

"So how do you plan to play this situation out?" Jamal asked

"I'ma give him what he want." Jihad said, holding the pot away from the stove. "He wants me to find out who took they shit then that's exactly what I'm going to do."

As he whipped the oil into submission, Jihad explained the details of his plan. They were going to monitor Vanessa's schedule for a few days then break into her house when she wasn't home and hide two kilos of coke. Once he reported back to Moe, it wouldn't take Jihad much to convince him that she had knowledge about the robbery.

"And knowing Moe, he'll have us double back with one of his soldiers to smack the broad around for some information. And after we rough her up a little bit, we're going to search the spot and get the bricks that we stashed to make her look guilty."

"I saw shorty last night." Jamal said.

"Who Vanessa?"

"Yeah, the hoe was up in Oak Room last night partying and shit."

"Are you serious?"

"Dead ass serious!"

"I guess the bitch haven't learned yet, huh?" Jihad smirked. "She's not going to be happy until she is somewhere slumped in a dumpster."

Stone walked into the kitchen and handed Jamal the remainder of the blunt. He leaned against the counter and exhaled, mixing the marijuana smoke with cocaine fumes lingering in the apartment.

"It sound like you got this shit all figured out." Stone insinuated. "How long have you been putting this thing together?"

Jihad paused and thought back to the day that he decided that he wanted to control the city's drug market.

"I've been lying on this shit for so long ya'll probably wouldn't believe me if I told you."

As he continued to twist and turn the oil inside of the pot, Stone and Jamal watched until it finally locked up. For the next two hours, Jihad repeated the process until all of the powder was transformed into crack and ready for the block.

CHAPTER 8

Meanwhile, Trina was at Exquisites beauty parlor, getting pampered for the evening. Leaned back in her seat, she received a pedicure from a loud mouth chick name Sugar while Candy put the finishing touch on her weave Salon Soar was like a woman's country club in the hood. This is where most baby mamas and mistresses of ghetto celeb's came to get glamorous while discussing the latest gossip around the town. This was actually the first time that Trina had stepped foot inside of the extravagant salon but she was familiar with many of the stories that were told by its patrons.

"Did you hear what happened to Kamesha?" Sugar asked Candy.

"Candy shook her head. "Nah, what happened?"

"You know that she just had a baby right?"

"I knew that she was pregnant by that sexy ass nigga who be pushin that Range Rover. What's his name?"

"Rick!" Sugar confirmed. "And he is not all that sexy."

"That nigga money is longer than train smoke so the mutha fucka is sexy to me, I don't care what you say." Candy reciprocated.

"I know that's right." Trina slapped hands with candy.

"Anyway!" Sugar emphasized. "Come to find out, the baby not even his. It's the boy Rondo's baby."

"Girl, you lyin!" Candy was marveled. "Isn't that supposed to be his right hand man?"

"Mmm hmm that's what I thought."

"I didn't think that Kamesha was all that scandalous the way she be coming in here flaunting around like her shit don't stink."

"Hmph." Trina huffed. "Those are the main ones.'

She hardly knew these women and Trina was already feeding into their bullshit.

Sugar wasn't surprised at how comfortable Trina was in their presence. Many of her clients felt secure enough to speak their mind in a room full of inquisitive women. In fact, Sugar and Candy rendered their services, expecting some type of gossip in return. They both had been working at Salon Soar since it opened and they loved the drama that came along with it. Sugar was a nail technician who stayed in everyone's business. She wasn't all that cute but was sexy as hell with some of the sweetest pussy that a nigga ever tasted.

Candy was cool as a fan but was quick to whip a bitch ass if came to that. She would entertain the chatter of the women around the shop but didn't let it interfere with her hustle. Candy was about her paper! She began doing hair in her grandmother's kitchen back when she was in junior high and been on the grind ever since.

By four o'clock in the afternoon, the shop was semi crowded with ladies all shapes and sizes. Some were getting their hair washed or sitting under the dryer while others were getting a sew in. Those who were waiting in the lounging area were either glancing through a magazine or watching the lifetime channel.

The telephone rang and one of the beauticians walked across the shop to answer it.

"Is it somebody in here name Trina?" She yelled with the cordless pressed against her ear.

"That's me!" Trina signaled with a raised hand.

"Jamal told me to ask you is everything cool?"

"Tell him that I'm almost done and that I'll call him as soon as I leave the shop."

As she relayed the message, the other beauticians exchanged glances at one another. They watched an uneasy expression spread across Sugar's brow as she wrinkled up at Trina. She quickly recovered but her co-workers had already noticed the disapproval written on her face.

Sugar and Jamal use to have a sexual relationship before he cut her off a few months back. To him she was nothing more than a piece of ass but Sugar had developed strong feelings and wanted to take their relationship to the next level. Seeing that she was getting caught up in her emotions, Jamal fell back from her without an explanation. He hadn't returned her calls in over a month and now he was calling her job for another bitch.

"Where do you know Jamal from?" Sugar asked.

"Excuse me?" Trina was caught off guard by the question.

"I asked you where do you know Jamal from." She repeated with a hint of anger in her voice.

Trina glared around the shop and observed a room full of women eagerly awaiting her response. Surrounded by sharks, she treaded the waters carefully.

"I know him from my brother."

"Ya'll messin around or something?" Sugar continued to press.

"Nah sweetie relax, it's not even like that. Jamal and I are just friends."

"Oh ya'll just friends huh? Well if you are fucking him, I hope that you don't think that he's going to settle down because the nigga ain't shit but a hoe."

"Come on now Suge." Candy intervened. "I'm not going to sit up here and let you talk bad about my boy Jamal like that."

"Don't even try and front Candy; you know that Jamal aint shit. All that nigga want to do is chase pussy and rob niggas. He doesn't give a fuck about nobody but himself."

Trina rose up out of her seat and examined her hair in the mirror. Candy had her looking like Jets beauty of the week, she thought to herself. Satisfied with Candy's work, she paid her for the services before responding to Sugars last statement.

"Apparently there are some issues that you need to bring to Jamal's attention." She spun around to address Sugar. "I am not the enemy sweetheart. Like I said before, I know Jamal from my brother and he suggested that I let Candy do my hair because she does good work from what I can see. Now if you have a problem with that, I suggest that you take that up with him."

"I don't have a problem with him or you; I'm just letting you know how the nigga get down before you get caught up."

"Well that's something that you don't have to worry about." Trina clarified. "Now how much do I owe you for my nails?"

"Fifty dollars." Sugar replied.

Trina handed her three twenty dollar bills from out of her pocket book. "Keep the change boo!" She told her as she left the salon.

CHAPTER 9

The evening approached slowly as the sun set into the western hemisphere. Incognito, Remy sat beside Stone inside of a tinted out Ford Taurus. In the rear seat, Lil P was shifting back and forth. He was on his third New Port within the last hour. The three of them had been camp out down the street from Vanessa's house for the better part of the day, waiting for her to leave. Although Jihad had instructed his young soldiers on what to do, Stone still went with them to make sure the job was done properly.

"When ya'll niggas go up in there, don't touch nothin." Stone spoke from behind the steering wheel. "Just stash the work somewhere that she would never look and come right back."

"C'mon Stone, you've been telling us the same shit all day." Remy said. "What do you think we're stupid or something? "

"Nah lil nigga, I'm just making sure that ya'll know what the fuck is going on because I don't want to have to fuck you up for not following instructions."

"Don't worry fam, we got this." Lil P puffed his cigarette, causing the tip of the tobacco to glare as he inhaled. "But I still don't understand the science behind us breaking up into shorty house to stash some work. I thought that we were supposed to be taking this type of shit not giving it away?"

"Word up!" Remy said. "I ain't never heard of no shit like that unless it was some police type shit and I know Family don't rock like that so I'm not going to question the method behind his madness."

While they were conversing, a car pulled up into Vanessa's driveway and blew the horn. Moments later, she came strutting out of the house holding a four year boys hand.

"There she go right there." Remy glanced down at the photograph that Jihad had given them.

Appearing to be in a hurry, she got in the awaiting vehicle with her son and pulled off. Once they were out of sight, Lil P and Remy gathered their burglary tools and hopped out the Taurus.

Still in the driver seat, Stone rolled the window down and said, "Yo don't touch..."

"We're not going to touch nothing Stone, chill out." Lil P cut him off.

"We'll be right back." Remy told him as they moved towards the house.

*****

Back on the block, it was the same hustle as any other day. Crack heads were scampering back and forth through the avenue, chasing a high and Zae had been out there since the crack of dawn to serve them. Out of all the young hustlers in the neighborhood, Zae was the most dedicated to the grind. He hugged the block morning, noon and night regardless of the weather. It didn't matter if it was rain, sleet or snow; he didn't take any days off and was always the first one outside and the last to leave.

Across the street Jihad and Jamal stood on alert as Zae distributed crack to the fiends from out of an abandoned yard. It was the first of the month so there was a consistent flow of the customers, stampeding the strip in search for a hit. The new product that they had put out there had the smoker's wide open.

A hype name Debra approached Zae as he was completing a transaction with another addict from up the block. She had been on a three day binge and she looked exhausted. If a person took a good look at her, they would be able to see that she had once been an attractive woman but the years that she spent addicted to drugs had took its wear and tear.

"Hey baby." Debra spoke in a course like voice. "Let me get a fifty."

Zae grabbed the money from her outstretched hand and replaced it with a ½ gram.

"If you come back and I'm not out here, call me and I'll come to you." He gave her a torn piece of paper with a number on it.

As Delores made her way up the street, Jamal shook his head at the pitiful sight before him. He remembered a few years back when she was a caramel colored bombshell sought after by every hustler within a thirty mile radius. Now as she disappeared around the corner he couldn't help but think back to when she was in her prime.

"Remember when Delores used to be fine as hell back in the day?" Jamal nudged Jihad.

"Yeah I remember nigga." Jihad replied. "You use to be in love with her mutha fuckin ass. You act like you wanted to marry the bitch and everything."

They both burst out laughing.

"Go ahead with that bullshit; didn't nobody want to marry that hoe."

Jihad cut his eyes at Jamal and sneered.

"Quit frontin cousin. You use to want to fight a nigga if they said something bad about Delores."

"I ain't gon front; I use to have a little crush on her when I was younger." Jamal admitted. "But don't act like I was the only one infatuated with her because if I remember correctly, you had a thing for her too."

"Not like you." Jihad defended. "And if my memory serves me correctly, Delores was one of the reasons that you wanted to start hustling."

"You crazy as hell; I was tryna come up on some paper."

"Nah, you was tryna come up on some pussy; you wasn't thinking about the paper until later on."

"Why you say that?" Jamal asked.

"Because you were like c'mon cuz put me on." Jihad mocked him in a childlike vernacular. "I'm tryna eat wit ya'll so I can get a girl like Delores."

Jamal Laughed at Jihad's exaggeration.

"I ain't never said no shit like that." He said. "But she was a star back then; I wonder why she started getting high?"

"I was just talking to Remy and them about this shit the other day. I was trying to explain to them niggas how the best get caught up in the allure of the streets but they wasn't tryna hear me."

"I've seen plenty go out bad but it fucked me up to see her go out like that. She could've done something with her life."

"You sound like you still in love or something." Jihad joked. "Let me find out that after all these years, pimpin ass Jamal still got a crush on his childhood sweetheart."

"There you go with that bullshit." Jamal uttered.

He looked down at his IPhone as it began ringing.

"Hello!"

"Where are you at?" Trina questioned.

He immediately recognized her sexy voice and replied, "I'm in the hood. Are you still at the salon?"

"No, I'm at the house but I had to check your little girlfriend at the shop today."

"Who?"

"Your girl Sugar!"

"Why, what happen?"

"After you called up to the shop, the broad had the nerve to question me in reference to you but I shut that shit down a-sap."

"The bitch is just mad because she's on dick restriction."

"Boy you are crazy." Trina giggled. "Are you coming to see me tonight or am I on restriction too?"

"Nah, I'm just getting started with you." Jamal told her. "When we hang up, I want you to text me your address and I'll be through there later on."

"Okay. Bye."

Jamal hung up and turned back to Jihad.

"Remember those bitches that we were chillin with up in Toronto last year?"

"The bitches we met when we were at the Caribana?" Jihad questioned.

Jamal nodded.

"That was the broad Trina who I just got off of the phone with."

"The little thick chocolate one?"

"Yep, I bumped heads with her and one of her friends last night at Oak Room She asked about you and said that her girl Nicky still be on your dick."

Every summer, Jihad and his crew drove up to Canada in the second weekend of August for the Caribana. The Caribana was a Jamaican festival held in Toronto, attracting a variety of different cultures. People throughout the world traveled to this extravagant event to get their freak on and party. Some of the most exotic women that Jihad had ever seen attended this Caribbean spectacle so he made sure that he was present whenever it popped off.

Their second night there, Jihad spotted a crew a female's loitering on Young Street, the strip where everyone congregated and introduced himself. After they conversed for a little while, Jihad was able to persuade the ladies to join him and his crew for a night on the town.

Trina was the most out spoken amongst the women and was automatically compelled to Jamal and his flamboyant style. Nicky had appealed to Jihad the moment that he laid eyes on her. She was a replica of the singer Lauryn Hill. His first objection was to set up some sex for the night but when he picked her brain, he found Nicky's conversation to be interesting. She didn't have any kids and was currently in her third year of college, studying law. The subjects she chose to discuss had substance. Jihad was use to females gossiping about who slept with whom or what neighborhoods were beefing, but those topics didn't seem to spark Nicky's interest. She seemed to be more into life; concerned with the real issues in today's society. The things that people seemed to ignore like the lack of education, employment and leadership in the black community. Jihad listened as she fumed about the absentee fathers in over 75% of the African American household across the United States. He was astonished that a woman his age spoke with such passion for the love of her people. This was the first time that he had been attracted to a female mentally. At the end of the night when everybody was drunk and ready to get their freak on, Nicky and Jihad dipped off to be alone. They walked hand in hand under the stars along the beach, talking until the early hours of the morning. That entire weekend, Jihad was the perfect gentleman. In the two days that they were together, he never tried to convince Nicky to have sex with him although that was the original objective. When it was time to leave she gave him her number but Jihad had already decided that he wasn't going to call when they got back to the town. He respected the fact that Nicky was a strong black woman with goals and aspirations so he chose to spare her the drama that came along with the lifestyle he led.

Jihad pushed the thoughts of Nicky from his mind when he noticed Chris coming up the block.

"What's good baby boy?" He said.

"I can't call it." Chris responded. "If I had your hands I'll cut mines off."

"You got the best hand lil homie. Just keep doing what you're doing and everything else will fall in place."

"That shit sounds good." There was frustration in his voice.

Jihad sensed the awkwardness in his demeanor and was about to acknowledge it but Jamal said, "I'm about to go and get me something to eat from the Jamaican spot; do you want me to bring you something back?"

Jihad reached in his pocket and handed Jamal a twenty.

"Get me some oxtails, rice and two beef patties." He then turned to Chris. "Do you want something to eat?"

"Nah, I'm cool." Chris replied in a dry tone.

"What's up with you?" He asked him. "I can see that you got something on your mind so tell me what's going on?"

After a long paused he looked Jihad in the eyes.

"I'm ready to get money out here with y'all niggas!" He answered.

Jihad was surprised at Chris's response.

"Now you're talking crazy! Keep your ass in school and get an education. This shit out here is not for you."

"No disrespect Jihad but I'm not trying to hear that shit that you're talking; I'm tryna eat and a nine to five isn't going to get it."

"I thought that you wanted to go away to school and play ball?"

"I do, but it's not a guarantee that I'm going to make it to the league. Plus I got another year before I can go to college and I need some paper right now!"

"And you think that selling drugs is the only way to get it?"

"What else am I going to do besides work at mickey Ds? I definitely am not going out like that."

"Why not; are you too good to flip burgers at McDonalds?"

"I don't even know why I told you?" Chris stood up to leave. "I knew that you wouldn't understand."

"Sit back down." Jihad stopped him in his tracks. "You're the one who don't understand. First of all, you see that your boys are out here doing they thing, getting to the money but everything that glitter ain't gold."

"It's not even about that."

"What is it about then?"

"She's pregnant."

"What?" Jihad was confused.

"My girlfriend is pregnant." Chris spoke softly.

Disappointment crept onto Jihad's face as he digested the bomb that Chris had just dropped on him. The fact that Chris had gotten his girlfriend pregnant wasn't the issue. What bothered Jihad the most was that this kid was ready to sacrifice his dreams to sell drugs. He'd witnessed so many prominent athletes get trapped off in the same predicament that the inevitable was almost predictable. Jihad hated to see a kid so talented willing to choose a path that had stolen the innocence of so many young brothers from the hood, including himself.

"Chris, there's other ways to handle this situation." Jihad told him. "Have you talked to your girl about having abortion?"

"She doesn't want to have an abortion; she wants to keep the baby. I told her that I wasn't ready for a baby and that I think we should wait until we finish school but she wasn't trying to hear that."

"I feel your pain when you say that you're ready to get some paper so you can provide for your seed. Trust me, I been there but it's a lot of bullshit that comes along with the game that I don't think that you're ready for."

"Yes I am fam, trust me!"

"Let me asked you a question." Jihad looked him in the eyes. "What would you do if you went to jail and was facing twenty years for conspiracy? Would you tell?"

"Hell nah, I'm gonna hold my on."

"That's what they all say until they're standing in the courtroom staring at the judge while their family is sitting on the back row crying. That's when they start thinking about who's in the street fucking their girl."

"I'll never go out like that." Chris defended. "I put that on everything."

"Okay let me ask you another question." Jihad said, keeping eye contact. "Would you pull the trigger on Remy or Zae if they were working with the police."

There was another long pause.

"That's how I know that you're not ready." Jihad broke the eerie silence hanging in the air.

"So you're telling me that you would kill Stone?"

"If he went against the grain; and he'd do the same to me if I was ever caught in a major violation."

"But you and Stone have been friends since ya'll were kids."

"And I live with that every day, knowing that it's a possibility that he might be the one to take my life. But I've accepted it because I know that's how the game goes sometimes." Jihad said. "Everything ain't for everybody and I don't think that you're built for this shit out here. You're a cool ass little nigga and I got crazy love for you but this is not for you. Go to school and do something with your life. Don't be like me or the rest of these knuckle heads around here and wind up dead or in prison. You deserve better than that."

He gave Chris a minute to absorb his words. Jihad wanted to see him break the curse that has kept the black generation in bondage over the years. Chris had a bright future ahead of himself as long as he made the right choices.

When his cellphone started ringing, Jihad snatched it off his belt and spoke into the mouth piece.

"Tell me something good."

"Everything is everything." Stone replied. "We're on our way back to the hood now."

"That's what I wanted to hear." A gigantic smile spread across his face, knowing that Remy and Lil P accomplished the job.

CHAPTER 10

The very next day, Vanessa moved around her three bedroom home, collecting the toys that her son had left scattered throughout the house. Earlier that morning, Malik's father had picked him up and taken him shopping for his birthday; that was the least he could do being that he never spent time with the boy.

Malik wasn't due back until later that night so Vanessa decided to clean up and catch up on some reading. She hadn't seen or spoken to Gamble since the night of the robbery and wondered if he was alright. She suffered from paranoia and didn't feel safe in his company anymore since the violent act had occurred. Her life flashed in front of her eyes when the masked men forced themselves into Gamble's apartment at gunpoint. The near death experience still had her shook up and the only time she wasn't thinking about it was when she was high on cocaine. Once she finished vacuuming the living room, Vanessa took a seat on the sofa and removed a sack of powder from her Gucci hand bag. She dumped the drugs onto a cd case and separated the powder into two lines before filling her nostrils. Immediately the cocaine took its effect, giving Vanessa a rush as she leaned back and began to drain. The euphoric sensation impelled her to relax as she opened an essence magazine. She focused on an article that was titled 10 reasons why men cheat. Suddenly there was a knock at the door. She wasn't expecting any company so she ignored it, hoping they would leave but then figured that it could be Malik's father bringing him back early.

"This is just like his dead beat ass." Vanessa stormed to the door. "This nigga is going to blow my high with his bullshit."

To her surprise, there was an attractive man holding a package beneath his arm when she peeked through the blinds. He stared back at her, revealing a friendly smile.

"Who are you looking for?" Vanessa screamed through the door.

"I have a special delivery for a Miss Vanessa Walker." The guy shouted back in proper English.

"Who is it from?"

He looked down at his clipboard and said, "Umm... it's from a Mr. Robert Gamble."

Skeptical about the situation, Vanessa examined the uniformed man from head to toe. She had to admit, his physical features were very alluring and seemed to be non-threatening but she wasn't about to opened the door for him.

"You can leave it on the porch and I'll get it later." She said.

"I'm sorry ma'am but I'm afraid that I'm going to need your signature." He protested. "It's company policy!"

"Well I don't feel comfortable opening the door because I'm not properly dressed so whatever it is that I need to sign, I'd appreciate if you could slide it through the mail slot."

"That won't be a problem."

A moment later some papers were shuffled through the mail slot along with a pen. Vanessa quickly signed her name next to the X then shoved the documents back to him.

"Thank you!" She said politely. "You can just leave the package on the steps and I'll get it later."

"Okay." He set the box down. "You can never be too safe nowadays. I wish that there were more women as cautious as you because there are a lot of sicko's in the world today."

"You can say that again."

"Alright now, you have a blessed day." The man casually walked to his delivery van and drove away.

When he was a good distanced up the street, Vanessa unlocked the door to retrieve the package. As she stepped onto the porch, two assailants emerged from the side of the house with pistols drawn. Out of her peripheral, she caught a glimpse of them rushing towards her and ducked back inside, quickly slamming the door shut. They burst in behind her as she took off running desperately trying to escape. Stone caught up with her in the bedroom and struck her with a clenched fist, sending her to the floor. The only thing covering her seductive body was an oversized tee-shirt. Roscoe got a peek of the goods beneath the shirt as she scooted backwards into a corner.

"What do you want?" Vanessa questioned in fear.

"Calm down Miss Walker, we're not going to hurt you" A third person walked into the room. "Just give us what we came for and we'll be on our way."

Vanessa looked up and saw the delivery man staring down at her.

"What are you talking about?" She asked confused. "I don't have anything."

Stone snatched her up by the throat and pressed the pistol to her temple.

"Bitch we don't have time to be playing with you. We know that Gamble got some coke and money up in this mutha fucka now quit fucking around and tell us where it's at."

"I swear that I don't know anything about any coke or money." Tears were streaming down her face. "Me and Gamble don't even mess around all like that. I haven't seen him in over a week."

"You wouldn't lie to me now would you?" Jihad stepped across the room.

Vanessa shook her head.

"I swear that there is nothing here." She whimpered, sensing something conversant about his conduct.

Instantly it hit her. These were the same individuals that had held her captive at Gamble's house. Another surge of fear swept through her as she wondered why he had allowed her to see his face. Thinking the worst, Vanessa released her bladder.

Jihad motioned for her to have a seat on the bed when he noticed urine discharging down her leg.

"Relax sweetheart." He stole a glance at Roscoe to see if he was buying into the façade then focused back on Vanessa. "If everything is like you say it is then you don't have anything to worry about. But if you're lying to me, I'm going to get very upset and there is no telling what I might do so this is your last chance to tell me the truth."

"I am telling you the truth; you can check for yourself. Please just leave. I promise that I won't call the police."

Jihad turned to Stone and Roscoe.

"Split up and search the house." He told them. "I'm going to keep our little sexy friend here company."

Roscoe and Stone separated. They explored various sections of the house while Jihad remained in the room with Vanessa. He felt somewhat guilty for having to sacrifice an innocent woman to implement his scheme but his conscious wasn't about to hinder him from following through.

After a ½ hour of searching the premises, Roscoe re-appeared in the doorway with the two keys of coke. Just like Jihad had anticipated, Roscoe had discovered the drugs that Remy and Lil P had planted in the bathroom ceiling.

The friendly smile that Jihad had displayed earlier was replaced with a sinister smirk. He stared at Vanessa sideways as Roscoe walked over and handed him the bricks.

"Mmm... mmm... mmm..." Jihad shook his head. "You lied to me Vanessa."

Her eyes shifted from Jihad to the objects in his hand.

"Wh-what's that?" She began to tremble as she stammered over her words. "That is not mine. I don't know where..."

"Bang!" Without warning, Jihad fired a shot into her forehead. The blast echoed throughout the room, causing Roscoe to jump as Vanessa's body tumbled to the floor.

At the sound of a gunshot, Stone rushed in with his pistol leveled.

"Oh shit!" He paused at the sight of the body. "You wasted the pussy."

They all watched her life seep into the carpet, forming a small pool of blood.

"Let's get the fuck out of here." Jihad said. "Aye Roscoe call Moe and tell him that we're on our way." He added stuffing the coke into a knapsack.

*****

On the eastside of town inside of a restaurant, Moe was seated at a table across from Blue discussing the weekly revenue of their operation. While waiting for the waitress to bring them their meal, they both nursed a shot of cognac, focused on everyone that entered the building.

Roscoe had called Moe earlier that day and informed him that the situation had been handled and he'd meet him at the El Morocco by 8:00pm. The El Morocco was a legitimate establishment owned by Moe and managed by his wife Florence. Many of their illegal schemes were orchestrated over dinner there.

Moe took a sip of his drink and noticed the place was crowded for it to be a Wednesday night. It was mostly occupied by couples in their mid to late thirties, enjoying an evening meal. They operated a tight ship and kept it conservative and didn't tolerate any miscreant behavior from the local riff raff. They preferred a mature clientele who conducted themselves properly.

"So have you been in contact with the connect?" Blue spoke just above a whisper as he removed a cigar from inside the pocket of his blazer.

Moe reached over and offered him a light.

"I talked to him this morning and he said that the next shipment should be in by the end of the week."

Blue inhaled the cigar and held the smoke in the back of his throat to savor the sweet taste.

"Good!" He released the smoke. "Is everything else in order?"

"Besides the little dilemma with Gamble everything is up to par. The Crew from Niagara Falls still owes us sixty grand but I spoke with the boy Vaughn and he assured me that he'll be up here tomorrow morning to take care of the bill."

"What about this kid Jihad? Do you really think that him and his crew are prepared for the load that you're willing to drop on them?"

"The kid is hungry." Moe assured. "He has the same look that we had in our eyes when we were hunting to come up."

Blue set his cigar in the ashtray and took another sip of cognac.

"I hope you're right about this kid because this is a huge responsibility that you're entrusting him with." He said in a skeptical voice. "I hope that your personal feelings for him won't cloud your judgment concerning business; because I don't care if he's family or not if he fucks up…"

"If he fucks this up, I'll deliver the bullet to his head personally." Moe declared without a hint of emotion.

A devious smirk emerged onto Blue's face. He knew that Moe was a man of his word and wouldn't hesitate to kill someone close to him if it needed to be done.

Finally the waitress appeared with their food. She rendered a seductive smile as she set the steaming plates on the table in front of them.

"Is there anything else that I can get for you gentlemen?" She asked flirtatiously and filled their glasses with water.

"No that will be all for now." Moe dismissed her with a reciprocating smile.

As she made her way across the dining area, both gangsters watched her ass sway from side to side.

"Where did you find that sexy young thing at?" Blue asked with lust in his eyes.

"That's my wife's niece, Roxy." Moe told him. "Her little hot ass got into some trouble with some guy that she was dating so Flo gave her a job to help her keep her nose clean."

"I wouldn't mind sampling some of that young pussy."

"Make sure that you pop a Viagra my friend because from what I hear, she's a super freak who has a thing for powerful men with money."

"Typical Bitch!" Blue snickered.

The mellow sound of Sade filled the restaurant as they attended to their meal. Moe chose the special of the day which was a porterhouse tenderloin smothered in onions and mushrooms, a loaded baked potato with a side of mixed vegetables. Blue was a bit more reserved, selecting the BBQ salmon and creamed spinach.

"This is delicious!" he shoved a fork full of fish into his mouth. "This may be some of the best salmon that I've ever tasted."

"The cook that Flo recently hired just graduated from Le Cordon Bleu." Moe replied, cutting into his steak. "And I must admit that the guy does know his way around the kitchen."

As Moe bit into his steak he spotted Roscoe enter the El Morocco followed by Jihad and Stone. He acknowledged them with a nod and they made their way over. When they reached the table, Moe stood up and exchanged greeting with them. Blue remained seated but noticed the knapsack that Jihad was holding over his shoulder.

"Aye Roscoe!" Moe addressed his protégé. "Go ahead and take our friend Stone over to the bar and have a couple rounds on the house; I need to have a word with Jihad."

When Roscoe and Stone stepped off, Moe motioned for Jihad to have a seat.

"I would like for you to meet Blue." He said.

Jihad's eyes were piercing and unmoving as he extended his hand. Staring back at the young man, Blue wiped his mouth with a napkin then embraced him with a firm handshake.

"I hope you don't mind but as you can see, we were enjoying a little dinner before you walked in." Blue said. "You're more than welcome to join us if you'd like; the food is quite delicious.

"I appreciate the offer but I'm cool." Jihad declined."

"Well, let me not waste anymore of your time than I have too." Blue spoke with authority. "I'm assuming that whatever it is that's in the bag belongs to me?"

"It's two keys in there. We got them from the house that we were sent to."

"And the girl?"

"I think a man in your position can respect it when I say that whatever is understood doesn't need to be discussed."

Blue nodded his approval.

"I hear a lot of good things about you, Jihad. Moe has been watching you with a close eye and he feels like you're ready to become a member of the family; but how do I know that I can trust you."

"You don't!" Jihad's eyes held steady. "That's one of the first rules that you learn in the game; not to trust a person. But I feel that as long as I'm an asset and not a liability, I can prove my worth, while you reap the benefits."

Blue studied Jihad for a moment without saying a single word. Finally he leaned back and cracked a crooked smile. He liked what he saw in the kid.

Jihad was well groomed and his words revealed wisdom beyond his twenty three years. There was a disciplined determination in his demeanor that separated him from the mediocre.

"I've seen a lot of hustlers come and go." Blue said. "The things that my eyes have seen would have driven the average man crazy and the places that my feet have taken me, others wouldn't dare go. I've been to the pits of hell and back and through it all, I still have my sanity. The eyes never lie and as I look into yours I see someone that may have traveled to some of the places that I speak of, seeking for a position of power."

"That's a possibility that I wouldn't doubt." Jihad responded.

"I can see the hunger in your eyes; but every so often a kid like yourself comes along and puts in a little work then thinks that he's ready for the major league without learning the instructions on how to play the game."

"I know what you're capable of and I wouldn't even be here wasting your time or mine if I didn't think that I was ready play with the big dogs."

"You're smart, but do you have the morale to remain loyal once you've become rich because loyalty is everything."

Jihad took a moment to think before answering.

"I'm a man of principles and I live by the code death before dishonor." He told him. "I laugh with the people that I cry with and eat with the ones that I starve with. I've never crossed my friends, I've never bitten the hand that fed me and I've never killed a man who didn't deserve it unless it was business. If it's loyalty that you're looking for then you don't have to look any further."

"You've taught this kid well my friend." Blue smiled at Moe impressed with Jihad's reply. "It sounds like he's been around the block a few times."

"I might've showed him a thing or two but he speaks from experience." Moe place his hand on Jihad's shoulder. "He did hop off the porch kind of early."

"Well I must admit that I do like what I've seen thus far so I'm going to give him a chance to earn himself a position in..."

Blue was interrupted by the vibration of his cell phone.

"Excuse me for a moment; I have to take this call.

He spoke into the receiver and nodded a couple of times before clasping it shut.

Looking Jihad square in the face he said, "I want you and your partner to take a ride with me." It was more of an order than a suggestion.

*****

Raindrops beat heavily upon the windshield of the 750II as the four men rode through the darkened streets in silence. Slowing the BMW to a steady pace, Moe turned into a parking lot where a dilapidated warehouse sat off into a cut. He pulled around to the back of the building and blew the horn as the car came to a halt. A few seconds past before the garage door was raised up, allowing them to enter.

Jihad sat back in his seat wondering what was going on. He peered over at Stone and shrugged then shifted his eyes on Blue.

"What's up in here?" He asked, inching towards his 9mm, preparing for the unexpected.

"Business!" Blue stated as he got out of the car.

The inside was dark and obscure like a dungeon. Moe led the way through a large corridor that reeked of gasoline. Various vehicles had been stripped and dismantled so Jihad assumed that it was some type of chop shop. He and Stone moved cautiously through the passageway equipped for any surprises. They pushed their way through the steel doors at the end of the hall and a mixture of emotions billowed inside of them as they took in the sight before them.

The concrete room was covered in plastic and sitting in the middle of the floor bound to a chair was Gamble. He was blindfolded without a stitch of clothing to cover his naked body. There was blood flowing from his open wounds and a rag was stuffed into his mouth to muffle the screams as two of Blue's henchmen tortured him. Both men were muscularly built and the ice grills on their face didn't show any emotion.

Blue looked at Stone and Jihad to catch their reaction as he walked over to Gamble and snatched the rag out of his mouth.

"Your time is up mutha fucka. Where is the rest of my shit?" His voice was cold and harsh.

Gamble tensed up at the sound of Blue's voice.

"C'mon Blue, I need a little bit more time to find out who did it." He pleaded.

"I already know who did it."

"Tell me who it is so I can go and handle it."

"Cut the charade you backstabbing son of a bitch!" Blue snatched the scarf down from his eyes. "You didn't get robbed, you've been playing on my intelligence; but you didn't really think that you were going to get away with it did you? Now you have approximately 30 seconds to tell me where the rest of my shit is before I cut off your dick and shove it down your throat."

Gamble squinted in confusion and began stuttering.

"W...what are you talking about? I would never cross you."

Blue signaled for Jihad to toss him the bag.

"Then how do you explain this?" He revealed the bricks inside of the knapsack.

"W...where did you get those from?" Gamble was baffled, recognizing the drugs.

"From your bitch Vanessa!"

"Hold on Blue, it must be some kind of mistake."

"It's not a mutha fuckin mistake." Blue struck him with a blow to the face. "You and that bitch tried to play me for a fool. And even if you're not in cahoots with the broad, you're too stupid to see when you're being rocked to sleep. Whatever the case may be, you're worthless to me."

In a devious way, Jihad was enjoying the spectacle taking place. Blue stepped up and handed him back the bag, containing the coke.

"Here's your chance to prove that you want to be a part of this family." He looked Jihad square in the eyes. "That's your startup kit. Tomorrow there'll be eight more inside the trunk of the car that you drove to the El Morocco. I want you to swing by the restaurant first thing in the morning and pick it up. Do you think that you can handle that?"

Jihad held his eyes steady and nodded.

"I'm going to be expecting for you to move ten of them a week at 24gs a pop." Blue told him. "Now hand me the keys to your car."

Jihad reached into his pocket and did as he was told. To no avail, Gamble continued to beg, refusing to accept that his fate was being sealed.

"Somebody's tryna set me up Blue!" He appealed. "Please don't kill me for something that I didn't do."

Gamble's plea went on deaf ears as Blue exited the room trailed by his two goons.

"The least you can do is have some type of dignity before you go." Moe looked at Gamble with disgust.

"Moe it's a set up; you know that I wouldn't bite the hand that's feeding me."

Moe turned to Jihad. "Do you believe that a man chooses his destiny or does his destiny choose him?"

"I believe that a man creates his destiny through his thoughts and actions." Jihad quickly responded.

"Welcome to the major leagues nephew. Don't fuck this up or you'll suffer the same consequences just like anybody else." Moe gestured towards Gamble to rectify his point. "Don't allow this to happen to you because regardless of our relationship, I won't hesitate to deal with you accordingly. Are we clear?"

"Crystal!"

Good! There's a van parked in the garage that you can use to get rid of the body. If I don't hear from you tonight, I'll assume that everything went according to plan and will speak to you tomorrow after you've picked up the package."

With that being said, Moe left Jihad and Stone alone with Gamble.

"Moe! Moe!" Gamble shouted out after him. "C'mon Moe don't let them do me like this."

"Save your breath playboy, nobody can hear you." Jihad spoke. "We're going to do you a favor and make it quick and easy."

Gamble's heart knocked against his chest rapidly as he looked up at the strangers. With every heartbeat, his fear escalated as every breath he took grew more urgent. His wrist and ankles were secured to the chair with duct tape, allowing no movement.

"C'mon dawg, I'll pay ya'll boys whatever you want if you let me go." He attempted to negotiate. "Blue wouldn't know shit. I swear, I'll be on the next thing smoking and I'll never step a foot in this town again."

Stone's laughter echoed off the walls.

"Cut the jokes Scarface, we're not trying to hear that shit."

Gamble shifted his eyes to Stone and a million thoughts jolted through his mind. There was something descriptive about his demeanor. As he studied the strangers who would decide his fate, a light bulb went off in his head.

"You the mutha fucka's that set me up!" Gamble distorted his face into a scowl.

"Scarface is smarter that he look." Stone Said sarcastically. "Too bad you couldn't figure it out before you got yourself all tied up. Maybe boss man Blue would've spared you."

"Fuck you bitch!"

Why do you have to be so disrespectful? The last time we spoke, I told you that we would see each other again but you don't look too thrilled; and I thought that you would be happy to see me."

"Fuck you!" Gamble repeated, struggling to free himself.

As Gamble contested ineffectively with the restraints, Stone flung open a switch blade with a flick of the wrist. He approached him with the sharp metallic object as Gamble eyed him with a cold stare. Despite the fear that he was feeling, he mustered up a chuckled from beneath the surface as death confronted him.

"I'll see ya'll bitch ass niggas in hell."

"I know the devil got a bed waiting for me but tell him to have a hot bitch waiting for me too so I won't be lonely when I get there." Stone remarked before plunging the blade into Gamble's torso repetitiously.

CHAPTER 11

It was a quarter past midnight by the time Stone and Jihad were finished rinsing down the warehouse. They wrapped Gamble's body in plastic, dumped him in a nearby alley and then drove in silence along the city's desolate streets. Jihad was exalted like a pit-bull tasting blood for the first time. Stone face was expressionless as he focused on the dark road ahead of them. A flash of lighting spread throughout the sky followed by a clash of thunder as a heavy rain poured from the heavens.

Stone pulled into a quiet residential neighborhood on the outskirts of the city and parked when he reached Jihad's house. After shutting off the engine he leaned his head against the seat and yawned.

"Today has been kind of crazy." He exhaled.

"It comes with the territory homie." Jihad replied. "But shit is really about to get funky in a minute."

"I already know that it's about to go down; I can feel it in the air."

"We still have to play it cool until Blue gets all the way comfortable with us."

Stone removed a pack of Newport's from his pocket and placed a cigarette between his lips.

"I need to stop smoking these squares before they kill me." He added fire to the tip, blowing smoke in Jihad's direction.

"If you keep blowing smoke in my face, you're not going to have to worry about them killing you because I'm go knock you off myself." Jihad playfully clutched his gun.

"Nigga, I've been holding you down since the summer program was giving out free lunches at the park. You wouldn't know what to do if something happened to me; you'd go crazy without ya boy."

Jihad grinned, knowing what his partner had stated was true. They'd been tight since high top fades and British Knights. Stone was the only person whom he considered a friend and if something was to happen to him, a piece of Jihad would be lost.

"And what would you do if something was to happen to me?"

"Kill the mutha fucka's responsible." Stone said seriously.

"You have always been my nigga." Jihad told him. "The streets don't make niggas like you anymore. You're a rare breed and you've never given me a reason to question your loyalty. We came into this game together and whatever is mines is yours; I'll never let this shit come between us. The money, the hoes, the shine, none of it! I won't only kill for you but I would literally die for you my nigga."

"I feel the same way." Stone nodded. "We've come too far to go out like Rich and Po shot up in the staircase over a couple of bricks."

"That's real talk!"

"You're the only family that I got Jihad. You are the only person that ever gave a fuck about me and showed me some love when my own peoples turned their back on me. I remember when I was in juvie, my mom's never came to check for me. She never even sent me a fuckin letter and protecting her ass was the reason that I was locked up. The only thing that helped me get through that shit was the letters and pictures that you sent to me. You kept me connected to the streets and when I came home your mom dukes embraced me and let me live with ya'll until I got my shit together."

"Because we got love for you and I know that you would've done the same thing if the shoe was on the other foot." Jihad said.

"No question." Stone replied. "All we got is us and I'll never let this shit go to my head and forget where I came from."

Jihad gave him some dap as they embraced. "Then let's get ready to make history homie."

"Let's do it!"

"Come and scoop me up in the morning so we can go and snatch that package."

"That's what's up." Stone exclaimed. "I'll be here to get you around 6:30."

"Alright then, I'll holler at you on the A.M." Jihad got out of the van.

Safely inside the house, he removed his boots and mounted the stairs quietly. He could hear the sounds of the television as he moved towards the bedroom. Entering the room, Jihad glanced over at Angela sleeping peacefully across the bed. The glow from the T.V. illuminated the darkness, radiating her lovely face, breathing softly. After he stashed the knapsack inside of the closet, he aimed the remote at the television and pressed power, causing the room to darken. Suddenly awaken, Angela sat up in the bed and reached over to click on the lamp.

"What are you doing?" She squinted, adjusting her eyes to the light.

"I'm sorry baby; I didn't mean to wake you up." Jihad replied.

"What time is it?" Angela yawned.

"It's about two o'clock."

"You want me to get up and fix you something to eat."

"Nah boo go back to sleep."

"Your mother called here looking for you."

"Why didn't she call my cell phone?" Jihad cringed.

"She said that she left several messages on your voice mail but you didn't return any of her calls."

Jihad dug into his pocket and pulled out his phone. It was turned off.

"Did she say what she wanted?" He pressed power.

"Why are you always cutting your phone off?" Angela ignored the initial question. "You must've been laid up with one of your other bitches."

"Girl don't start with that bullshit, I had a long day today."

"Mmm hmm, I bet."

"I'm serious Ang, save that shit for another time. I'm tired and I don't feel like going through this with you tonight. I got to get up in a couple hours so miss me with the sucka shit.

Angela didn't respond immediately. She heard the tension in Jihad's voice and wondered what had him so uptight. He usually fed into her jealous accusations until they argued and reconciled with passionate sex, but being that he didn't take the bait, she knew that there was something on his mind.

"I'm sorry baby." Angela apologized. "I know that you got a lot on your mind and you shouldn't have to come home and hear my mouth but I swear if I catch you with another bitch, I'm going to fuck you and that hoe up."

"You trippin!" Jihad chuckled.

"You can take it as a joke if you want to but I'm going to mess around and hurt you." She threatened. And no, your mother didn't say what she wanted; she just said that you should call her when you get a chance."

"I'll stop over there tomorrow and check on her." He took a seat on the bed.

Angela scooted behind him and massaged his head in an effort to sooth his mental strain.

"Is that better?" She fingered his temples.

Jihad closed his eyes, enjoying her gentle touch.

"You think you're slick."

"What are you talking about?"

"If you want some dick all you have to do is ask; you don't have to beef with me to get you some lovin."

She smiled bashfully, embarrassed that he had seen through her front so easily.

"Shut up boy, I'm not thinking about you and your little thang.

"That's what your mouth says but your body is telling me something different." He pushed her onto the bed and mounted her.

She looked up at his chest and pointed to the blood on his shirt.

"What is that?"

Jihad looked down at the crimson stain and said, "I was fighting one of my pit-bulls today and I got some blood on my shirt when we was breaking them apart."

"Don't lie Jihad; you hurt somebody didn't you?"

He got up from the bed and walked towards the bathroom. Angela followed behind him.

"Don't walk away from me." She grabbed his arm.

"Don't put your fuckin hands on me." He snatched away. "Every time I come in the house, you're up in my face bitching about something or another. I answered your fuckin questioned, if you don't like it then stop asking me shit that don't concern you."

"You coming in here with blood on your shirt don't concern me?"

"I said what I had to say, I'm through with it.'

"No you're not through with it; you're going to tell me what going on."

"I'm not telling you shit." Jihad barked."

"Is this how it's going to be?"

There was no response.

"Is this how it's going to be Jihad?" Angela repeated. "What about me and the baby?"

"We already talked about this so why are we going through this again?"

"So I'm supposed to run up to Virginia while you're up here playing cowboys and Indians with these niggas. I don't think that is fair! Why should I have to put my life on hold while you do whatever you want?"

"Ain't nobody holding a gun to your head, making you stay with me Ang. If you feel like I'm holding you back then bounce."

"Oh it's like that? These streets are more important than your family?"

"You knew what type of nigga I was before you started fucking with me so don't try to switch up on me now."

"But there's going to come a time when you're going to have to grow up and become a man."

"So now I'm not a man?"

"You know that is not what I am saying. All I'm trying to tell you is..."

"I'm out there in the streets every day and night, risking my life tryna make something happen so we can live comfortable and you say that I'm not a man. Bitch I'm more of a man than you'll ever know and don't ever forget that." Jihad walked out of the room, leaving Angela speechless.

CHAPTER 12

Six o'clock had quickly rolled around and Jihad hadn't had a wink of sleep. After arguing with Angela he'd tossed and turned on the sofa until the sun began to rise. Once he finally managed to nod out, the phone started ringing, awaking him from his slumber.

"Yo!" He answered groggily.

"Nigga get ya ass up and come on, I'm outside." Stone informed him.

"Alright, I'll be out in a minute."

Stretching his limbs, Jihad struggled up off of the couch and stumbled to the bathroom to relieve his bladder. He peeked in on Angela as he walked past the bedroom. She was already awake, surfing the channels on the television. She looked as if she hadn't slept much either.

"Morning." Jihad dryly uttered.

"Good morning." Angela's tone was evenly matched.

She never looked up from the screen as she flicked through the channels. Her eyes were swollen from crying all night and if she were to look at Jihad, the tears were sure to wail up again. To avoid another confrontation, Jihad continued to the bathroom. He took a shower, dressed quickly and left the house without any further discussion.

Stone cranked the ignition once he saw his boy coming out the building. He pointed to the clock on the dashboard as soon as Jihad got in the car.

"What happen to six o'clock? I've been sitting out here for an hour waiting on yo ass."

"That's my bad Fam. Fucking around with Angela and her bullshit; I didn't get any sleep last night."

"Excuses… Excuses … Excuses…"

"Whatever nigga, take me to get my truck." There was a touch of irritation in Jihad's voice.

Stone recognized the irritability and attempted to lighten the mood.

"Today is s'posed to be a good day; don't get in here on your period and shit." He humored. "Take the thong out of your ass and clear your head before we go and pick up this package."

"I'm good."

"Nah, I'm serious dawg. Clear your head and get focus, I can see the aggravation all in your face. Tighten up and leave whatever it is that you and Angie got going on here until you get back."

"You're right." Jihad said. "I'm not going to let her throw me off of my square and I'm definitely not about to let her keep me from getting this paper."

For the remainder of the ride, they talked about their plans to gain control of the drug market. When they arrived at the El Morocco, Stone pulled up next to Jihad's Expedition

"You want me to follow you to the Honeycomb? He asked.

"Yeah ride behind me so the police can't jump in back of me." Jihad replied. "And call Jamal and tell him to meet us at the spot.

*****

The alley was ribboned off with yellow tape and the police was everywhere. Gamble's body had been discovered at the crack of dawn by two kids taking a shortcut to school. The press had dispatched it to be top story and news vans were aligned along the alleyway. Fox, CNN and local news reporters were facing the cameras with their backs towards the crime scene, giving an account on what they believed to be the facts.

Detective Barnes arrived at the scene in a blue Crown Victoria. He pushed his way through a crowd of spectators to where another Detective was talking to a uniform officer.

"What do we got here boys?" Barnes approached them.

Detective Lee looked up from his notes at the sound of his acquaintance.

"Hey lieutenant!" He shook hands with Barnes. "We got an African American male in his late twenties with multiple stab wounds to the upper torso.

It seems that he was stabbed to death somewhere between nine and eleven o'clock last night and dumped here in the alley some time during the early hours of the morning. Some kids found him on their way to school."

"This guy looks familiar." Barnes looked down at the naked body. "Did you get a positive ID on him yet?"

Not quite but one of the officers over at E district seems to think that his name is umm..." Lee flipped through his notes. "Robert Gamble."

"Gamble... Gamble... Gamble..." Barnes searched his memory. "Oh shit, I know this guy. We've been trying to catch him for years but he always seemed to slip through our fingers."

"Well it looks like someone finally caught up with him."

"Yeah, I guess we weren't the only ones that were after MR Gamble."

Over the years the two Detective had worked together on a couple of cases so they were very familiar with one another. Lieutenant Barnes was a veteran who had come up through the ranks of the police force during the war on drugs. He was a hard nose cop with old school morals who did what it took to get the job done. At 49 he carried around an unwanted 30lbs due to lack of exercise and a bad diet, not to mention the alcohol that he consumed religiously. Although his salt and pepper hair was balding at the top, Barnes was still sharp as a whip and one of the best homicide detectives on the city's police department.

Detective Lee was 20 years younger than his predecessor and was determined to rid the streets of crime. All the men in his family were either cops or parole officers so he was predestined to work in some type of law enforcement. His hard face matched the 5'10 physique of solid muscle that he wore confidently and unlike Barnes he jogged every morning to keep it that way.

"Did he have any beefs with anyone that you know of?" Lee inquired.

"Not to my knowledge but it is a good possibility." Barnes replied. "Over the last two years, Gamble has become a major player in the drug game and I'm pretty sure he has stepped on some toes along the way. I want you to check with all of your informers and find out whatever you can about MR Robert Gamble and anybody he may have had problems with."

"I'm on top of if lieutenant."

"And keep me updated on all the information that you come across." Barnes stepped away.

He pushed aside the police barricade and walked into barrage of questions followed by flashing lights from the camera.

"What can you tell us about the murder?"

"Do you have any suspects?"

"What is the victim's name?"

"Is it true that his genitals were severed from the body?"

Another bulb flashed as Barnes held up a hand to block the blinding light. He sighed heavily. He hated talking to the press but it came with the job.

"We have an unidentified African American male, approximately twenty eight years old with multiple stab wounds. As of right now, we don't have any suspects but we are leaning towards a couple leads."

"Is the murder drug related?" A red headed female reporter asked.

"We don't know that for sure but that's a possibility that we're going to investigate. Now if you will excuse me, I have a job to do. No more questions."

After giving the reporters a short briefing, Barnes returned to the primary scene where Lee was talking to another detective. He examined the guy and noticed that he was dressed in a navy blue suit over a white shirt and burgundy tie. Judging from his appearance, Barnes concluded that he wasn't a detective but a federal agent.

"I'm Lieutenant Barnes, homicide division." He extended his hand to the man. "And you are?"

As they shook hands, the guy flashed his badge.

"I'm agent Richard Wright from the federal bureau of investigations and I'll be assisting you on this case."

"This is a state case." Barnes stiffened. "What interest do the FEDS have in this matter?"

"Well like I was explaining to Detective Lee here before you walked up; the corpse that you have laying there was a C.I. who was cooperating with me on a very important case that I've been investigating."

"Robert Gamble was a confidential informant for the FBI?

"Yes, MR Gamble has gathered a substantial amount of evidence on one of the government's most targeted crime figures in the city. And we have reason to believe that his cooperation with the bureau may have been the cause behind his demise."

"And what reason do you have to believe that?"

"Off the record?" Agent Wright suggested.

"Off the record!" Barnes agreed.

"The last time we had contact with the C.I. he was a bit shaken up and disorientated about following through with the operation."

"Do you think his cover was blown?"

"Not exactly, you see MR. Gamble was a lieutenant of organization led by a gangster name Benny Blue Johnson and his underboss Big Moses Grant. You may know them."

Barnes nodded, allowing Wright to continue.

"From my understanding, Gamble had gotten himself robbed for some drugs and money that belonged to Blue. After leaving a nightclub one morning, he and a female acquaintance were surprised by three gunmen when he returned home. After they were assaulted and bound, Gamble gave the assailants what they came for but was afraid of what Benny Blue and Big Moe were going to do once they found out that he didn't have their money or product."

"So that gives us a motive and a suspect." Lee spoke as he recorded the info onto his notepad.

"And this is at least the second homicide that we believe to be connected with our case."

"Is that so?" Barnes raised a brow.

"Remember the young lady that I mentioned was with Gamble the night that he was robbed?" Wright questioned.

Both detectives nodded.

"Well last night her ex-boyfriend and five year old son found her shot to death inside of her bedroom."

"You gotta be shitting me!" Barnes stated.

"I wish I was lieutenant but unfortunately I'm not. However MR Gamble has already provided us with enough information to build our case but these two homicides would put the icing on the cake."

"I'll have to get it approved by my superior but I don't have a problem assisting the bureau with their pending investigation."

"We would really appreciate it." Wright shook Barnes hand. "I know our divisions don't always see eye to eye but at the end of the day, we're all on the same side of the law so if you scratch my back, I'll be willing to scratch yours."

CHAPTER 13

Joyce sat alone at her kitchen table drinking a hot cup of coffee while reading the morning newspaper. Despite a couple strands of grey hair in her head, she didn't look her age. She was a slim petite woman in her early forties with a beautiful refined skin tone. All her adult life she had viewed the dangers of the streets first hand. She had lived it then disregarded it when her husband was killed but it wasn't long before her son had picked up where his father had left off. Jihad was her first born and it hurt Joyce to watch him travel the same path that had stolen the love of her life. She constantly warned her son about the perils of the underworld but her pleas went on deaf ears. Jihad was allured to the streets as a preteen. He hit the block with nickel bags of marijuana without Joyce's knowledge and by the time she became aware of his activities, he had already advanced to crack cocaine. By fifteen he'd started giving her money to help pay the bills and keep food on the table. Although Joyce didn't approve of the lifestyle that he lead, she accepted the dirty money and soon afterward depended on it to support her youngest child, Kareema.

When Zeak had gotten murdered, Joyce was eight weeks pregnant with a second child that he was unaware of. She was oblivious to where he kept his stash so by the time Kareema was born the funds that she saved up herself had been extinguished. Over the next couple of years, Jihad watched his mother struggle, trying to provide for him and his sister so he began hustling to relieve the pressure. Now over a decade later, drug money was still the primary income for their family.

Joyce took another sip of her coffee as she read about the rising crime rate in the city. She looked up from the paper when she heard the lock on the side door unfasten. Jihad appeared in the doorway, looking his usual stoic self.

"I've been calling you for two days." Joyce started as soon as he stepped into the kitchen. "Why haven't you returned any of my calls?"

"Good morning to you too Ma!" Jihad replied sarcastically.

"Don't come in here with your smart ass mouth boy; just answer the question.'

He walked over and opened the refrigerator.

"I didn't get your message until this morning so I thought I'd come by and check on you."

"Do you want me to cook you something to eat?"

"Nah I'm cool, I just wanted to stop by and make sure everything was alright because Angela said that you had an emergency."

"Have you spoken to your sister lately?" Joyce asked.

"I haven't spoken to Kareema in couple of days. Why, what's up?"

"She's out of control and you need to talk to her before I break her neck."

"What has she been doing?" Jihad questioned.

"I don't know what has gotten into Kareema but for the last couple of weeks she has been very disrespectful." Joyce responded. "She's been coming into this house in the middle of the night smelling like weed and when I tell her to do something, she always trying to have the last word."

"Where is she at now?"

"She's upstairs in her room."

"Let me go up here and see what this girl got goin on."

On the way to Kareema's room something on the television caught Jihad's attention. He stopped in the living room and increased the volume so he could hear what was being said.

"Authorities have discovered a dead body early this morning. Resources tell us that two seventh grade students were on their way to school when they stumbled across twenty eight year old Robert Gamble stabbed to death in a nearby alley. The police do not have any suspects at this moment but they do believe the crime is drug related. The residences of the community are outraged at the violence submerging the city and demand justice. We've tried contacting lead detective Lieutenant David Barnes but he was unavailable for comment. This is Karen Kauffman reporting live from channel 7 eyewitness news; more on this story at five."

"Thank you Karen. Yesterday, president Obama traveled to china to discuss foreign..."

Jihad switched the T.V. off and ascended the stairs. He knocked on Kareema's door before easing it open. When he entered the room, she was seated at the desktop computer surfing the internet. Her invisible braids were pulled into a ponytail as she typed away at the keypad.

"What's good baby girl?" Jihad spoke.

Kareema looked up from the monitor and swiveled around in her chair at the sound of her brother's voice. She was a young replica of her mother.

"Hey Jihad." She smiled. "How long have you been here?"

Kareema was Jihad's baby sister as well as the pride of his life. He was the only father figure that she had ever known so he made it a priority that she didn't want for anything. As long as she did what she was supposed to do, he spoiled her with whatever she desired so he couldn't understand why she was acting out towards Joyce.

"I got here about fifteen minutes ago and I've been down stairs talking to moms and she said that you've been bugging out lately; what's up with that?"

"Mommy still thinks that I'm a little girl Jihad. I'm seventeen years old but she treats me like I'm a kid. I'm practically grown."

So that gives you the right to be disrespectful?"

"Mommy is blowing the whole thing out of proportion." Kareema said.

"What happen?" Jihad questioned.

"I missed my curfew a couple times this week and before I could explain why, she started screaming and yelling at me as soon as I walked in the house."

"Did you come in here smelling like weed?"

"Yeah but I wasn't smoking." She huffed.

"If you weren't smoking, why did you smell like weed?"

"Tasha's brother Rock gave me a ride home and him and his boys were puffing a blunt when they dropped me off but mommy wasn't trying to hear that, she just jumped to all types of conclusion when I came through the door."

"And you didn't hit the blunt at all?" He probed

"No I didn't hit the blunt; I couldn't smoke if I wanted to."

"What do you mean by that?" Jihad prepared himself for what she was about to say.

Kareema's eyes automatically dropped to the floor.

"Pick your head up and look at me when I'm talking to you.'

When she looked up, her eyes were moist.

"Promise me that you're not going to get mad."

"Kareema you know that I'm going to hold you down regardless so talk to me and tell me what's going on."

She continued to stare at him without speaking. Her eyes were soft and filled with tears.

"You're pregnant aren't you?" Jihad questioned in a jeering tone.

The tears began to flow as Kareema confirmed his inquisition with a nod. Jihad paced the room back and forth.

"Damn Reema!" He scoffed. "I warned you about letting these little niggas go raw. If you're going to be out there having sex, the least you can do is use protection. How do you expect to go to college with a baby? And you already know mom is not about to raise your child while you run the streets."

"Jihad, I know that I messed up but I can still go to school." Kareema responded. "I'll just stay close to home until I get on my feet."

"What about the dude that got you pregnant? How does he feel about the whole situation?"

"He wants me to have the baby; and he said that he'll do whatever he has to do to make sure that we're alright."

"Don't be so damn naïve girl; a nigga will say whatever you want to hear as long as he is hitting the pussy."

"Come on now big bra, you know that you taught your baby sister better than that. I might be young but I'm not stupid, plus Chris is not even like that."

Jihad stopped pacing the floor.

"Chris?"

Kareema nodded.

"Lil Chris from the neighborhood?" Jihad questioned.

"Christopher Cunningham!" She confirmed.

He sat on the bed and thought back to the day when Chris had told him that he'd gotten his girlfriend pregnant.

"How long have you and Chris been seeing each other?"

"A little over a year."

"And I'm just now finding out about it?"

"I wanted to tell you but Chris was afraid that you wouldn't approve of us being together. He idolizes you and he didn't want you to think that he was being disrespectful by talking to me."

"I don't give a fuck about him talking to you, it's him getting you pregnant is what I have a problem with. You have your whole life ahead of you and I don't think that you and Chris are ready to bring a child into this world."

"You were my age when you started messing around with Angela."

"But we weren't making babies back then." Jihad quickly countered. "And this isn't about me; this is about you."

Kareema put her hands on the arm of the chair and pushed herself erect.

"Jihad, I love Chris and you might not believe it but he loves me too." She declared.

"I do not doubt the love that you think that Chris has for you baby girl. He's a good dude and I do believe that he'll do whatever he has to do to take care of his responsibilities and that's exactly why you shouldn't have this baby."

"What, you want me to get an abortion?"

"I think that would be the best thing for you to do. I'll pay for it and mom will never have to know about it."

She looked at Jihad and frowned.

"I don't care what you say; I'm not getting an abortion."

"That's your emotions talking." He told her. "How are you going to provide for a child and you can't even provide for yourself? And if you really love Chris like you say you do then you wouldn't put that type of pressure on him."

"Pressure?"

"Yeah pressure! Chris is a very talented dude and he has an opportunity to get up out of the hood and do something with his life; don't take that from him. I've seen too many gifted kids who should've gone off to school and played ball get trapped off with a baby and wound up selling drugs instead."

"I'm not trying to trap him with a baby." Kareema protested. "I want him to go away to college and pursue his dreams."

"But I guarantee if you have his baby he won't leave." Jihad said. "He'll feel obligated to stay here and help you out with the baby. He's already been tryna convince me to put him on but I won't let him get down because I see something special in him. There's something special in you too and I don't want my little sister stuck in the hood raising a bunch of babies."

"Jihad you're my brother and I respect what you're saying because I know that you are only trying to protect me from getting hurt but I'm keeping my baby no matter what you say."

All he could do was shake his head and smile at the fact that his little sister was becoming a young lady.

"Whatever you choose to do I'm going to support your decision but I still think that you should give it some thought." He told her

"There's nothing to think about, my mind's already made up." She clarified.

"It is what it is then. Let's go down here and tell Ma Dukes the good news."

"She's going to trip out ain't she?"

"You already know what time it is." Jihad led the way to the door. "But I'll talk to her as long as you promise me that you'll finish school."

"You have my word big bra."

"I'm going to have a talk with Chris too so don't worry about him; I'll make sure that he's alright."

Kareema stood up and hugged him around the neck while kissing him on the cheek.

"Thank you Jihad, I knew that I could depend on you."

"As long as I'm breathing you'll be able to depend on me. Now let's go and tell mom what's going on so she can help you find a good pediatrician."

Back in the kitchen, Joyce was on her second cup of coffee while eating a bagel smothered in cream cheese. She looked up as Jihad and Kareema entered her presence.

"Kareema has something that she needs to tell you Ma." Jihad took a seat at the table.

Joyce bit into the bagel and shifted her eyes towards her daughter. Kareema took in a deep breath and searched her mind for the proper words before she spoke.

"First of all, I want to apologize for the way that I have been behaving lately." She began. "I've been going through something and I should've come and talked to you instead of acting out."

Joyce rinsed the bagel down with a drink of coffee and said, "Kareema you know that you can come and talk to me about anything so there is no excuse for being disrespectful. I've done everything I could as a mother to make your life comfortable so why are you treating me like I'm the enemy?"

"I'm sorry mom but I didn't know how to come and tell you…" Kareema paused.

"Tell me what?" She looked at Jihad then back to Kareema. "What do you want to tell?"

Kareema looked away and said, "I'm Pregnant!"

"What?"

"I'm pregnant!" She repeated.

Her mother stared at her with piercing eyes, clenching her jaws.

"What do you mean you're pregnant?"

"Mom before you start screaming let me explain…"

"What is there to explain Kareema? We've talked about this and I've told you over and over again about the struggle that I faced being a teenage mother so why in the world would you go and repeat the same idiotic mistake?"

"It just happened!"

"What do you mean that it just happened?" Joyce raised her voice. "That is not something that just happens. How could you be so irresponsible after everything we discussed?"

There was no response as Joyce stood up and continued to scold her.

"How do you expect to take care of a baby? I hope you don't think that I'm going to be around here raising a baby while you're ripping and running behind some nappy headed little nigga. If that's the plan, you got another thing coming!"

"I didn't ask you to do anything for me." Kareema shouted in her mother's face. "I can take care of myself."

Smack! Joyce open handed her across the face.

"You better check your tone when you're talking to me." She struck her again. "I don't know who you think you're dealing with but you better check yourself before you get hurt."

Jihad quickly jumped between them.

"Hold on ma!" He restrained her. "I know this is a lot to digest but you can't do it like that, she pregnant."

"Uh... uh... Kareema what to act like she's grown then I'll treat her like she's grown. If she don't like it, she can get out."

"I'll get out of your house!" Kareema barked. "I planned on getting my own apartment anyway."

"Shut up and go upstairs." Jihad instructed. "You talk too much."

Kareema stormed off to her room, mumbling something beneath her breath. Joyce crossed the kitchen and returned to her seat.

"I don't know what I'm going to do with her? She looked at Jihad. "She listens to you but when I tell her to do something, it's a problem."

"She's just going through that rebellious stage right now; she'll be alright."

"I'm tired Jihad, I don't have the energy to be fooling around with that girls nonsense."

"I know ma but you can't kick her out."

"I'll never put your sister in the streets but she is not going to be disrespectful under this roof as long as I'm paying the bills. I've done my job as far as raising her so if Kareema feel like she's ready to go out on her own then I'm not going to stop her."

Jihad answered his cell when it started vibrating.

"I'll be there in a minute family; I'm building with my Ma Dukes about something important." He paused then consulted his watch. "Give me fifteen minutes and I'll be around there."

After Jihad ended the call, he turned and faced Joyce.

"Go ahead and take care of your business." She said before he could get it out. "Don't stress yourself out about Kareema; it'll be alright. We'll get through this.'

Jihad dug into his pocket and came out with a wad of cash. He peeled his mother off a couple of dollars and said, "I'll be back through here when I'm done making my runs. Call around and see if you can schedule an appointment for Kareema to see a pediatrician tomorrow."

A smile crept its way across Joyce's lips

"I swear that you remind me so much of Zeak."

CHAPTER 14

On the Westside of town, three members of the Gibson Street crew were having a meeting inside of a small café, discussing who they thought was behind Gamble's murder. The café was a mom and pop establishment used to launder the dirty money they'd obtained in the streets.

Occupying the back office, Stacks, Shabazz and Y.G was devastated as they attempted to figure out what happened to their comrade.

Stacks was a short and stocky man with a bald head and long beard. He wasn't a stranger to pistol play but avoided it as much as possible if it wasn't about a bankroll. Shabazz on the other hand was a true pistoleer. Ill-mannered with a quick temper, he looked for trouble and was always ready to pop off. Young Gamble or Y.G for short was the younger brother of the late Gamble and the ringleader of this group of bandits. A few years back, they gained a reputation as the enforcers for Gamble after a sequence of murders helped establish him in the neighborhood. Now that Gamble was dead, Shabazz and Stacks knew that it was only a matter of time before they set the town on fire.

Y.G. couldn't believe that his brother was gone. Despite his unruffled exterior, he was fuming inside and determined to kill everyone responsible for Gamble's demise. He downed a double shot of Tequila as Shabazz suggested how they should approach the situation.

"Anybody that had a problem with big homie got to get it." He stated. "If I even think that a nigga had anything to do with what happen to G, they got to go."

"We probably need to go and get at them niggas from Broadway!" Stacks responded. "Gamble had some words with the boy Lo a few weeks back and them Downtown niggas is known to be on some grimmey shit."

Shabazz pounded his fist on the table.

"What the fuck is we waiting for? Let's get it poppin."

Stacks turned to Y.G. for a response. He seemed to be well composed under the circumstances but his silence signified the quiet before the storm. There was something dangerous simmering inside his mind, longing to come out.

Noon was approaching and Y.G. was already working on his third shot of liquor.

"I think I know who killed my brother." He finally spoke.

"You think you know?" Stacks shift positions.

Y.G. nodded before guzzling his drink.

"And it wasn't Lo and them niggas from Downtown." He slammed the glass on the table.

"Are you sure?"

"I'm almost certain."

"Then why in the fuck are we sitting here talking about it." Shabazz burst out. "Let's get it poppin!'

"We're definitely about to get it poppin" He slurred in a harsh tone. "And when we set this mutha fucka on fire I'm not sparing nobody. If they're not in the circle, they can get it."

"Who do you think did it?" Stacks questioned.

Y.G. leaned across the table and said, "Blue killed him. Blue killed my brother."

Shabazz nodded, flexing his jaw muscles as he gritted his teeth. Perplexed, Stacks shook his head in disbelief.

"Are you sure?"

"Yeah, I'm sure!" Y.G. assured him. "That fat mutha fucka probably didn't do it himself but I know that he put out the hit."

"Gamble earned them a lot of money, so why would Blue get him knocked off? It doesn't make any sense."

Y.G. rose and poured himself another drink as he spoke, "Two weeks ago somebody hit Bra up for a buck eighty and a couple blocks of coke and Blue was poppin some shit about what he was going to do if G didn't come up with the money that he owed him for the work."

"Gamble got robbed?" Shabazz questioned. "Why didn't he say something?"

"Because he wanted to make sure that it wasn't an inside job before he showed his hand."

"So what's up? What are you trying to do?"

"You already know what I'm trying to do. I'm going to make that fat bastard bleed and then I'm going to find out who robbed my brother and I'm going to make them mutha fuckas suffer a long and slow death because they're the reason that this shit went down the way it did."

"I'm with you my nigga; all you gotta do is give me the word and I'll lay the murder game down for you because G was like my big brother too."

"Hold up, we can't go at Blue on some shoot and miss type shit." Stacks reminded them. "If we're going to put the murder game down, we're going to have to do the shit right because we might not get a second chance if we fuck up the first time."

"Nigga you acting like you're talking to an amateur or something." Shabazz said. "I've been doing this shit for a while and I ain't never been on that studio bustin shit. When my guns go off, I'm tryna hit something."

Y.G. sipped his drink. "Stacks is right! We can't be sloppy when we approach this nigga. We're going to have to do our homework and and come with our A game!"

CHAPTER 15

Spring had quickly approached, causing the city to blossom to life. Every neighborhood was vibrant with hustlers, aligning the pavement of the street corners.

Posted up on Bailey and Berkshire, Jihad stood front and center alongside Stone, watching everything moving. They kept track of every package sold on the block as their young boy's directed traffic.

Everything was going according to plan. Jihad and his crew had managed to establish themselves into Blue's organization without suspicion. They started out with a weekly obligation of 10 kilograms but double that order within 90 days. At Twenty eight thousand a pop, they were able to pay Blue and still split a fifty thousand dollar profit amongst the team, yet Jihad was dissatisfied. He was always thinking of ways to build his own empire. Depending on his wits was something that he had learned to rely on as a youth and although he'd expanded his hustle since the days of slinging nickel bags of marijuana at the park, Jihad wanted more. Having control in the hood was one thing but reigning over the city was another ball game that he was determined to play.

Jihad scanned his watch and noticed that it was a quarter before noon.

"The block doing numbers today!" He spoke to Stone. "It's not even Twelve o'clock and we've already downed a quarter joint."

"I know!" Stone replied. "That last pack that Moe blessed us with was some fire! That shit got these fiends going bananas."

"How many of them things do we got left?"

"Last night, we had three bricks but I think Jamal hit them boys from the Cold Springs with two of those joints this morning so we should have at least one left."

That's what's up!" Jihad remarked. "Get him on the horn and see where he at."

Before Stone could reach in his pocket and retrieve his cell phone, Jamal turned the corner and parked.

"What's good?" He hopped out the SUV and exchanged dap with his partners.

"I was just about to call you." Stone shot back. "Did you handle that business with them boys from Central Park?"

"Yeah, I slid through there about forty five minute ago and hollered at the boy Marco. He only copped a half joint but I'm supposed to go back through there around three o'clock and get at his man with the whole thang."

"Who is his man?" Jihad interjected.

"Mike!" Jamal confirmed. "The nigga that's always with him."

"Are you talking about the brown skinned nigga that just came home about a year ago?"

"Yeah!"

"When did that nigga start getting bird money?" Jihad frowned.

"Homeboy had a little bit of bread before he left."

"We'll make sure that you count that paper before you put anything in those dudes possession because you never know what's on these niggas minds now a day."

Jamal gave his cousin a look as if he was offended.

"You're talking to me like I'm a rookie or something." He barked. "I know how to handle my business."

"Nah bra, don't take it the wrong way; I just want you to stay on point like an icicle because mutha fuckas is thirsty as hell and that crew don't always play fair."

"Yeah, them boys will definitely shake something if given the opportunity." Stone stated.

"I know how those dudes rock." Jamal replied. "But trust me; they'll never play them type of games with me."

"I hope you're right because we don't have any room for mistakes," Jihad told him. "We got too much on the line to fuck up now."

For the remainder of the afternoon, the three young men conversed amongst themselves while their protégés continued to interact with the crack fiends. The traffic had been non-stop all day due to the addicts from the neighborhood and other surrounding areas with an appetite for getting high. Everyone was so absorbed into what they doing that no one noticed the two individuals parked up the block in a utility van, watching their transactions.

Agent Richard Wright had been studying the young men for the better part of the day through a set of binoculars while his partner, Agent Patricia Daniels watched from surveillance cameras connected to a laptop. Agent Wright was a clean cut, fair skinned man with a muscular build and all 5ft 11inches demanded respect. Agent Daniels on the other hand was more of a mild mannered intellectual. She was a young, ambitious officer fresh out of the academy that also demanded respect but had to earn it the hard way, being that she was an attractive black woman with Spanish features.

She poured two cups of coffee, handing the first one to Agent Wright.

"So what are your thoughts about our boy's here?" She sipped from her cup.

"I think that we're onto something here." Agent Wright blew the steam from his cup, "And I am willing to bet that these are the perpetrators behind the murder of Robert Gamble."

"What makes you say that?"

"A hunch!"

"What type of hunch?" Agent Daniels pushed. "Don't keep me in the dark, go ahead and fill me in."

Agent Wright removed the binoculars from his eyes as he turned to face his partner.

"Well, I don't have anything solid to prove my theory but my instincts tell me that these guys were involved because they are the most recent group of individuals that have been inducted into Blue's organization. And the information that I have received from many informants is that Blue doesn't allow anyone to become a member without proving their loyalty."

"So you think that these guys killed Gamble to prove their loyalty?"

"That's exactly what I think!" Agent Wright stated firmly.

"But why would Blue have Mr. Gamble murdered, I thought that Robert worked for Blue and Moe?" Agent Daniel questioned.

"I don't know, maybe he caught wind that Gamble was a Federal informant who has been supplying us with evidence. You know he has crooked cops on his payroll that is feeding him information."

"That is a possibility!"

"Or maybe Gamble stole some money or fucked his wife, I don't know but I will put up a dollar to a donut that these are the ones behind it. I can feel it!"

"Do any of them have a criminal history?" Agent Daniels continued to question.

"None of them has a serious criminal background except for Stephens Jacobs and he was only a minor when he was charged so we can't use it against him."

"Which one is Stephen Jacobs and what were his charges?"

Agent Wright pointed to one of the many pictures that were placed upon a chart.

That's Stephen Jacobs but he's known as Stone in the streets." He emphasized. "And he was originally charged with murder but it was reduced to manslaughter, being that he was a youthful offender. Plus, I think that the person that he killed was his mother's boyfriend and the guy had a history for beating on her so the district attorney had some compassion for Stephen."

Agent Daniels diligently jotted notes onto her pad as her mentor spoke.

"I think it would be a good idea if we put a little bit of pressure on him and see what we can come up with.

"I agree!" Agent Wright replied. "I'll put someone on it right away."

"What about the others?" She continued writing without missing a beat.

"I don't really have too much information on the others except for this one." He pointed to a photo of Jihad. "He's a problem!"

"What do you mean by a problem?

"Jihad Smith has been raising hell in this city since he was in his early teens but the authorities have never been able to make anything stick on this kid."

"Why not?" Agent Daniels asked.

"Because he's smart." Agent Wright admitted.

"Or just lucky!" She countered.

"But what he fails to realize is that we have more time then he has and it's only a matter of time before he slip up."

"And as soon as he does, we will be there to make sure that he will never see the sun from this side of the fence again."

CHAPTER 16

Back at EL Morocco, Moe was seated at his desk in his office across from Blue, counting their earnings from the previous day. Cigar smoke filled the air as the electrical money machine flipped through the currency at a rapid pace. Business had slightly increased since adding Jihad to their roster, so both men were in a vibrant mood.

"What's the count?" Blue inquired, releasing a ring of smoke.

"Nineteen!" Moe replied as he removed the stack of bills from the machine.

Blue quickly jotted the number onto a notepad as Moe placed another bundle of hundreds into the electrical device.

"Seventeen five!" Moe announced once the machine came to a stop.

Again, Blue recorded the number into the notepad as his partner retrieved some more cash from a duffle bag beneath them. They repeated this process until every dollar was counted and wrapped in a rubber band.

"What's our bottom number?" Moe asked, pouring himself a shot of crown royal.

Blue grabbed the calculator and began adding up the figures that he had documented.

"Two thirty four!" He displayed the screen on the calculator.

"Two thirty four?" Moe repeated as he leaned back in his seat. "That's a good way to begin the week!"

"That's a wonderful way to start the week, especially when we still have money out there that needs to be collected."

"Speaking of money that need to be collected; I spoke with Jihad yesterday evening and he said that they would be ready later on today or first thing in the morning."

Blue thumped the cigar ashes into a nearby tray then allowed the smoke to dance around in his mouth as he relished the flavor.

"Your nephew and his crew are some hustling mutha fucka's!" He exhaled. "We just gave them that package three days ago and they already need another one? We might have to double up their assignment again."

"Let's not jump the gun just yet, but I do want to have a sit down with them and see where their head is at."

"That's your call! Whatever you decide to do, I'll roll with it."

"Yeah, I just want to make sure that he remains focused and doesn't allow the money to get to his head because you know how these young boy's get down once they start seeing a little paper."

"You're absolutely right!" Blue agreed. "We can't have the little nigga runnin around here, getting too big for his britches."

"Nah, Jihad is too cautious for that." Moe admitted. "It's his crew that I'm worried about. They're known to get a little reckless, so we need to make sure that he keeps his wolves on a short leash."

"I understand! Like I said, it's your call."

Suddenly there was a knock at the door.

"Who is it?" Moe shouted with authority.

"It's Roxy!" a voice returned from behind the door.

"Alright, give me a minute." They began stuffing the money into the duffle.

After zipping the bag, Moe instructed Roxy to enter his office; and she sashayed her way into the room with the sex appeal of a runway model. The Vera Wang dress that hugged her hips left very little room for the imagination as it inched up her thighs with every step that she took. The sweet smell of Chanel fragrance rising from her flesh held the two gangsters captivated as they stared at her exposed breast.

"What can I do for you?" Moe quickly regained his poise.

"Oh, excuse me, I didn't mean to interrupt you." She glanced over at Blue. "There is a young man here to see you."

"What's his name?

"He didn't give me a name, but he did say that he was your nephew."

Moe leaned over to the security monitor, hanging from the wall and noticed Jihad at the bar.

"Thank you Roxy. Tell him that I will be with him shortly."

"Okay."

As she moved towards the door, Blue stopped her short.

"Excuse me Miss Roxy; do you mind if I have a word with you?

"Sure." Roxy spun around. "I don't mind if it's alright with Moe."

"I don't mind." Moe stood up as he finished his drink. "I'll let you two speak in private."

"Don't let us run you out of your office boss man." Blue responded. "I'm not saying anything that you can't hear."

"I know it's all good. I'm about to go out here and see what nephew is talking about."

"Alright, I'll be out there in a couple of minutes."

As Moe exited the room, Blue arose from where he was seated and made his way over to the mini bar located across the room. He was elaborately dressed in a brown sport coat and matching slacks, held up with an ostrich skin belt that complemented the shoes on his feet. Blue poured himself a glass a Remy Martin VSOP mixed with a splash of coke then turned towards Roxy.

"Have a seat." He motioned to the leather upholstered sofa against the wall. "Would you like something to drink?"

"That would be nice, but I am on the clock and time is money." She spoke in a flirtatious tone.

Blue cracked a devilish grin as he reached down in his pocket and pulled out a roll of hundred dollar bills. He peeled off a crispy Benjamin Franklin and set it down on the bar.

"You let me worry about the time and money." He looked her deep in the eyes. "You just need to relax."

Roxy eased over to where he was standing and rubbed her manicured hands across the back of Blue's cleaned shaven head.

"What is it that you want from me Mr. Blue?" "

"Only time will tell."

"Well in that case, I'll take a Cîroc on the rocks with a splash of pineapple juice."

For the next hour the two of them sat in the office and shared dialog but Roxy did most of the talking. Blue sipped his drink and listened, occasionally puffing his cigar while she told him her life story. Roxy explained in detail how her promiscuity had gotten her mixed up into some illegal activities, concerning a guy that she was dating in Philadelphia. Although she had grown up the suburbs and lived somewhat of a sheltered life, she had it rough. At thirteen years old Roxy had begun getting molested by her father who was a prominent judge in the city of Buffalo; and when she pled to her mother, Roxy's cries fell on deaf ears. As a young girl, she became very insecure and started exploring the dangerous parts of the city, searching for attention. By age fifteen, she had been turned out by the magnetism of the streets and quickly learned what it took to thrive in the ghetto. A variety of young hustlers would cater to her with shopping sprees in exchange for sexual desire. Gradually, the trips to the mall turned into trips to Atlanta GA and before Roxy knew it, she was trafficking cocaine to several states. For the next five years things were going smooth and Roxy was living a life that she had always imagined until it all came crumbling down.

It was the 4th July weekend when Roxy and a guy by the name of Wes, one of her many companions travelled to Philly for a Meek Mills concert. Being that Wes was from the city of brotherly love, he knew where all the entertainers, athletes and local ballers dwelled. The entire weekend, they splurged at the finest shops and boutiques on Chestnut Street; and attended every hot night spot from club Onyx to the Vango Lounge where Roxy got a chance to meet Cassidy and take pictures with the Broad street bully. As the night dwindled into the morning, they decided to get a Philadelphia cheesesteak from Geno's before heading to their hotel room. As they pulled to the intersection of 9th street and Passyunk Avenue, Wes let Roxy out of the rental while he found a place to park.

The restaurant was filled mostly with young adults who had just left the club, so the ambience was a bit louder than usual. As Roxy approached the counter to place an order, Wes came through the doors accompanied by two unfamiliar faces. By the look written across his brow, she could tell that he was uncomfortable as he conversed with the men. A minute or two past before the conversation flared into an argument. Suddenly, one of the guys caught Wes with a hard right cross the chin, sending him to the floor. Quickly rolling to his feet, Wes removed a 380 from his waist line and fired a shot into the person who had just punched him. It was pure pandemonium inside of Gino's as the patrons rushed towards the exit. Roxy was frozen with fear as the chaos unfolded right before her eyes. In an abrupt haste, Wes snatched her by the arm and hurried outside. By the time they made it to their vehicle, police had already swarmed the scene, apprehending them both. Wes was charged with attempted murder and possession of a weapon while Roxy was accused of accessory to a crime.

"So do you still have a case pending?" Blue asked her.

"Yeah, but my lawyer said that the next time that I go to court that the charges are supposed to get dropped." Roxy responded.

"That's good news." He sipped his Remy. "Does Moe know about the trouble that you got yourself into up in Philly?"

"Yes, he is aware of what happened." She replied. "He and my aunt Flo have been a blessing to me. They helped pay for my attorney and allowed me to work here until I get back on my feet."

"Well how can I be a blessing to you?"

Roxy's eyes shot down to the diamond encrusted Rolex that decorated Blue's wrist. She then looked up into his face and seen something in his eyes that she had never witnessed in a person before. This man had an aura about himself that was difficult to duplicate and the confidence that he displayed had actually turned her on, causing her panties to become moist. For a brief moment, she had forgotten that the objective was business and became slightly attracted to the older gentleman. Roxy had come across many ballers and gangsters in her short existence in the game and at that second, sitting in the back office of the EL Morocco, she knew that she was in the presence of a true boss.

"How would you like to be a blessing to me?" She regained her composure.

Blue placed his hand on the side of Roxy's face and rubbed her cheek gently, sending electricity through her body.

"I'm going to give you the world if you'll let me." He spoke in a deep baritone.

"You probably say that to all the young girls you deal with."

"For one, I don't deal with girls, I attract women! And two I only engage in someone if I see something special I them."

"So now you think that I'm special?"

"You don't think so?"

"I think that I am not as naive as I look so you don't have to stroke my ego just to get inside of my pants."

Blue laughed.

"I'm not going to sit up here and act like it hasn't crossed my mind. You're an attractive young lady so any man in their right mind would love to have sex with you, but that's not my only intent."

"Well what are your intentions?"

"My intention is to put a smile on your face if you'll allow me too."

"Do you know how many guys have come at me with this same song and dance?"

"This isn't a song or dance and I'm not the average guy that you're going to come across."

Roxy took a drink from her cup as she digested the words that had just escaped from Blue's mouth.

"Why me?" She questioned. "You can have any woman in the city that you want; why do you want to toy around with me? I have a lot going on right now and the only thing that I want to do is get my life back on track and getting involved with you would only complicate things."

"I'm not here to complicate things for you or bring any type of confusion into your life; I'm just trying to help you get through whatever it is that you're going through. And I promise that if you give me the opportunity to guide and give you some direction, your life will change overnight and most of your problems will go away."

"But you don't even know me!"

"I thought that we were getting a chance to know one another right now?" Blue re-lit his cigar. "And I hope as time progress, we get a chance to know each other a little better."

Roxy smiled, impressed with how he expressed himself.

"You're smooth." She admitted. "I know this is all game that you are running but a part of me still wants to believe you."

"And you know what I believe?"

"What might that be?"

"I believe that if anyone is running game here it's you." Blue took a puff of the cigar.

"What makes you say that? She asked a bit confused.

"Do you think that I'm crazy or stupid?" His demeanor turned ice cold.

"Neither?" Roxy voice exposed a hint of fear. "I actually think that you're rather brilliant."

"Then why in the fuck are you playing on my intelligence if you think that I'm so brilliant?"

"You're trippin!" Roxy got up to leave. "I don't have any idea what you are talking about."

Blue moved quickly alongside of her and blocked the doorway.

"Bitch you think I'm crazy." He became loud. "These last few weeks, I've been watching you parade around here in your mini skirt and short shirts, trying to get my attention so now you got it."

"I think that it's time that I get back to work."

Suddenly, Blue grabbed her by the throat and pressed her against the wall.

"I'm going to ask you this one time and one time only, who sent you, the feds or some niggas?" He inched the cigar close to her face.

"No one sent me!" Roxy panted in fear.

"Bitch, I've been around too many hoes that were seasoned prostitutes not to recognize when some amature bitch is trying to run some elementary game on me so cut the shit."

"Okay okay okay please don't hurt me." She pleaded. "No one sent me but I haven't been completely honest with you."

"Go ahead and talk." He continued inching the cigar closer.

Roxy mind began to race as she conjured up a story. She knew that she was in danger and if Blue didn't believe her, he might burn her face with the cigar or even kill her.

"I was just trying to get in position." She quickly spoke. "I know that there aren't too many men as powerful as you and Moe in the city and I just want to be a part of that. I'm tired of dealing with these broke ass niggas who swear that they are balling. I need a real man in my life that I can learn from."

Blue studied her with a close eye to see if she was lying.

""Why, didn't you just say that in the beginning?" He released her. "Why are you playing these mind games like I'm one of these young punks out here?"

"I'm sorry; I didn't mean to play mind games with you." Roxy's eyes began to wail up in tears as she rubbed her neck.

"There isn't any reason for you to be sorry, if anyone should be apologizing it should be me so don't go getting all emotional on me now." Blue reverted into his cool demeanor. "I think that you are a very attractive and smart young lady but I can never be too sure because sometimes people aren't who they say they are so I have to be careful."

"I understand!"

"Good!" He reached into his pocket and peeled off another c-note and passed it to her.

"No you don't have to….."

"Take it!" Blue pressed. "Then after you get yourself cleaned up, I want you to tell Moe that you're taking the rest of the night off because you're coming with me.

*****

Meanwhile, Moe and Jihad were at the bar, discussing business.

"So how is everything on your end of things?" Moe got right to the point.

"Everything is lovely." Jihad responded. "Those thangs moving like hot cakes. That last pack that you hit me wit was that thing; I hope you still got some of that left."

"Yeah, it's still around."

"Good! I need thirty of them in the morning."

"Thirty?" Moe chuckled. "That's ten more bricks than what we've been fronting you. Do you think you can handle it?"

"I know me and my team can handle it." Jihad emphasized. "Plus, I only want you to front me twenty, I'm going to put up the money for the other ten."

Moe took a moment before answering. He was impressed with Jihads ambition but there were some things that concerned him. As he leaned back into the bar stool, Moe studied the person in front of him. There was a look on Jihad's faced that Moe was very familiar with but only a few people possessed. Hunger mixed with a lot of determination lingered in the pupils of the young man's eyes. Moe smiled as he recognized the appetite that dwelled inside of him twenty years ago. Going against his better judgment, he dismissed all of the anxieties that he felt about his nephew. He just hoped that he wasn't allowing his emotions to supersede his intelligence.

"Give me the keys to the car that you drove." Moe finally spoke.

Without hesitation, Jihad recovered the keys from his pocket and set them on the bar as Moe continued his statement.

"Tomorrow morning at seven o'clock your vehicle will be located at the LaSalle train station parking lot with your request in the trunk. I expect you to meet me here with the money an hour after you retrieve the package."

"You don't have to wait until tomorrow." Jihad smiled. "I can have Jamal bring the money down here now."

"That'll work even better!" Moe nodded in agreement.

Quickly dialing Jamal's number, Jihad listened as the phone rang in his ear.

"What's poppin?" Jamal answered on the third ring.

"Yo, I need you to go through the spot and snatch that bag and bring it to me."

"Okay, where you at?"

"I'm down here kicking it with Unk."

Reading between the lines, Jamal knew that he was referring to Moe.

"I'm on my way." Jamal replied. "Give me about a half an hour!"

"Alright, I'll see you in a minute." Jihad ended the call.

As he hung up the phone, Moe signaled for the woman serving drinks at the other end of the bar. She quickly stepped to his assistance once gaining eye contact with him.

"Hey Moe, What can I get for you?" She spoke in the sweetest voice.

"Yeah, Shawna let me get my usual."

"Crown Royal and coke?"

"Yes, thank you!"

"And what can I get for you Jihad?"

"Let me get a fish sandwich and a ginger ale."

"Okay, I'll be right back with your order." Shawna stepped off.

Once she was out of earshot, Moe turned his attention back to Jihad.

"I hope you're not always that reckless when you're on the telephone?"

"What are you talking about?" Jihad cringed. "I wasn't talking reckless!"

"When you were on the phone with Jamal, you told him to go through the spot and snatch the bag and bring it to you. And when he asked you where you were, your response was that you were kickin it with Unk."

"Yeah, but I never said an address or anyone's name so how was I talking reckless?"

Suddenly, Shawna reappeared with their drinks.

"You're sandwich should be out shortly." She assured Jihad.

"Okay, thank you." He responded.

Moe smiled at the waitress then waited for her to walk off before he continued.

"Go through the spot... Snatch the bag... Kicking it with Unk... These are all key phrases that the Feds can use to build a conspiracy case against you." He explained. "If the government is watching and you better believe that they're watching and listening to every word when you're playing this game, they can build a drug case from a simple word or two, especially if the people talking are known for that specific crime."

"That's some real shit!" Jihad spoke with concern.

"Look nephew, I've been at this thing now for at least thirty years so I know how the game is played and I know that they're watching and waiting for me to slip up. Why do you think, I don't use phones? Every time we talk we talk in person never over the phone because I know that one word will get me nailed to the cross."

"Damn Moe, do you really think that they are watching us like that?"

"Jihad, you're too smart to be asking me such a naïve question like that." Moe chuckled as he drank his liquor. "Even if they're weren't watching and listening, you should always think and navigate as if they were."

"You're absolutely right." Jihad nodded in agreement.

Just then, the waitress returned with a Haddock fish sandwich and placed it in front of Jihad alongside a ginger ale and another shot of Crown Royal for Moe.

For the next half an hour, the two men involved themselves in small talk as they ate, drank and waited for Jamal to bring the money.

"Where the fuck is this nigga at?" Jihad mumbled to himself.

He glanced at the call log on his cell phone and noticed that an hour and fifteen minutes had gone by since he had spoken to Jamal. Just as Jihad felt himself getting agitated, the door to the tavern swung open and in came Jamal with a black Louis Vuitton duffle bag draped across his shoulder.

CHAPTER 17

Across the street from the EL Morocco, lurking in the shadows of the night, Stacks, Shabazz and Y.G. sat patiently inside of a black Jeep Cherokee with tinted windows, surveying the premises. The music played at a low volume as cigarette smoke escaped the vehicle through a cracked window. For the last couple of weeks, they had been doing their homework, trying to get a schedule on Moe and Blue's daily routine but the two gangsters were unpredictable.

"I'ma kill one of these niggas tonight!" Y.G. stated through clenched teeth.

"Be cool my nigga." Shabazz replied. "I know you want these dudes head but we have to catch them right because we might not get a second chance if we jump the gun."

"Shabazz is right." Stacks included. "When we get at these niggas, we gotta make it count."

"Y'all act like y'all scared of these muthafuckas or something!" Y.G. exploded. "These niggas aint untouchable like everybody thinks and if anyone of them walks out this bar, I'm popping they top off."

"Aint nobody scared." Shabazz countered. "All I'm saying is that we got to be cool and do it right."

Six months had gone by since the demise of Gamble and Y.G. was beginning to allow his emotions to get the best of him. Day and night he strategized ways to seek revenge and now that the time was drawing near, he felt his crew was backing out on him.

"Gamble was like a brother to both of you niggas so don't front on him now that he's gone." Y.G. continued. "He always had our back so it's only right that we put this work in so he can rest in peace."

"I feel everything that your saying bra but we still have to be smart." Shabazz reasoned. "Blue and Moe is connected like a muthafucka and would have each one of us knocked off if he even thought that we were plotting on them."

A sinister grin spread across Y.G. face as he removed a package of cocaine from his pocket. Casually dipping his pinky nail into the bag, he powdered both nostrils. Shabazz and Stacks sat there in silence, watching their partner as the venom took its effect. They understood that Y.G's. behavior was abnormal due to his brother death but he was beginning to get out of control.

"Y'all see this?" He grabbed the 38 revolver from off of his lap.

Both men continued to stare as he emptied the chambers, replacing only one bullet in its slot. After spinning the barrel several times, Y.G. aimed the gun at his temple, pulling the trigger. (Click)

"I can't even kill myself." He emphasized. "So how in the fuck do you think I'm going to let these pussy ass niggas kill me?"

"You're trippin now Fam!" Shabazz became angry. "Don't be doing that bullshit around me."

"Well quit acting like a bitch then."

"If you keep runnin your mouth and I'ma show you who the bitch is."

"Hold up!" Stacks interjected. Look!"

They ceased the commotion and observed a familiar vehicle pull to the curbside of the bar. Y.Gs. blood really began to boil once he noticed Trina in the driver's seat of the cherry red E class Mercedes Benz accompanied by a male companion. A minute or two later, the guy in the passenger seat exited the sedan carrying a duffle bag across his shoulder.

"I know that nigga from somewhere." Shabazz searched his brain as he watched the man enter the El Morocco.

"That's the boy Jamal." Shabazz confirmed. "He be uptown with that nigga Stone."

"That is him."Stacks recollected. "We used to play ball in the summer leagues together back in the day."

"Fuck all that!" Shabazz barked. "What's this nigga doing with Trina and what the hell is in that bag?"

Y.G had a diabolical look in his eyes as he focused on the woman in the luxurious red vehicle.

"I don't know but I'm damn sure about to find out."

CHAPTER 18

Around two o'clock the next morning, Trina entered into her two bedroom apartment and tossed her fur coat across a chair in the dining area. The studio was fully furnished with all the amenities that a woman could desire: wall to wall carpet, entertainment center, suede furniture throughout the living room and a stocked bar. Her vision was a little distorted due to the darkness mixed with the alcohol that she'd been consuming so she stumbled over to the lamp and flicked on the light. To her surprise, Y.G. was sitting on the sofa gripping a pistol inside of his hand.

"Shit!" She stumbled backwards startled.

Y.G. didn't say a word; he just stared at Trina with intimidating eyes as she attempted to gain her composer.

"What the fuck are you doing in my house? Her fear turned to anger

Slowly rising up from where he was seated, YG walked over towards Trina and gently rubbed his free hand against the side of her face. She slightly jumped from the touch of his fingertips brushing alongside her cheek because she knew what Y.G. was capable of doing.

"What are you doing in my house?" Trina repeated.

"Where is my son?" YG finally spoke.

"He's at my sister's house." She replied. "Now answer my question."

"I'm not allowed in your home anymore?"

"I'm not about to play these games with you. What do you want?"

"I want some answers." YG responded in a controlled voice.

"What do you want the answer too?"

YG pointed his gun at a chair in the kitchen, gesturing for Trina to sit down. She cautiously followed instruction never taking her eyes off of the revolver. Once she was seated, he pulled up a chair and sat next to her.

"Are you fucking that nigga?"

"What nigga?" Trina snapped.

"Don't play stupid with me." Y.G. stared her in the eyes. "The nigga Jamal."

At the mention of Jamal's name, Trina became uneasy as she sat up in her chair.

"Wh... what are you talking about." She began to stutter.

"You know what the fuck I'm talking about!" YG retorted. "Now stop playing with me and answer the fucking question before I get upset."

"Why are you questioning me about who I'm fucking, you're not my man anymore!"

YG smacked Trina violently across the face with the back of his hand, sending her tumbling to the floor.

"You're always going to be my bitch rather you like it or not." He stood over her still gripping his pistol.

With blood trickling from the corner of her mouth, Trina looked up into YG's threatening eyes and smiled.

"Mmm, you know I like it rough!" She licked her wound.

Expressionless, YG watched her closely as she slowly crawled to him on her hands and knees. Once she was at his feet, Trina carefully grabbed the hand holding the gun and placed the weapon to her temple at the same time unzipping his pants. He allowed his jeans to fall to the floor as she reached into his underwear, searching for his manhood. The erection, staring her in the face let Trina know that YG was willing to fulfill her desires. She gently caressed his dick as she placed it in her mouth and began going to work. Her silk tongue licked every inch of his chocolate staff until he was brick hard.

"Fuck me!" Trina pleaded.

With the snub nose still to her temple, YG clutched a fist full of hair and pulled Trina to her feet. Abruptly bending her over the kitchen sink, he ripped her skirt down to her ankles and entered her from behind. With every stroke, he smacked her on the ass with the gun. Trina's excitement grew more intense as the cold steel beat against her warm flesh. The moist juices from the pussy felt like some sticky water and with each thrust it became wetter. Trina could feel him in the pit of her stomach as he continuously lunge into her with anger.

"This is what you want, you funky bitch?" YG shouted.

"Yessss." She panted back. "Fuck this pussy baby. Yeah, do it just like that."

After a few more strokes, YG pulled his dick out and replaced it with the barrel of the pistol. As he slid the blue steel in and out of her, Trina screams became louder as she began to reach her climax.

"Oh, I'm about to cum…. I'm about to cum!"

YG watched as the fluids from the pussy started squirting recurrently onto his weapon. He quickly re-entered his dick and went back to work, pounding her from the back. Besides the moaning all you could hear was his thighs slapping against Trina's voluptuous ass as she eagerly threw herself back into him. This lasted for about twenty minutes before YG finally exploded inside of her. Once it was over, he buckled his pants and instructed Trina back into the living room. She wiped herself with a paper towel and did as directed. Once she was seated, YG placed the gun onto the coffee table and took a seat across from her.

"We are going to try this again." He spoke in a more relaxed voice." What's up with you and the nigga Jamal?"

Trina let out a long sigh as she began to speak.

"I met Jamal a couple of months ago at the Oak room." She admitted. "We get up once and awhile but it isn't anything serious."

"Do you love this nigga?"

"Dude is cool but it's nothing like that. He's just something for me to do from time to time."

"You got to have some type of feelings for the nigga." YG barked. "He riding around here driving your car like it's his and shit."

"Why do you care about who I'm fucking or who is driving my car." Trina replied." You don't give a fuck about me because if you did, you wouldn't've left me to raise our son by myself."

"Bitch, you jumped ship on me when I went to prison so if anybody should feel some type of way, it's me."

"Ain't nobody jump ship on you." She defended. "You left me out here to fend for myself."

Trina, I can count on one hand how many letters you wrote me and the only time that you came to visit me, was when I was downtown in the holding center so don't sit up here and act like you're the victim. I did everything for you when we were together; you didn't have to worry about shit."

"You didn't have to worry about shit either; I played my position. I cooked, I cleaned, I sucked and fucked you on command, and I even set niggas up for you so don't act like I never held it down."

"Yeah, you held it down while everything was sweet but as soon as shit got a little hectic for a nigga, you jumped ship and left me for dead."

Tears began to wail up in Trina's eyes as YG reprimanded her about their past.

"Besides my brother, you were the only person that I trusted." He continued. "So how do you think I felt when I was upstate, fighting for my freedom and I'm hearing that the mother of my only child was out here freaking off with these suckas?"

"I'm sorry Darius." She referred to him by his government name. "I'm sorry that I didn't hold it down like I was supposed to but I was young, stupid and five years had seemed like forever when you first got locked up. I was lost and confused out here without you, especially when people began getting in my ear telling me about all the other bitches that you were fucking. My intentions was never to shit on you, I just got caught up in my emotions and started doing me. Again, I'm sorry"

While listening to Trina tell her side of the story, YG removed a cigarette from a pack inside of his jacket pocket and lit it up.

"I already know that you're a sorry, funky, no good hoe." He blew a ring of smoke into her face. "But you're my sorry, funky, no good hoe, right?"

With tears still in her eyes, she shot him an evil glare without responding to that last statement.

"You're still my hoe, Right?" He repeated.

"Yes Darius, I'm still your hoe." She dried her eyes.

"And I can still depend on you right?"

"I would like to think so, just tell me what it is that you want me to do."

"I want you to keep doing what you've been doing."

"And what is that?"

"Fucking and sucking that nigga Jamal."

"You don't have to say it like that." She frowned.

"Just keep doing you."

"Okay and then what?"

"I'll let you know but for the meantime, I want you to find out everything that you can about that nigga because I think him and his crew had something to do with my brother's murder."

"Are you serious?" Trina gasped.

YG nodded, confirming his assumptions.

"So you dealing with homeboy may be a blessing in disguise because you're going to help me rock this nigga to sleep.

"I'm willing to do whatever it is that you need me to do under one circumstance."

"What's that?

"That you spend more time with your son."

"Man listen…"

"No you listen." Trina cut him short. "I know that I fucked up, I'm woman enough to admit that but D.J. shouldn't suffer because of my carelessness. So if I do this thing with Jamal, You have to promise me that you'll spend some time with D.J."

There was a brief silence in the air as YG stared at the mother of his child with mixed emotions. On one hand, he couldn't stand the sight of her, being that she left him while in prison. Then there was something inside of him that still loved her, especially seeing that she was still willing to put in some work for him.

"I got you!" He cracked a smile. "I'm going to start coming to get my little man at least once a week."

"I'm serious Darius; DJ needs his father in his life."

"I said that I got you." YG picked his gun up off of the coffee table. "Now go and wash yo ass so I can fuck you again before I bounce."

Trina stood up from the couch and began walking towards the bathroom. As her naked body glided past him, YG smacked her across the ass with the pistol.

"Bitch get yo ass in there and get ready for round two."

CHAPTER 19

The next night Jamal cruised through the city, smoking a loud pack while listening to a new mixed CD by Young Jeezy. The music had him in a zone as the lyrics from Atlanta's number one trap star blared through the speakers. He felt as if every verse was speaking directly to him. The last six months had gone according to plan and he felt like he was living the American dream. Money, cocaine, women and the best marijuana to choke on; what else could a nigga asked for? He turned onto the Chippewa district and observed the streets alive with partygoers every shade and color. For three blocks, there were nightclubs and restaurants arranged on both sides with an array of people scattered around. As his Escalade came to a standstill in front of The Lodge, it seemed as if everyone was frozen with anticipation of who was behind the tinted windows of the cream colored S.U.V. After reducing the volume on his music, Jamal lowered the passenger side window to get a better view.

"Aye beautiful, what it look like in there?" He yelled to a female standing in line.

"I don't know I haven't been inside yet." She smiled.

Jamal eyed her from head to toe and was impressed with what he saw. Her deep dimpled, butterscotch complexion was flawless.

"Come here for a minute."

"No, you get out and come here." She swiftly shot back.

Luckily there was an empty parking space across the street in front of the mighty taco so Jamal quickly bust a U turn before anyone could get it. Once the Escalade was secure, he tucked the 40 Cal on his hip, exited the vehicle and began walking towards the club. The woman and her friend watched Jamal as he strolled in their direction.

"Mmm, girl that nigga is fine as hell." Butterscotch friend expressed. "If you don't want him, I'll see what he's talking about."

"I bet you would!" Butterscotch nudged her playfully.

Jamal approached them dressed in a pair of True Religion jeans and a Brand New Life T-shirt.

"Y'all ladies don't have to wait out here, come on." He gestured for them to follow him.

With no hesitation, the two women fell into stride as he led the way to the door. Once the heavy set bouncer recognized that it was Jamal, he allowed them to skip the line and enter the club without being searched. Jamal reached into his pocket and pulled out a bankroll intentionally for Butterscotch to see.

"They're with me." He pointed to the females trailing behind him as he handed security a C-note.

"Good looking Jamal." He gave him dap. "Enjoy yourself tonight."

"No doubt!"

"As they walked through the party, Butterscotch and her friend noticed all the attention that Jamal was receiving. He was revered by both man and women as they made their way to the V.I.P. section. Jamal entered the roped off area, shaking hands with many of the major hustlers as the gold diggers eyeballed him with lust.

"What are y'all drinking?" He asked as they took a seat at a booth overlooking the dance floor.

"You didn't even tell us your name." Butterscotch said, slipping in beside him.

"Jamal." He extended his hand. "And you are?"

"My name is Fatima and this is my girl Erica." She shook his hand.

"How you doing Erica?"

"I'm doing well and you?" She eyed him seductively.

Jamal smiled and told her that he was good as he picked up on the enticing vibes that Erica was sending. The dress that she had on was screaming that she wanted to get fucked and if the night went as planned he would be the one fulfilling that desire.

"You still haven't told me what y'all wanted to drink." He curved his attention back to Fatima.

"I guess we can drink whatever it is that you're drinking." Fatima responded.

Jamal looked over at Erica and she nodded in agreement.

"Then that's what it is then."

A minute or two had passed before Jamal could get the attention of a waitress working the V.I.P area. The club was alive with a collection of people from various parts of the city along with some Canadians from Toronto.

"Hey Jamal!" The waitress appeared with a flirtatious grin. "What can I get for you?"

"How you doing Lisa?" Jamal returned with a smile of his own. "Let me get a bottle of patron and a triple order of wings with fries."

"How do you want your wings?"

"Let me get half of them hot and the other half BBQ."

"Is that all?"

"Yeah, that'll be all for now. Thank you!"

"Okay, I'll be right back." She sashayed off into the crowd.

The two women picked up on the chemistry between Jamal and the waitress.

"Is that one of your girlfriends or something?" Erica was the first to speak.

"Nah, what makes you say that?" Jamal laughed.

"Apparently there's something going on between y'all the way she came over here skinning and grinning," Fatima countered.

"It's nothing like that." He assured them. "I come here quite often and I flirt with the ladies that work here sometimes but it's nothing serious."

"Mmm hmm, I'm pretty sure you've fucked a few of them too." Fatima stated.

Jamal shook his head. "I'm not about to do this with y'all! I'm starting to feel like I'm in a relationship or something."

They all began laughing at Jamal's last statement just as the waitress returned with the bottle of liquor sitting in a bucket of ice. She eyeballed them as she dressed their table with the alcohol and glasses.

"Can I get you guys anything else?" Lisa asked politely.

"Yeah, can you make sure those wings are extra crispy?" Jamal replied.

"Sure." Lisa continued to eyeball him. "I'll be back shortly with your food."

Jamal snatched the bottle of liquor from the ice and filled the glasses halfway to the rim. Once everyone possessed their drinks, Jamal raised his glass. The ladies were in awe as the diamonds surrounding the watch on his wrist sparkled off the lights in the club.

"To success and new friendships." He toasted.

"To success and new friendships." The ladies replied in unison.

After drinking their shot, Jamal refilled their glasses. Two hours later the platter of food was empty and they were working on their second bottle of Patron as they engaged in small talk. The results from the alcohol were beginning to take its effect as the two women practically threw themselves onto Jamal. It was clear that they were ready to have sex and he picked up on it quick. His hands fondled Fatima's bare legs, exploring beneath her skirt as Erica brushed against him, whispering seductive comments into his ear.

"What's up with you tonight?" Erica asked him.

"Y'all already know what's up?" Jamal responded in a drunken slur

"Where are we going?" Fatima questioned.

"We can go and snatch a room somewhere downtown." He continued rubbing her thighs.

"That's cool." She glanced over to Erica.

"I'm game for whatever!" Erica confirmed. "You already know how I get down."

30 minutes later, they were staggering into room 432 at the Adams Mark hotel across from the skyway. They didn't waste any time stripping off their clothes once they were inside. Jamal led the way over to the king size bed as he and Fatima's lips intertwined. She pushed him on to the mattress and continued to kiss him passionately, working her way down to his manhood. Slowly undressing, Erica sat on the edge of the bed and began playing with herself. Jamal locked eyes with her and signaled for her to join them. She quickly complied and crawled over to where he was laying and mounted his face. In a circular motion, Jamal commenced to tickle her clitoris with the tip of

his tongue, causing Erica to moan with pleasure. Once his manhood arose to the occasion, Fatima straddled him and eased down gently. Jamal was so caught up in the moment that he never attempted to put on a condom.

"Damn baby." She squirmed back and forth in a rhythm like motion. Jamal clutched her ass and pulled himself deeper inside until Fatima felt him in the depths of her stomach. A moment or so later Erica switched places with her friend, allowing Jamal to take her from behind while she licked the walls of Fatima's pussy.

Over the next hour, the three of them switched positions numerous times as they aimed to please one another. They were exhausted as they collapse onto the bed, dripping in sweat. Besides the air blowing from the dispenser, the only sound in the room was the heavy breathing coming from the bodies sprawled across the mattress. Jamal smiled to himself as he laid there intertwined between the two dime pieces, pondering on what just took place until they dozed off.

*****

Early the next morning, Jamal woke up to a hangover and an empty bed. His eyes searched the room for any signs of the girl's but there wasn't a stitch of clothing or anything else indicating their presence. He quickly jumped up and snatched his jeans off of the floor, checking its pockets. To his surprise, the wad of bills was still in place. As he began counting the money, Jamal walked into the bathroom and noticed something written in lipstick on the mirror.

Hey Boo, Sorry we had to leave but I had some business to take care of this morning…..we really enjoyed ourselves last night and look forward to doing it again soon. Give me a call. 716 603 4237 (FATIMA)

He grabbed his cell phone and began dialing the digits left on the glass but was interrupted by an incoming call flashing across the screen.

"What's good?" He answered, recognizing the number.

"Where are you at?" Trina questioned.

"I'm downtown at the Adams Mark hotel."

"What the fuck are you doing at a hotel?" She snapped.

"Bitch don't be questioning me about where I'm at!" Jamal shot back. "I'm relaxing, trying to get my mind right."

"Well, do you still want me to follow you to drop your truck off at the shop or not?"

"Damn, I forgot all about that." He told her. "Come down here and pick me up."

"What's the room number?"

"I'm in room 432."

"I'll be there in 15 minutes

"Okay."

Shortly after the conversation, Trina arrived at the room carrying three breakfast sandwiches and some coffee from the café adjacent to the lobby. To her astonishment, the door was slightly cracked as she approached. Without a second thought, she pushed it open and cautiously stepped inside. Immediately Trina took note of the scattered clothing on the floor along with the disheveled bedding. Jamal wasn't anywhere in sight but she could hear the running water coming from the bathroom so she assumed that he was in the shower. She walked deeper into the room and took a seat in a lounge chair against the wall. As she opened her bag and began eating her egg and cheese croissant, Trina noticed Jamal's watch sitting on the nightstand and picked it up. She was fascinated by how clear the diamonds was, thinking that it must've cost him a fortune. Through her observation, a touch of fear jolted through her body once she reached the inscription on the back reading GAMBLE.

"Oh my goodness." She mumbled to herself.

The words of YG resonated into her mind as she thought back to what he said about the possibilities of his brother's murder. Once she heard the shower come to a stop, she quickly arranged the jewelry back in its place to avoid suspicion. Minutes later, Jamal appeared in the doorway with a towel wrapped around his waist. Beads of water dripped from his torso as he strode towards her.

"What's up?" He examined her. "How long have you been sitting out here?"

"I got here about five minutes ago." She quickly responded.

"Did you bring me something to eat?"

Trina reached over and grabbed the bag off of the nightstand.

"Here." She handed it to him. "There are two turkey bacon, egg and cheese sandwiches in there."

"Good looking out." He opened the bag.

"No problem."

Jamal took a bite into his sandwich. "After we dropped the truck off down here on Genesee Street, I need you to take me to the block real quick. I was supposed to meet Jihad at nine o'clock this morning so I hope this nigga don't get on some bullshit."

"Well maybe if you wouldn't've been in here freaking off with one of your whores all night, you would've been able to get up and be on time." Trina expressed with an attitude.

He grabbed her up by her arm. "First of all bitch, don't worry about what the fuck I'm doing or who I'm doing it with."

"Get the fuck off of me." She snatched away.

"Who the fuck do you think you talking to?" Jamal attempted to take hold of her again.

Trina shot him an evil glare. "I'm serious Jamal don't put your fucking hands on me again."

"Or what?

"Put your hands on me and find out!"

"Whatever bitch!" He walked over and picked his clothes up off of the floor. "Don't make me beat ya ass in here."

"You're not going to do nothing to me."

Jamal laughed as he began getting dressed. "You're real tough this morning ain't you?"

"I'll be downstairs in the car waiting for you." She walked towards the door. "And I have something else that I need to do so could you please hurry up?"

"I don't know what your problem is but you better get ya mind right before I fuck you up."

"Whatever!" She stepped into the hallway.

When she reached the elevators, Trina recovered her cell phone from the hand bag draped across her shoulder and quickly dialed YG's number.

"Yo!" He picked up on the second ring.

"Hey, it's me." Her voice trembled as she spoke. "I think that Jamal did have something to do with what happen to your brother."

Why, what happened?" YG responded with anger.

"I went to pick him up from the Adams Mark this morning and while he was in the shower, I was searching around and came across a watch with Gamble's name inscribed on the back."

"What it look like?"

"It's platinum Franck Muller with diamonds throughout the bezel"

"Where are y'all at now?"

"We're still at the hotel but I'm about to follow him to Geneva's on Genesee to drop his truck off."

"Okay, try to stall him for a minute so I can get my people in position." He instructed. "Text me when you get close."

"Okay!" She ended the call.

Ten minutes later, Trina was in the E Class trailing behind Jamal, headed east on the 33 expressway. Her stomach turned with apprehension as she contemplated the event about to take place. Once Jamal veered off onto the Best Street exit, she texted YG as ordered, letting him know that they were nearby. He instantly responded with a thumbs up emoji, signifying that he was all set. As they came to a stop at the Bailey and Genesee intersection, the anxiety that Trina was feeling worsened. For a brief moment, she was establishing a change of heart as thoughts about the consequences flashed through her mind. She quickly dismissed these emotions the second the light turned green and continued towards the destination. Pulling into the parking lot, Trina scanned the area. There wasn't any sign of YG or his crew at first glance; but as soon as Jamal placed his vehicle in park and killed the engine, two masked men wearing hoodies appeared from behind the building with machine guns and opened fire.

  Rat ta tat... tat... tat... tat... tat... tat...

  Jamal never saw it coming. The first shot shattered the driver side window and ripped through his face, decorating the dashboard with parts of his brain. The rounds that followed were just to make sure that the job was complete. Bullets pierced the metal doors into the motionless body, sprawling it onto the passenger seat. Boiling with rage, YG continued squeezing the trigger until the clip was empty. His partner Shabazz felt a sense of satisfaction as he watched the corpse shudder with every bullet. In a panic, Trina shifted her car into reverse and backed up into oncoming traffic almost causing an accident. Horns blared from every direction as she sped off. Oblivious to the bystanders across the street, YG raced over to the Escalade and opened the door once the shots ceased. He stared at Jamal's body momentarily before releasing a glob of spit onto him.

  "C'mon Fam, we gotta go!" Shabazz shouted.

  At the sound of his partner's voice, YG moved swiftly, confiscating the watch from the dead man's wrist before disappearing back into the cut from where they had emerged.

CHAPTER 20

Jihad clutched his new born baby in the pit of his arms as he stared at her with admiration. Earlier that morning, Angela had given birth to an 8lb, 7oz little girl which they named Imani. All morning the both of them had been marveling over the small bundle of joy with angelic features and Jihad was still in awe that he had participated in bringing a life so beautiful into the world.

"Thank you." He kissed Angela on the forehead.

"What are you thanking me for?" She questioned.

"I thank you for not giving up on me. I know that it's not easy putting up with my bullshit and sometime I wonder why you even bother at all."

"I'm never going to give up on you Jihad. And I put up with you and your foolishness because I love you. I've already told you that I don't care about the money and everything else that comes along with it. All I want is for you to love me back and be here for your family."

Angela's words were filled with compassion as she raised the back of the hospital bed with the hand held remote. The delivery had been a long procedure and she was exhausted. Her body ached from the incision across the bottom of her stomach, making it hard to get comfortable.

"Now that you have a daughter, what are you prepared to do?" She rested her head onto a soft pillow.

"What do you mean; what I am I prepared to do?" Jihad looked at her with a puzzled expression. "You already know what I'm going to do. I'm going to make sure that you and my baby girl don't want for nothing."

"And how are you going to do that?"

Jihad gazed down at his daughter resting in his arms then back into the eyes of Angela.

"Don't start this right now Ang." He shook his head. "This is supposed to be a pleasant moment that we're experiencing together and I don't need you breathing down my throat right now. I just want to enjoy my first day, being a father without the drama.

"I'm sorry baby." Angela apologized. "I don't mean to stress you out; I just want what's best for Imani."

"I want what's best for Imani too, but it's still some things that I need to do before I can make that transition."

There was a long pause in the conversation as they both became absorbed in their thoughts. All Angela wanted to do was to settle down and live a normal life but Jihad wasn't content with living ordinary. He had always desired more and was willing to do whatever it took to get him to the next level but was prepared to make some changes if that's what it took to create some peace for his family. The more he stared into his daughter's eyes the further he could see into the future and if he continued to travel the road that he was on, it was certain to end in one or two ways.

"So what happens now?" Angela broke the silence.

"Once you're back on your feet, you're going to start making preparations to make that move to Virginia with your sister." Jihad replied.

"Jihad, I'm not trying to..."

"We've already talked about this!" He cut her short. "And as far as I'm concerned this isn't an option. I need you to go down there and set the foundation so everything will be in place by the time I get there."

"Okay jihad." She let out a long sigh. "I'm going to go down there but you have to promise me that you're going to square all the way up when we get there. No schemes or scams. Everything has to be legit."

"Once I liquidate and cash out everything is going to be square business, I promise you that. One of my mans that I grew up with moved to Norfolk V.A. and opened up a small car lot about a year ago and he said that it is sweet and I can come down and sell used cars with him whenever I get ready. It's just a couple more things that I need to take care of before I bounce."

"That's a good idea because, I heard that the car business is very lucrative and I think that you would be good at it because you like dealing with people."

"And it still allows me to be a hustler." He emphasized. "Because to be a successful car dealer, a person has to have a hustler's mentality"

His phone echoed throughout the room, interrupting their conversation.

"Hello!" Jihad quickly answered the phone.

"Where you at?" Stone asked in a frantic tone.

"I'm at the hospital with Angela." He responded. "Why, what's the matter?"

"Somebody just ambushed Jamal at Geneva's"

"Hold up!" Jihad was perplexed. "What do you mean somebody ambushed Jamal?"

"My man at Geneva's just called me and said that some niggas ran up on cousin and air his joint out."

"Is he dead?"

"I don't know but my people said that they hit him up pretty good. We need to get down there and see what poppin?"

"Alright, I'm on my way."

When he hung up, Jihad set the baby in its bassinet and looked up at Angela with fire in his eyes. She could tell that something was wrong from the conversation but by the expression on his face, she was afraid to ask.

"Jamal just got shot!" He confirmed her fears. "

"Oh my god, no!" She gasps. "What happened?"

"I don't know, I'm about to go up there now and try to find out what's going on. I'll be back up here within the hour or two but if you need something before then, call me and I'll send somebody to get it."

"I'm fine." Angela told him. "You just be careful out there because I don't need you doing anything crazy."

"No doubt." He responded in a dry voice.

"I'm serious Jihad. I know you and I know how you feel about Jamal and I don't want you to go and get yourself in any trouble."

"I understand your concerns baby girl but I still need to see what's going on. I don't even know if my cousin is dead or alive."

"Okay, I love you."

"I love you too!" He said as he exited the door.

*****

Police cruisers explored the eastside of Buffalo for the remainder of the morning in pursuit of any evidence, concerning the 26th homicide of the year. They checked every alleyway and backyard, searching for footprints or anything else that would give them a break in their case. The crime scene was barricaded and sectioned off with yellow tape while the detectives questioned the nearby spectators who may have witnessed anything irregular before or after the shooting. By the time Jihad and Stone pulled up to Geneva's, the paramedics were placing Jamal onto a gurney. They were able to get a peek at him right before the EMT covered the body up with a white sheet, leaving nothing but one of his sneakers exposed. Jihad attempted to push through the fortified area to get a better look but was stopped short by an officer securing the scene. Tears began flowing down his face as he and Stone watched his cousin get stationed into the back of an ambulance and hauled off.

"Hell nah, not my nigga!" Jihad cried out at the top of his lungs.

"Damn!"." Stone punched the side of the ambulance. "We're going to paint the town red behind this one."

Jihad led his disgruntled friend to the car; locking eyes with each individual he passed by. As they got in and pulled off Agent Daniels recognized their faces and jotted down the license plate number after snapping a quick photo of them with her phone. By this time the crowd had double in size and assembled around the auto mechanic service station, attempting to catch a glimpse at what was happening,.

"Excuse me sir!" Agent Daniels yelled out to her superior. "Can you give me a minute?"

Agent Wright slowly made his way over to where his underling was scribbling onto her notepad.

"What do we have over here?" He questioned.

Agent Daniels displayed the picture on her cellular to Agent Wright and instantly his wheels began spinning.

"I knew that this Cadillac truck looked familiar." A lightbulb went off inside of his head. "The victim and Jihad are related."

"Do you think that this is some type of retaliation for what happened to our friend Mr. Gamble?"

"It's definitely a good possibility." Agent Wright declared. "But we don't have any strong evidence to go on at this point. The victim wasn't robbed and from the looks of things, he never even seen it coming. Whoever did this wanted him dead!"

"What about the other vehicle that was trailing him at the time that he was ambushed?" Agent Daniels checked her notes. "Witnesses say that there was a female in a red Mercedes Benz driving behind him when he pulled up and then sped from the scene once the shot were fired."

"Yes, I need you to see if the witness was able to get a positive I.D. on the license plate number and then put an APB out on that vehicle."

"I'm on it!" Agent Daniels nodded.

"Meanwhile, I'm going to run a background check on the target and see what I can come up with."

"Okay, just keep me up to date on whatever you dig up on him."

"Will do!" Agent Wright agreed. "And it probably won't be a bad idea if we go and pay our boy's Jihad and Stone a Visit over the next couple of days to shake them up a bit."

"Alright, let me wrap things up around here and I'll meet you back at the office." Agent Daniels said.

Agent Wright turned around and walked to the unmarked vehicle parked on the sidewalk. He was determined to get to the bottom of this investigation and put an end to all of the major players involved but to do that, he was going to have to disrupt some circles.

CHAPTER 21

Back at the projects in the downtown of Buffalo, Y.G. and his gunmen were invigorated with adrenaline. They sat around the small apartment smoking on a loud pack while discussing the details of their latest atrocity. Once the sunset into the skyline, they had intentions on hitting the streets once again on the hunt for those responsible for his brother's demise. Stacks and Shabazz were fulfilled by the work that they had put in on the behalf of their comrade, however Y.G. wouldn't be satisfied until everyone involved was buried. He took a long pull from the swisher sweet as he removed a large desert eagle from his waistline and placed it on the table. He disassembled the metallic object within a matter of minutes and began cleaning it with lubricating oil. By the time the firearm was reconstructed, they were on their second blunt of sour diesel.

"I'm not playing with these niggas." Y.G. cocked the slide back and set the dessert back on his hip. "I'm going to catch each one of them faggots one by one."

"Say no more my guy!" Stacks inhaled the smoke. "When we get through laying the murder game down, the town is going to be too shook up to come outside."

"I don't give a fuck about the town being shook up. All I want to do is make the niggas responsible for what happened to my brother to suffer."

Stacks took another pull then thumped the ashes into the tray in front of him. He glared over at Y.G. and understood his friend's frustration.

"I'm with you family. Anybody we even think had anything to do with what happened to Gamble is going to get it."

"Without question." Shabazz confirmed. "My gun ain't never on safety."

"I'm not going to front, y'all boys was on point today." Y.G. announced. "By the time he put his whip in park, we was already up on him."

Yeah, Jamal never seen that shit coming." Stacks declared.

"Don't you ever say that nigga name again, you hear me?" Y.G. snapped.

"My bad G, I was just tryna…."

"I don't care what you were trying to do Just don't let that shit happen again, you understand me?"

Stacks locked eyes with Y.G. "I got you

"What's up with Trina?" Shabazz attempted to change the subject.

"She's a little shook up but she'll be alright." Y.G. responded. "I just have to coach her through it so her emotions don't get the best of her."

"No question! Because we don't need her to develop a conscious and find religion because that can cost us"

"We're not going to have to worry about that." Y.G. assured them. "Trina is as thorough as they come. Trust me!"

Stacks nodded in agreement as he inhaled the weed smoke.

"Trina is definitely official when it comes to staying quiet.

"I hope so." Shabazz declared. "You know that her car was on the scene when it went down so don't be surprise if the ds come knocking on her door, asking questions."

"This isn't Trina's first rodeo." Y.G. replied. "She knows how to handle herself under pressure."

"Did she tell you anything about the boy Stone or any of them other niggas that homeboy run with? Shabazz questioned.

"Yeah, she gave me the resume on Stone and how he gets down and mentioned something else about a nigga named Jihad that supposed to be his cousin. Sounds familiar but I can't put a face with the name."

"Yo G, you know them nigga's when you see them." Stacks claimed. "Jihad is kind of quiet but he's getting a little bit of money with a crew uptown and Stone is his right hand man who jive known for playing with them hammers."

"Them six deuce niggas?"

"Exactly!"

"Oh, those dudes are light work!" Y.G. exclaimed. "Do you know there exact location?"

"Nah, but it shouldn't be hard to find, the town is only but so big."

"Yeah, because we need to get at them bitch ass niggas ASAP." Y.G. spoke with malice in his heart.

"It's whatever!" Shabazz retorted. "If we apply enough pressure, the pipes will eventually bust!"

"Then let's apply the pressure to these fuck niggas." Stacks added.

Y.G. looked at both of his partners with menacing eyes and smirked. "We definitely about to apply the pressure to their whole crew but we can't forget about Blue and Moe, they set this whole thing in motion and I'm not going to be content until they suffer the same fate that Gamble suffered.

Both men didn't even feel the need to respond. They just grabbed their weapons and followed Y.G. to the tinted out jeep in back of their building. Once inside, they fired up the engine and hit the town on a mission for blood.

CHAPTER 22

The word on Jamal's murder spread rapidly throughout the city and every street corner was wondering who the individuals were behind the latest slaying on the eastside. The funeral was held in the fruit belt community at St. John's Baptist Church. The parking lot was filled with an array of people who had come to show the young player some love for his home going. Inside of the sanctuary, gangsters, hustlers and some of the finest females that the town had to offer were congregated inside of the pews, crying and thinking about the better times that they shared with the deceased. Jamal laid in the casket dipped in a pure white linen suit with a pair of leather Ferragamo shoes to match. Besides the complexion due to the makeup, he looked like himself. Dressed in all black, Jihad sat alongside Stone on the front row, observing the crowded room around him. He recognized many of the faces that came to pay their respect but there were a lot of people in attendance that he'd never seen before. When Trina entered the room, his heart skipped a beat as he watched her closely. She passed by the casket to view the corpse and locked eyes with him momentarily as she took her seat. He acknowledged her with a nod of the head and she returned the greeting with teary eyes and a weak smile. A flash of guilt jolted through Trina's body, causing her to become a bit uncomfortable as the Pastor began to preach.

"I know that it is a sad day for you all but this is no time to be sad." The preacher began. "This is a time to rejoice so I want everyone in this room to dry their eyes and stay encouraged. Hold your head up high because we're not here to mourn the death of Jamal James Wright, we're here to celebrate the young brothers home going.

Applause broke out around the room.

Now it's a lot of talk about our brother in the media and I'm not here to play judge to say what is or what is not true." The preacher continued. "But I do know that no one passes through this life without committing sin. I am a sinner!... And if I did not commit sin, I wouldn't need the mercy or the forgiveness of The Most High GOD! Now as I look into the crowd, I see the anger on many of your face and I understand that you all want revenge but vengeance is the lord.

A collection of praises vibrated the throughout the church as the people raised up and started clapping their hands. The Pastor preached for another twenty minutes before family and friends began heading over to the gravesite to say their last goodbyes to the fallen soldier.

As the coffin was lowered into the ground, tears began flowing down Jihad's face nonstop. His heart was heavy at the thought that his cousin had lost his life to a game that he'd introduced him to. Once everyone had dispersed from the cemetery, he approached the burial site with a bottle of Hennessy to speak his last words to Jamal.

"I never thought that it would go down like this cousin!" He said, pouring the liquor into the dirt. "I thought that we would make it out of this shit as old men rich as hell, laughing and reminiscing about the times we shared as young boys. I know that you used to think that I was kind of hard on you when we was growing up but the reason that I pushed you so hard is because I always expected you to do something better for yourself. I never wanted you to get caught up in these streets with me. This was my thing, the ladies and playing ball was your thing and if I would have pushed you a little bit harder, I know that you would've made it to the league. I hope that you accept my apologies Bra! And if it's the last thing that I do, I promise you that I'm going to kill whoever did this. Until we meet again, stay up and stay fly and look after my pops while you're up there. Peace!"

He poured the remainder of the liquor onto the burial ground then returned to the vehicle where Stone was patiently awaiting in the driver seat.

"You good brah? Stone asked as he pulled from the cemetery.

"I'll be alright." He replied in a somber tone. "I just need a little bit of time to get my head together."

"I feel you. It's going to take some time to get used to my nigga not being around. This shit feels surreal. It still hasn't really hit me yet."

"This shit is definitely unbelievable."

Stone reached into the ashtray and grabbed a half burned blunt and fired it up. He took a long pull and deeply inhaled the smoke when his phone began to ring. He scanned the screen and noticed that it was Jamal's friend Dog from Goodyear St. Although they were from two completely sections of the city, Jamal and Dog developed a mutual respect for one another during a short stint in the county jail that conceded over into the street.

"What's good fam? Stone answered the phone.

"Peace King." He replied. "I'm good and you?"

"To be honest with you brah, my head is all over the place right now. I'm jive going through it but I'll figure it out."

"Yeah, the homies death is a little too much for all of us to bare right now" Dog was sympathetic. "Tell Jihad that I send my condolences. I saw him at the funeral and I wanted to come over and holler at him but I didn't want to seem too intrusive."

"It's all good, you fam but we do appreciate your consideration?"

"I do need to scream at y'all boys in person though. You know these phones are filthy."

"No doubt. Give us about an hour and we'll hit you back."

"Nah King, I need to holla at y'all now." Dog emphasized.

"It's like that?" Stone quizzed.

"I got some information that I think y'all need to be privy to."

"Where you at?"

"I'm at the Tea Cup, getting something to eat. Swing through so we can chop it up."

"We're on the way." Stone ended the call.

Who was that? Jihad questioned.

"That was Dog." He replied. "He said that he needs to scream at us ASAP."

"Where is he at?

"He's at the Tea Cup, getting something to eat."

"Go over there and see what it is that he's talking about."

Stone bust a U turn in the middle of Main St. and headed north up the block. A couple minutes later he pulled up to of the small café on Oakgrove St. When entering the restaurant they immediately noticed Dog, sitting off to the left at a table, watching Sportscenter on the television above him while eating a sandwich.

"What's good family?" Dog stood up and embraced Stone and Jihad with a handshake.

"Same fight, different round!" Stone Replied.

"I feel you bro. As long as we keep fighting we'll be alright."

Dog then turned to Jihad. "You good fam?"

"I'll be alright.' Jihad declared.

"I know Jamal was your cousin but that was my man and I'm going to do whatever I need to do to even the score."

"I hear you."

"Let me buy y'all something to eat

Jihad and Stone both refused as they all took a seat.

"So what was so urgent that you needed to see me right away?" Stone questioned.

Dog took a deep breath and exhaled before he spoke.

"Yo, you know the Trina broad that Jamal was fucking with?" He quizzed.

"Yeah, what about her?" Stone retorted.

"She was there the day that Jamal got murdered."

"How do you know that?" Jihad asked.

"This broad that I've been creeping with name Chanel told me." Dog confirmed. "Her and Trina are best friends and last night while I was over her building, she told me that Trina was stressed out about what happened to Jamal and also explained to her how she was following him to get his car fixed when some guys ambushed him and started shooting."

"Did she see who did it?"

"She told me that Trina said that it was two dudes with masks and black hoodys."

"I saw shorty at the funeral today, I wonder why she hasn't tried to reach out and say anything?" Jihad questioned.

"I don't know." Dog answered. "But Chanel also told me that shorty has a kid by some wild ass nigga name Y.G. who just came home."

"Y.G.?" Stone was bewildered. "Are you serious?"

"Who the fuck is Y.G.?" Jihad inquired.

Stone turned to Jihad with a disturbed look on his face.

"That's the nigga Gamble younger brother.

CHAPTER 23

Over the next couple of days, Trina isolated herself to her apartment. The sun peeking through the blinds was the only light illuminating her bedroom as she lay sprawled out across the bed crying. She felt a sense of remorse as she played the shooting over and over in her mind. Although it wasn't Trina's first time setting someone up for Y.G., she was undergoing a case of anxiety due to her feelings for Jamal. Even though they weren't a couple, Trina had begun to develop some type of love for the young hustler and didn't feel like he deserved to die. Suddenly there was a continuous knock at the door, causing her to roll over and check the time on her cell phone which read 8:28am.

"Who, the hell is this coming to my house this early?" She questioned herself as she rolled back under the covers.

The knocking continued for another five minutes before Trina finally got out the bed to see who it was. She strolled across the hardwood floor and stopped at the door to look through the peephole.

"Damn!" She said quietly once she noticed YG

Trina's thoughts raced as she tried to figure out what she should do next.

"Open the door Trina; I know that you're in there." YG yelled through the door.

"Give me a minute." She responded.

Turning the lock on the door, she tried her best to gain her composure. Once Trina opened the door, she allowed YG to enter the small studio apartment, carrying two shopping bags.

"What took you so long to answer the fucking door?" He barked.

"Don't come in here with all that noise." Trina replied. "It's eight o'clock in the morning; I was in the bed sleep."

"And why haven't you been answering my calls? I know that situation don't have your head all fucked up?"

"Boy please, you already know that I'm not sweating that. I've just been trying to play it cool until I figure out my next move because I know the streets is talking and being that my vehicle was identified leaving the scene, I know it's only a matter of time before those people come knocking on my door asking questions."

"Are you prepared for that?"

"I don't even know why you would even have to question that?" Trina sneered.

"I know you know how to handle yourself under these types of circumstances but the fellas are worried about your mental and if you cool under this type of pressure?."

"And why would they be worried about that?"

"Because you were jive feeling that nigga!" Y.G. declared. "And don't try to deny it."

"I'm not going to act like I wasn't digging Jamal." She admitted. "He was cool and all that. But at the end of the day, he was just something to do so tell your boys to relax. My loyalty begins and ends with you."

"I'm glad to hear you say that." He handed Trina the shopping bags.

"What's this?" She accepted.

Y.G. made his way over to the couch and took a seat.

"It's just a small token of my appreciation." He leaned back. "Open it!"

Trina reached into the bag and pulled out a black rectangular jewelry box. She cracked it open and was astonished by the diamond studded necklace, shinning in her face. She gazed up into Y.Gs eyes and smiled.

"This is nice Darius, but you don't have to do this to keep me quiet." She handed the box back to him.

"Don't insult me like that." Y.G. replied. "It's the least that I can do for you putting your life on the line for me once again. I know that we have had our differences in the past and since I've been home we haven't actually been seeing eye to eye but that doesn't negate our history together. There was a point in time when I would've done anything for you and I know that you would've done the same for me; and the other day showed me that you're still down for a nigga and I was hoping that we could rekindle some of what we had."

Trina searched his face to see if Y.G. was being sincere and to her surprise, he was. "In despite of our differences; I am always going to have your back." She said. "I miss what we had and if you are willing to give me another chance, I promise to make it right."

"Oh don't worry about that, we're definitely going to make it right." Y.G. told her. "Now go in there and run you some bath water while I put us some breakfast together."

"Are you Okay?" Trina checked his temperature with the back of her hand. "You must be sick!"

"Nah, I'm not sick." Y.G. chuckled. "Why you say that?"

"First you come in here with shopping bags and now you're about to go in the kitchen and cook me something to eat? Yeah something is definitely going on; where is Y.G at?"

They both shared a laugh as Y.G. stood up and began walking towards her. The closer he got, the faster her heart raced. The years spent lifting weights while incarcerated had His physic powerfully built and Trina horny as ever. Y.G cupped her face with his hands and kissed her passionately. She didn't show any resistance as her tongue danced around in his mouth. In an abrupt motion, Y.G. swooped Trina from her feet as they continued to osculate. She wrapped her legs around his waist and he carried her into the bedroom. Falling on to the queen size mattress, Trina began removing his clothing as he explored beneath her nightgown. His fingertips rubbed against her soft skin down to the hot and wet center between her legs. He relentlessly moved his tongue up and down her inner thighs until finding himself face to face with her vaginal area. After enticing her with the tip of his tongue for a few minutes, Y.G. buried his face into her pussy and began sucking her clitoris. Moaning with pleasure, she pulled him in close as he continued to satisfy her orally. Another ten minutes went by before Trina began shaking uncontrollably.

"Damn Darius, What are you trying to do to me?" She screamed

After the orgasm, Y.G. climbed on top of Trina and eased into her slowly. It seemed like the pussy had gotten better with time. He stroked her long and hard, causing her to pant heavily. She could feel him in the pit of her stomach, the deeper he pushed inside of her.

"I missed you!" She whispered into his ear.

"I missed you too!" He replied.

Trina's manicured nails dug into his back as he plunged away. The sex lasted for about twenty five minutes before Y.G. released his load inside of her and buckled on to the bed.

An hour later, Trina awoke to the aroma of turkey bacon and eggs coming from the kitchen. As she lay there fully exposed, she pushed her thoughts of Jamal aside and imagined how life would be different this time around for her and Y.G. Taking a glimpse at the clock, she noticed that two hours had gone by. As she made an effort to get up out of the bed, Trina reminded herself to call her mother's house to check on her son D.J. After covering her body with a terry cloth robe, she wandered into the kitchen where YG was preparing a delicious breakfast. Trina stopped in the foyer and admired his physique as he stood over the stove in nothing but his boxer briefs.

"Ahem!" She cleared her throat.

Gaining His attention, YG spun around and smiled.

"I see that you finally decided to wake up?" He said.

"Whatever it is that you're in here putting together woke me up." She admitted. "It smells wonderful; what is it?"

"A little light nourishment to get the day started."

"Well I'm already sold if it's half as good as your sex game is."

"Maybe better!"

"I seriously doubt that." Trina sneered.

"Just have a seat and relax." YG countered. "I hope you're hungry."

"I'm starving."

"Trust me, I got you."

Trina smiled as she took a sea t at the island placed in the middle of the kitchen floor. Moments later, YG placed a steaming plate of food in front of her and watched as she began eating.

"Bon appetite." He said

Within a matter of minutes, Trina began feeling dizzy and her breathing rapidly increased. Immediately, she became paralyzed with fear as a demonic grin spread across, YG's face. The Cyanide that he used to poison Trina's breakfast was causing her to go into Cardiac arrest and he enjoyed watching her foam from the mouth, gasping for air. In an attempt to make it to the phone to call an ambulance, Trina dropped to the floor wheezing. Right before she fell unconscious, she looked into the eyes of her child's father and seen the devil. He didn't have any compassion or remorse in the window of his soul, only hatred. As she lay lifeless in the kitchen, YG grabbed the jewelry that he'd given Trina and began wiping down everything that he touched before exiting the apartment.

*****

Later on that evening, YG and Shabazz drove through the city with intentions of murder. They were adamant about finding Gamble's killers and didn't plan on resting until the mission was complete. The streets were talking and the more they talked the more they were listening. YG had already gotten some information on Stone and Jihad concerning the block that they hustled on so it was only a matter of time before they surfaced from the shadows and into a barrage of gunfire.

YG was silent as he rode in the passenger seat lost in his thoughts. The idea of his son growing up without a mother weighed on him a little bit. He and his brother had grown up in unstable conditions, bouncing from relative to relative after their mother had overdosed on heroin, leaving them to fend for themselves. A major reason that he gravitated towards the street life was due to the lack of love he found at home and nine time out of ten his child was going to suffer the same fate. He quickly dismissed those emotions once Shabazz broke him from his thoughts.

"Yo brah." He spoke in a raspy voice. "This might be them nigga right there."

"Where?" YG leaned back in his seat.

"Over there shooting dice in the driveway."

"Pull around the corner."

As they drove passed the house, Stone stood in the cut, watching everything coming through the block. Noticing two shadows behind the tinted windows of a Cherokee looking extra hard, he alerted his crew to get on point. Jihad placed his hand on his weapon as the young boys stopped shooting dice and looked up at the passing vehicle. Everyone's eyes were locked in on the black Jeep until its tail lights disappeared from their sight.

"Who the fuck was that?" Jihad questioned.

"I don't know." Stone responded. "But whoever it was, they were looking hard as hell."

"Y'all nigga keep your eyes open." Jihad instructed.

A collection of agreements went out from the squad in unison as they went back to gambling. Chris walked up on the porch dressed in khakis and a polo shirt. After greeting everyone properly he took a seat next to Jihad on the steps. By the look on his mentor's face, he could sense that something was bothering him.

"What happened?" Chris inquired.

"It ain't nothing." Jihad replied, examining his outfit. "Where are you coming from?"

"I'm coming from this pre-collegiate business internship program that I'm taking at UB."

"Oh, that's what's up." Jihad gave him dap.

Chris smiled. "It's alright too. I'm learning a lot of information that supposed to prepare me for my major once I began school in the fall."

"That's what I'm talking about little bra. I'm proud of you!"

"Thanks Jihad."

"You don't have to thank me Chris; you're the one that put the work in."

"I know but you're one of the only ones that believed in me from the beginning. If it weren't for you I would probably be on my way to jail instead of college."

"You're giving me too much credit." Jihad told him. "Like I said, you're the one that put that work in. I just tried to get you to maximize your potential. You just make sure that you don't forget about us little people once you make it to the big leagues."

"Never that big bra." Chris assured. "Never that."

They shared a quick laugh and embraced. Meanwhile YG and Shabazz had parked their vehicle the next street over and were now watching them from a yard directly across the street. Pulling a ski mask over their heads, they stepped into the street and opened fire.

Rat tat tat tat tat tat…..

Chris never saw it coming. The first shot from the Tech 9 tore through the side of his neck, sending him to the ground. The bullets that followed pierced into the house as Jihad and his crew took cover.

"Get that muthafucka!" YG gestured.

He and Shabazz began closing in on Jihad when suddenly, Stone emerged from the cut and backed them up with the Mac 10.

Pap… pap… pap… pap… pap… pap… pap…

At the sound of the machine gun, they ducked behind a parked car and returned shots.

YG fired his forty caliber weapon with intensity and struck another one of the young boys in the upper torso as they ran for cover. The force from the ammunition caused him to fall to the ground in pain. He screamed in agony. Lil P removed his weapon from under his shirt and attempted to let loose when he was struck in the shoulder. A surge of bullets was exchanged for another 20 seconds before YG and Shabazz made a run for the yard that they had appeared from. Suddenly, Shabazz felt an explosion in his back as he collapsed face first into the pavement. YG watched his partner stumble to the ground as bullets ripped through the air, whistling past his head.

"Come on bra, let's go!" He shouted as he continued to bust shots.

In the midst of the confusion, Shabazz struggled to get to his feet.

"Fuck!" He screamed back. "I can't move."

YG turned to assist his friend when he noticed Stone running down on them gripping a machine gun with the look of a mad man. Without giving it a second thought, he made his way into the backyard and disappeared over a wooden fence as Stone let off a couple more shot, missing him by inches. Interrupted by the sound of a yelling voice, Stone turned to see Chris cradled in Jihad's arms. Blood was leaking freely from the wound in his neck.

"Breath little bra." Jihad coached him. "It's going to be alright.

Jihad tried not to panic as he spoke to the young boy bleeding in his arms.

"Somebody call an ambulance." He screamed out."

Fuck an ambulance; we got to get him to a hospital now." Stone declared as he rushed to his aid.

"What about Zae?" Remy pointed to the bloodied body in the driveway.

"Only one that can help him now is GOD." Stone replied. "He's already gone."

With that being said, they lifted Chris off of his feet and carried him to the nearest vehicle.

"Keep your eyes open boy." Jihad instructed Chris "Don't you die on me."

"I can't feel my toes." Chris responded as tears streamed down his face.

"Just be cool. You're going to be alright. You got a lot more livin to do.

Meanwhile, a wounded Lil P grabbed his gun and walked over to where Shabazz was attempting to crawl to his feet. He began kicking the man several times in the face before placing the Ruger to his head.

"Look at me you punk son of a bitch." He kicked him again.

"As he rolled over, Shabazz looked Lil P in the eyes and smiled.

"You better kill me mutha fucka."He spit blood onto Lil P's feet.

Lil P looked over to Jihad and Stone, placing his friend in the back of Stones sedan. They were both covered in Chris's blood. He focused back on Shabazz and raised his gun, emptying five shot into his face.

"C'mon on P!" Shouted Stone

Police sirens could be heard at a distance as Lil P dashed over to the car, holding his shoulder. He climbed in the passenger seat while Jihad got into the back with Chris. Stone started the engine and pulled off into the night, speeding through the streets until they reached the hospital.

CHAPTER 24

The very next morning, Roxy awoke to the sound of Blue's voice, coming from the kitchen. She sensed that he was displeased by the tone in his speech. Quickly arising from the King size mattress, she made her way across the room and placed her ear to the door to clearly hear what was being said.

"So this is what you call, being quiet?" Blue spoke in an irritated manner.

"What are you talking about?" Moe responded.

Blue tossed the morning newspaper onto the kitchen table and watched as Moe read the headlines on the front page of the city & region section.

"What the hell is this?" He questioned with a frown.

"I'll tell you what it is." Blue said. "This is bad for business. Two bodies found in the middle of the block where business is supposed to be conducted isn't good."

"You're right. We definitely don't need this type of attention around us right now."

"First one of their boys get murdered at the car shop and now this?" We need to call a meeting with Jihad and his crew to see what the hell is going on because we can't afford this type of attention."

"I agree." Moe nodded. "I'm going to make a call and get him down here so we can get to the bottom of this."

"Please!" Blue leaned back and rubbed the bridge of his nose. Tension had built up from this unforeseen situation, causing him to have a slight headache. He leaned forward and looked Moe in the eyes.

"I know that's your boy and all that but if Jihad or any of those guys around him become a cancer to us, you know what we're going to have to do right?"

"I don't even know why you would even have to ask me that after all these years?" Moe firmly stated.

"I'm just making sure." Blue declared. "Because, I know that you really like this kid."

"Like I told you before, if he becomes a problem, I will pull the trigger myself." Moe confirmed.

The conversation came to an end once Roxy entered into the kitchen but not before she caught that last statement. A feeling of mixed emotions overcame her after hearing the remark about killing Jihad. Roxy and Jihad had known one another since grade school and she felt a sense of loyalty to him. They had been through alot together and although her original mission was to play up on Blue for Jihad's benefit, she was beginning to fall in love with the target. Blue was the type of man that Roxy had always yearned for; intelligent, rich and powerful.

She walked over to where he was seated and wrapped her arms around the large man's neck.

"Good morning babe." She kissed him on the cheek. "Would you like for me to make you guys some breakfast?"

"No thank you sweetheart." Moe interjected. "I was just about to leave."

"I'll take some salmon croquettes, grits and eggs baby, thank you!" Blue told her.

"Coffee or orange juice? Roxy asked.

"Coffee!" Blue replied.

Roxy swayed over to the refrigerator and began to retrieve the items she needed to prepare the meal. Moe glanced at Blue with confusion because he didn't know that she was in the apartment with them. They never discussed business matters in the presence of company so why didn't Blue give him the heads up on her being there he wondered. He hoped that his partner wasn't developing a soft spot for this young tramp. Blue read the expression on Moe's brow and dismissed it with a wave of the hand. He was sure that Roxy hadn't heard any of their conversation so she didn't pose a threat.

"Moe, are you sure that you don't want anything to eat? Roxy closed the fridge. "It won't take but a few minutes to throw it together."

"Yeah, I'm sure but thank you anyway." Moe was still focused on Blue.

As he prepared to leave, the men shook hands.

"Call me with an update." Blue said.

"I will call you as soon as I hear something!"

A couple of minutes after Moe left, Roxy was over the stove, stirring a small pot of grits while scrambling some cheese eggs. The smell from the salmon croquettes drifted throughout the condo as they sizzled in the skillet.

Patiently waiting for his food, Blue sat at the table reading the remainder of the Buffalo News. He occasionally sipped on his coffee between segments of the paper then glanced up as Roxy set a steaming hot plate in front him.

"Do you need anything else babe?" She sat across from Blue.

"No thank you, this is more than enough." He said.

There was something different about his demeanor today. Not only did Blue appear to be physically tired, he seemed to be mentally drained. Roxy accredited his disturbance to whatever was written in today's paper and made it priority to purchase one as soon as possible, especially since it may have had something to do with Jihad.

"Is everything alright Baby?" Roxy probed. "You seem to be a little distracted this morning."

"I'm okay." Blue replied as he dug into his food. "Just a little tired, that's all."

"Well maybe you need to take a vacation before you get burnt out. As hard as you work, you deserve some time to yourself.

"That might not be a bad idea. When you're finished eating, get on the internet and book us a flight for the weekend."

Between bites, Roxy looked up and smiled.

"Are you serious? Don't be playing because you know that I will jump on the computer right now and put that together."

"Yeah, I'm serious. " Blue validated. "When have you known me to play games?"

"Where do you want to go?"

"I don't care. Anywhere! As long as it's somewhere where I can sit by the water and relax with you by my side."

Okay, I'm going to book us a room at the Marquesa Hotel in the Key West. Roxy stated.

"Fuck that!" Blue Uttered. "I don't want to go to any of those hole in the wall resorts that one of your little boyfriends done wooed you with. Book us a two week getaway at the Ritz Carlton in Aruba."

"Two weeks?" Roxy questioned. "I don't think that Moe is going to let me take off from work for two weeks."

"You let me deal with Moe. And if he doesn't let you get the time off then fuck it. My lady doesn't need to be working in a juke joint, serving niggas drinks anyway."

Roxy hopped up from the kitchen table, squealing like a schoolgirl, during recess as she ran over and jumped into Blue's lap. She began kissing him passionately in the mouth. He reciprocated by lifting her petite frame around his waist as he stood up and carried her into the next room. The living room was flawlessly furnished with an acorn brown tuscano leather sofa and matching loveseat. The Bose CineMate home theater system brought life to the high definition 60 inch flat screen television covering the entire rear wall. Transporting her across the hardwood floor, they dissolved in front of the fireplace onto a Brighton gray and gold area rug. Their thirst for one another grew by the moment. Roxy treasured the way Blue's strong hands felt caressing her soft figure. He reached underneath her cotton robe and cupped her from behind, pulling her on top of him. She straddled his face and began to gyrate her hips as he slid his tongue inside of her. As he licked her clitoris, the desire increased, bringing her to a light orgasm. After she came, Roxy climbed off of him and countered the sexual act by placing the head of Blue's dick in her mouth and started sucking it sensuously.

Mmmm, you like that?"

Blue moaned with pleasure as she took him in and out of her mouth while giving him a hand job.

"Damn baby!" He whined. "Suck that dick."

Once he was rock hard, Roxy rolled over and allowed Blue to go to work. He climbed into the pussy nice and slow, moving his hips in a circular motion. She looked up at him and seen the passion in his eyes. They continued for another forty five minutes before Blue finally burst inside of her. Fatigued, they laid in front of the burning fire place, breathing heavily as the flames illuminated off their sweaty bodies. Blue nose was wide open and Roxy knew that she had the man right where she wanted him but she was beginning to have second thoughts. In all of the years that she had been rocking out with Jihad, Roxy never allowed her emotions to get the best of her but she was really feeling Blue. She stared down at him as he snored lightly, wondering how she was going to play the whole thing out because at the end of the day, she had to come out on top.

CHAPTER 25

When Jihad arrived at Buffalo General Hospital the next morning, Chris was still in the intensive care unit, recovering from surgery. The emergency waiting room was filled with distressed family members and friends concerned about his circumstances. He was expected to live but was still in critical condition due to the bullet that penetrated his neck.

"What are you doing here?" Chris mother screamed at Jihad. "You need to be out there trying to find out who did this to my baby."

"I promise you that I'm on top of it Ms. Diane." Jihad replied. "Chris is like my little brother and I'm not going to be satisfied until whoever did this suffers."

"I trusted you with my boy's life Jihad!" She cried. "You were supposed to protect him."

The spectators in the room observed as she descended into Jihad's arms wailing uncontrollably.

"Why did they have to shoot my baby? He is a good kid! Why lord, why?"

Tears formed up in Jihad's eyes as he embraced her with a firm hug. He glared across the room and locked gazes with Stone and Remy who were sitting off in the corner, fighting back tears of their own. He nodded his head with the indication that he was about to get on some shit. Stone and Remy both returned the gesture, understanding what was running through his mind.

"Don't worry Ms. Diane, Chris is a strong dude and I know that he's going to pull through this. " Jihad spoke in a soft voice.

She didn't respond. She just rocked back and forth in the pit of his arms sobbing. It broke Jihad's heart to see her like this. Ms. Diane was usually a vibrant woman with such a beautiful spirit. Although she was 5ft 2inches, her heart was comparable to a giant. She was like a mother for all the kids that were from the neighborhood but took on a special relationship with Jihad, being that she grew up with his father, Zeak.

Story has it that, Ms. Diane used to mule Heroin from New York City for Moe and Zeak sometime in the eighties but squared up after having Chris.

She would often reminisce and tell Jihad stories about how thorough his pops was. She even shared her suspicions and speculations about what happened the night Zeak was murdered. Ms. Diane would always express to Jihad how treacherous the streets were and how he shouldn't trust anyone. Once she learned that he had chosen the same path as his father, Ms. Diane made Jihad agree that he would look after her only son and keep him away from the streets and up until this point, he had made good on his promise.

"Ms. Diane, please stop crying." Jihad pleaded. "Chris is going to be alright and back home in no time."

She looked up and wiped her eyes. "I hope so Jihad. Really do hope so because he doesn't deserve this. Him and Kareema is about to have a baby and Chris need to be there to raise his child."

"What is the doctor saying?

"He said that Chris was lucky because if the bullet that hit him would've been a couple centimeters to the left, it would've hit his spine and paralyzed him."

"Damn!" Jihad shook his head.

"I know, baby. All we can do now is pray and hope that his recovery is successful."

"Are you going to be okay?

"Yeah, I'm going to be okay." Ms. Diane released him. "I just want what's best for my boy and I don't understand why this had to happen to him."

"It's going to be alright." Jihad hugged her again. "Let me go over here and holler at Stone but I want you to quit worrying. We got everything under control."

She nodded then made her way over to the vending machine for a cup of coffee. Jihad approached Stone and Remy with a pound and then signaled them into the hallway.

"What's the story on Lil P?" He inquired.

"He's good!" Remy confirmed. "It was a clean shot. The bullet went in and out of his shoulder. Doctor discharged him about an hour ago."

"How about Zae's mother, how is she holding up?"

"Not good! I spoke to his sister this morning and she said that Ms. Jacobs was taking it kind of hard. I don't even know what to say to her."

"Find out how much the funeral arrangements is and get the bill to me." Jihad instructed him. "And if his mother needs anything else, let me know."

"Done!" Remy established.

What's the word on the nigga Y.G?" Jihad turned to Stone.

"I haven't heard anything yet but I got the goons on it." Stone answered.

"Make sure that you tell them that I got a bounty on the nigga for ten. A dub if they bring him to me alive."

"Trust me; these niggas ear is to the concrete." Stone proclaimed. "The next time that faggot show his face anywhere in these streets, we on his ass bra."

"Yeah, we cannot give him another opportunity to touch anybody in the crew. And we probably need to fall back from the block for a minute until we find this dude."

"Fuck that Bra!" Stone snapped. "I'm not hiding from this nigga. I'm going to keep rocking out how I've been rocking out and when I see homeboy, we holding court in the street, Straight like that!"

This nigga know our movements so we have to switch it up on him fam" Jihad reasoned. "He's up right now and I don't' want to lose nobody else because of my pride."

"I hear what you saying family but I'm not hiding from this nigga. You can do whatever you feel that you need to do but I'm out here."

"I don't see why I have to go through this with you?"

"Go through what with me!" Stone raised his voice. "This mutha fucka done touched two of our soldiers, got Chris laid up in here in critical and Lil P on bed rest with his arm in a sling and you want me to hide."

"I didn't say hide." Jihad felt his blood boiling. "I said fall back from the block for a minute until we figure this thing out."

"If you want to continue to parade around here on some diplomatic shit be my guest bra but that's not what I do." He lifted his shirt and showed him his gun. "This is what I do! So let me handle shit the way that I know how to handle shit and if I got to play in the jungle to catch a snake then that's what I'm going to do!"

"I know how you feel. And I know that everyone's emotion is running wild right now but I need you to keep your head in the game. We have to be smart."

"Nah, we got to be proactive my nigga. The streets is watching and waiting for our next move and if we don't send a message immediately then niggas is going to think shit is sweet out here."

"Are you listening to yourself?" Jihad frowned. "First of all, I could care less what these niggas think and second if they watching and waiting on our next move then the police are too. And I'm not about to go out here on some cowboy shit and wind up in prison just to prove a point to some niggas that don't give a fuck about me or you."

Stone stared at him with a sneer. Deep down inside, he knew that everything that Jihad was saying was the truth.

"You're right bra, my bad." He apologized. "I'm just ready to get it poppin. This YG nigga is not playing and I'm not trying to be walking around here on pins and needles, wondering what rock he going to crawl from under and pop my top off."

"Don't worry fam, I'm about to take the muzzle off and let you get busy." Jihad assured him. "Just give me another day or two to figure this thing out."

"You got two days to figure out whatever it is that you need to figure out and after that, I'm setting the city on fire."

"Cool!"

They clapped hands and embraced when Jihad's phone began vibrating. He quickly grabbed it off his hip and knew that it was an emergency once he saw who number it was flashing across the screen.

"Hello!" He answered.

"We need to have a sit down as soon as possible." Moe spoke in a controlled voice.

"When?"

"Tonight at 9 o'clock on the roof top."

"Alright, I'll be there."

"Make sure that you bring your man with you too." Moe referred to Stone. "And don't be late."

Jihad could sense impatience in Moe's speech as they ended the call.

"Damn!" He turned his attention back to Stone.

"What happened?" Stone inquired.

"That was Moe. He wants to have a meeting with us."

"When?"

"A-Sap"

"You think it's about this situation?"

"From the irritation in his voice, I know that's what it's about." Jihad said.

Suddenly the bell sounded from the elevator and two federal agents stepped off towards the security desk. Instantly Jihad presumed them to be law enforcement but really didn't pay them any attention until they began walking in his direction.

"Good morning Mr. Smith." Agent Daniels extended her hand. "My name is Agent Daniels and this is my partner Agent Wright. "Do you mind if we ask you a couple of questions?"

"Do you mind if I ask you what this is about?" Jihad shot back.

"Just take a ride with us and we'll explain everything to you when we get down to headquarters."

"Headquarters!" Jihad winced. Am I under arrest?"

"No you're not under arrest, Mr. Jones but we do believe that you may be helpful to us in our investigation."

"Well, if I'm not under arrest anything that you need to say to me, you can say right here."

"Let's not waste each other time, Mr Smith or should I say Jihad." Agent Wright was more aggressive. "I think we both know why we're here. Now we can do this our way or the hard way, it's your call but I believe it's in your best interest that you take a ride with us."

Jihad glanced over to Stone and handed him his phone.

"Call my lawyer and have him meet us downtown." He instructed

Upon arriving at the Federal building, a million thoughts raced through Jihad's mind. Seated beneath a clock in a freezing interrogation room, he waited impatiently for his lawyer to walk through the doors. Instead, Agent Daniels followed by her partner Agent Wright entered the room, carrying a large portfolio. She placed the folder on the table and took a seat opposite from Jihad. Agent Wright remained standing while sipping on a cup of coffee.

"Now let try this again.' Agent Daniels began. "What can you tell us about the shooting that occurred on Berkshire yesterday?"

"What makes you think that I know anything about that?" Jihad responded.

"You were the attended target weren't you?"

Jihad leaned back in his chair and snickered. "What do y'all want from me?"

Agent Daniels opened the folder, retrieved two photos and faced them towards him.

"Do you know these two gentlemen?" She sat back and watched Jihad reaction as he scanned over the pictures of Moe and Blue.

He remained poised as he examined the photographs. "I think that you already know the answer to that question but I don't understand what they have to do with me."

"Let's not play stupid Jihad." Agent Daniels inclined forward with her hands crossed. "I get paid to gather information on guys like you so nine times out of ten if we're sitting here, I already know who you are and what you do for a living. Now it's on you if you want to help yourself or continue to play this cat and mouse game but trust me, we have more time than you do. It's only a matter of time before we catch you and place you somewhere where you will never see the sun from this angle again."

"Are we through?" Jihad asked

"Not quite." She removed another picture from the file. "What about this one?"

Jihad's expression grew serious once she laid a visual of Gamble on to the table. Her eyes assessed his body language as he shifted in his seat. Agent Daniels could sense that he was becoming uncomfortable.

"Looks familiar but I don't know him." He shook his head.

"Are you sure?" Agent Wright interjected. "Look a little closer."

Jihad pressed his lips together as he glared at him. "I said that I don't know him."

There was something about the look in eyes that let Agent Wright know that they weren't dealing with your average street punk. This kid was a little more seasoned.

"That's funny!" Agent Wright continued to press. "Because this guy was one of Blue and Moe's top guys and shortly after he was murdered, you emerge out of thin air as one of their... correct me if I'm wrong, lieutenants. And everyone knows that in order to become active in Blue's organization, you have to prove yourself. So what did you do to prove yourself Jihad?"

"I don't know what you're talking about." He shot Agent Wright a menacing look.

His uneasiness suddenly turned to anger but Agent wright refused to let up on this thug.

"Here's what I think," He resumed. "I think you and your crew killed Gamble for these low lives and in return they provided you with the opportunity to earn a lot of money. But in the process, your plan backfired because now you have someone out there that doesn't give a damn about you, Stone, Moe or Blue. This person doesn't even care about money, all he wants is revenge and your name is at the top of his list."

"Oh yeah?" Jihad smirked.

Agent wright shook his head. "Oh yeah, and because of you, Zaquan and your cousin Shawn is dead, and now a promising athlete, little Christopher is fighting for his life in the intensive care unit."

A silence fell on the room as Agent Wright allowed his words to register into Jihad's brain. No matter how calm and collected he seemed to be on the outside, he knew that he had struck a nerve in the young man's mind. The two men stared at one another as they played a mental chess game. Moments later the doors to the interrogation room swung open and in walked Jihad's lawyer, carrying a black leather briefcase.

"If you're not going to place my client under arrest, this charade is over." He spoke with self-confidence.

Your client is free to go." Agent Wright said eyes still locked in on Jihad. "But we'll see him again very soon."

An enormous smile spread across Jihad's face as Attorney Hurley escorted him out of the room.

"I'm pretty sure we'll see each other again." He remarked, walking out the door.

CHAPTER 26

On the way to meet with Moe and Blue, Jihad explained to Stone in detail about his discussion with the feds. He tried his best to remain cool but his thoughts were scattered in fifty places at once. He was overwhelmed by the information that they had disclosed during the interrogation. First Shawn gets murdered then Zae, Chris gets shot and now the Feds is breathing down his neck, trying to link him to Gamble's murder. Was somebody in the camp snitching? Were they under investigation by the Feds and if so how long have they been watching their movements? When it rain it definitely pours.

He pulled up to the Jefferson Projects around a quarter to 9 and killed the ignition. They exited the whip and approached the building with caution. Once they were inside, they made their way to the roof top. As usual, Blue and Moe were already in position accompanied by two of their gunslingers. Moe acknowledged them with a nod of the head but Blue never turned around. His back was facing them as he overlooked the projects with his hands behind him.

"This is where it all started for me." Blue spoke without looking at them. "Many nights, I sat up here envisioning how I would become a millionaire. I didn't know exactly how I would do it but I pictured myself becoming one of the most successful distributors that this city has ever seen and I've accomplish that. But I also pictured the many pitfalls and obstacles that I would face on my way to the top. The jealousy, the robbers, the funeral of loved ones, the betrayal of those closest to you, the snitches and investigators that's out to destroy everything that you've built from the ground up. Not to mention the blood that has to be shed to maintain this position of power. Do you see where I'm going with this?"

"I think so." Jihad responded.

"If I called y'all up here, it must be for a good reason, right?"

"Absolutely."

"Do you know what that reason may be?"

"I have a good idea what it is."

"So what's the problem?" Blue still wasn't facing them. "Our objective is to get money quietly not to be in the trenches on some cowboys and Indians shit, that's bad for business. Now I understand that your cousin got murdered a few weeks back and I'm sorry for your lost but you can't allow that to affect business."

"With all due respect Blue." Jihad said. "But I think that this problem that has occurred stems from your business."

Blue spun around and faced them for the first time.

"What do you mean that this problem stems from my business?" He moved toward them.

Well when my cousin Jamal first got killed, we thought that he had got caught slipping." Jihad told him. "Then we found out that the girl that he was with was actually Gamble's little brother baby mother."

"Wait a minute." Moe interjected. "YGs home?"

"Yep, and this dude is not playing."

"Well how did he know to come and target y'all."

"I don't know I'm still trying to figure that part out."

Blue's temperature began to rise as he paced the rooftop. "Do you think that your cousin put the girl in his business and she went back and told YG?"

"It's a possibility but I doubt it very seriously. Jamal was too thorough to put us at risk pillow talking with a broad."

"He couldn't've been that thorough because now we're all at risk." Blue shouted. "There's no telling who else knows about that situation with Gamble. Moe, I told you that these little niggas was going to become a cancer to us."

"Little niggas?" Stone spoke up. "Who do you think you talking too?"

"You, little nigga." Blue walked up on him. "Do you have a problem with that?"

Before Stone could react, the two goons drew their pistols and pointed them in his face. Jihad quickly pulled his weapon and aimed it at Blue. Neither man flinched. They just stared at one another with a heart cold as ice.

"Whoa, hold up!" Moe intervened. "Everybody put down their guns and let's figure this thing out."

A wicked smile spread across Blue's face as he ordered his men to lower their weapons.

"I like these boys." He nodded his head. "They're not afraid to die."

Jihad lowered his gun as well. "In order to live, you have to be willing to die."

Stone never took his eyes off of Blue.

"Chill fam, be easy." Jihad patted him on the chest.

"Is everybody Good?" Moe asked.

Everyone nodded in agreement as they allowed Blue to speak

"If this thing blows up in our face then we all lose." He told them. "So I need y'all to take care of this problem and do it quickly and quietly. No more headlines. Do you think that you can handle that for me?"

"We're already on top of it." Jihad said.

"Good!" Blue turned his back towards them and began lover looking the city again. "And until you get control over that situation all activity is dead."

"What do you mean all activity is dead?"

"It's exactly what it sounds like." Moe declared. "We're pulling the plug until you get a handle on YG."

"Moe, you can't..."

"You're hot!" Moe cut Jihad short. "You need to tie up these loose ends and cool off. You should have enough capital to hold you over until we get this resolved."

"Alright." Jihad huffed. "Where should I bring that bread that we owe you?"

"I'll have Roscoe get in touch with you for a time and a place."

"Okay." Jihad made his way over to the roof top exit.

Stone followed suit never taking his eyes off of the gunmen.

Once they were out of earshot, Moe walked over to Blue and looked over the edge of the building, inspecting the area below. By the somber look on his longtime friends face, he could tell that something besides the matter at hand was bothering him.

"What are your thoughts?" He asked.

"I'm tired Moe!" Blue spoke in a low tone. "I think I need a break from this shit."

Moe turned towards the henchmen and waved for them to fall back. "Give us a minute."

"Talk to me." He brought his attention back to his partner.

Blue motioned him over to the two milk crates sitting against the wall. As they took a seat, he removed a bottle of Hennessey from the inside pocket of his blazer and took a swig.

"Remember when we came home from prison, we used to come up here sip a little something and strategize on how we were going to take over the city?" He passed the bottle to Moe.

He took a long swig and passed it back.

"How could I forget?"

"We had some triumphs as well as some tragedies and through it all we were able to accomplish what we set out to do, would you agree?"

"Definitely."

"Then why in the hell are we still playing a game that we're destined to lose." Blue questioned.

"I've asked myself that same question many of nights." Moe admitted. "And the only conclusion that I could come up with is the adrenaline rush that comes along with playing the game. It keeps us coming back for more. Sometimes I think we become more addicted than the dope fiends."

"I think it's time for us to settle down and square up."

"Come now Blue, guys like us are not the settling down type." Moe chuckled. "We need some type of action in our lives."

"Well for the next two weeks, I'm going somewhere quiet and I'm going to need you to hold it down." Blue took another drink from the bottle.

"That's not a problem. Where do you plan on going?"

"Me and Roxy is scheduled to leave for Aruba this weekend."

"Roxy?" Moe looked at Blue as if he was crazy. "I know that you're not getting a soft spot for that young whore?"

"It's nothing like that my friend." Blue snickered. "We're just going to go down to relax and have some fun so I can clear my head from all this bull shit around here."

"Okay. Go ahead and clear your head and enjoy yourself for a change and I'll make sure that everything gets handled on this end. Just promise me that you're not falling for this little young bitch. She is just a piece of pussy."

"That should be the least of your worries."

"I'm serious Blue!" Moe stressed. "This bitch is trouble. The only reason that she's this close to begin with is because she's Flo's niece. Have your fun and get rid of her little ass."

"I got it under control my friend." Blue assured him. "Now what are we going to do about this YG issue?"

"I'm going to give Stone and Jihad a chance to rectify this matter before we intercede. YG can become a serious problem if we don't get a grip on it."

"Okay keep me posted." Blue stood up to leave.

He extended his hand and pulled Moe to his feet.

"Alright." Moe exhaled. "Get outta here for a couple of weeks and go clear your mind. Don't worry; I'll get things back in order while you're gone."

"Thank you my brother." They embraced. "I don't know what I would do without you?"

"Let's hope that we never have to find out!" Moe told him as they exited the rooftop.

CHAPTER 27

Holed up in an apartment across town, YG sat with a bottle of gin at the kitchen table, cleaning his pistol. A week had passed since the death of Shabazz and it was truly troubling him. His thoughts went back to the day that his partner was murdered and envisioned different scenarios that could've taken place to prevent his demise. Suddenly his cell phone rang snapping him from his trance.

"What's up?" He answered the phone. "Where you at?"

I'm outside in front of your building." Stacks replied.

"Alright, I'll be down in a minute." YG said, ending the call.

He tucked the burner onto his waistline and threw a hoodie over his head. YG left the apartment and quickly hopped into the car with Stacks after checking his surroundings to make sure that the coast was clear.

"What's so important that you needed to see me face to face?" YG questioned his partner Stacks. "You already know that these niggas is lurking for me."

"That's the reason that, I came to holla at you." Stacks admitted.

"Talk to me playboy."

They rode east down Best street headed towards the expressway. As they merged onto the 33, YG lit up a cigarette and cracked the window. He removed his pistol from the small of his back and placed on his lap as the night air circulated through the vehicle.

"What's the word on those boys?" YG questioned as he blew out a ring of smoke.

"Since that situation popped off, it's been real quiet uptown." Stacks declared. "And word on the vine is that homeboy put up a couple dollars for ya head."

"Who, Jihad?"

"Yep! My young boy told me that them niggas ain't been hustling or nothing."

"Who's ya young boy?" YG inquired.

"My lil nigga Reef." Stacks replied. "He originally from down the way but he's been getting him a little bit of money up top for about a year now. He might be able to play up under them niggas for us"

A light bulb went off in YG head. "How well do you know this dude?"

"That's my lil man. I practically raised the little nigga"

"Do you really think that he can play up under them boys for us?"

"I'm pretty sure that he can pull that off for us."

"Word!" YG flicked the cigarette butt out of the window. "See if he can put that shit together for us but he better not fold under pressure."

"Don't worry about that, I got this."

"You better." YG pointed his finger in Stacks face. "Because I'm holding you accountable if ya man fuck this shit up."

"We got this." Stacks declared. "But on another note, what happened that night?"

YG turned to towards Stacks and cringed up his face. "What you mean what happened that other night?"

"The night that Shabazz got killed, what happened?"

YG continued to stare at his friend with an incredulous expression written across his face. Stacks returned a skeptical glare of his own as they took the Suffolk St exit off the expressway. Neither man had spoken much about the incident since it had taken place and YG didn't want to talk about it now.

"What the fuck is you asking me that for?" He snapped. "You got a wire on or something nigga?"

"You know that I don't get down like that bra." Stacks eyeballed him. "I just want to know what happened to Shabazz and how that shit got so funky?"

YG placed his head against the headrest and stared off into space.

"We had the drop on they ass." He began "Then all of a sudden the Stone nigga came up out the cut with a Mac 11 or some shit and started letting that thang go."

"Damn!" Stacks huffed.

"I know!" YG reciprocated. "But this shit ain't over, especially if ya man can make that shit happened like you said."

"I'm about to swing through there right quick and see if the little nigga out there."

On the way uptown, Stacks continued to check the rearview mirror to make sure they weren't being tailed. It had become habit, considering the line of work that they were in. YG lit up another cigarette and inhaled deeply as they entered into the Kensington Bailey district. It was like a ghost town. Every corner and side street was clear; the only thing missing was the tumbleweed rolling through the streets.

"Ain't nobody out in this mutha fucka!" YG emphasized.

"I told you that Jihad supposed to have shut everything down until this thing blow over or you come up missing." Stacks replied.

"So that's how the nigga want to play it huh?" YG blew out a ring of smoke. "We need to find out where he lay his head at?"

"I've been on top of that since this thing popped off but nobody seems to know how this nigga is moving and shaking. It's almost like he has all the angles covered."

"Everybody has a weakness." YG told Stacks." It's just a matter of time before we find his and expose it!"

CHAPTER 28

A quarter past 1 o'clock in the morning, Jihad awoke to the sound of his phone vibrating on the coffee table. Before he reached over to answer it, he grabbed the remote and turned the television down.

"Hello!" He picked up in a raspy tone.

"Where you at?" Roxy was wide awake.

"I'm at the building, why what's up?"

"What are you doing?" She questioned. "Are you coming out?"

"Ain't nothing out there," Jihad yawned. "I'm laying here on this couch watching T.V. or should I say it's watching me?"

"What you watching?"

"Some documentary called hidden colors that I got from the old head, selling DVDs at the store.

"Nigga put some clothes on and meet me somewhere we can have a drink."

"You know that I don't be drinking." He reminded her. "But you must have some good news for me or something?"

"Sort of kind of." Roxy replied. "Throw something on and meet me at the Groove. They got a live band tonight."

"I can't afford to be on front street like that. Meet me at Swings on Fillmore."

"Okay, how long?"

"Give me about twenty minutes."

"Don't have me sitting in there, waiting on your ass all night."

"I'll be there in a minute girl, bye!"

Half an hour later, Jihad pulled up to the small pub located on the corner of Rodney St. and Fillmore and parked. He cocked his weapon, placing one in the chamber before exiting the vehicle. He tucked the Magnum on his hip and made his way to the door after checking his surroundings. Roxy was already seated at the bar when he walked inside.

"Aye, Jihad what's happening?" The owner greeted him with love. "I'm sorry to hear about your cousin. Jamal was a cool dude. He didn't deserve to go out like that."

"I appreciate that fam." Jihad embraced him with a pound. "You know they say that the good die young!"

"No doubt." He nodded. "I'm going to go ahead and let you chop it up with your lady friend. If you need anything, I'll be in the kitchen, frying up some wings."

As the owner disappeared into the back, Jihad gave Roxy a hug then took a seat on the stool next to her. She was sipping on an apple Martini with a shot of Crown Royal to smooth it out.

"Now what's so important that you got to pull me out of the house at damn near two o'clock in the morning?"

"You act like I'm not worth coming outside for." Roxy stood up and posed.

She was sporting a black Moschino handbag to match her embellished wool mini skirt. Jihad studied her from head to toe and thought that the Zanotti leather sandals on her feet must've cost a fortune.

"You definitely worth coming outside for." He nodded. "You see I'm here, don't you?"

"You better act like you know!" She teased as she took her seat.

"For real tho, what's poppin? I see that nigga got you looking like a million dollars in small bills."

"Yeah this nigga Blue is a different type of nigga." Roxy admitted. "If it wasn't for the business at hand I might find myself really liking this dude."

"Keep your head in the game ma, don't get dick dizzy on me now."

"Boy please, you know me better than that. All I'm saying is that I like how the old man moves. He's very meticulous! You better be real careful with this one Jihad."

"Fuck all that! Jihad dismissed her statement. "What do you got for me?"

"I've been staying at one his lofts downtown for the past few weeks and there's not much traffic coming in and out but the other morning I overheard him and Moe talking."

"About what?"

"About you!"

"About me?" Jihad winced. "What were they talking about?

"I didn't catch the entire conversation but I know that Blue was upset about what happened on your block the other day and told Moe that they couldn't allow you and your crew to become a cancer to them."

"And what did Moe say?"

"He said that if you didn't get a handle on the situation that he would pull the trigger himself."

"Oh yeah!" Jihad shook his head. "That how he feel?"

Roxy sipped her drink. "I supposed to be going to Aruba with Blue tomorrow night. He said that he needed some time to get away from everything that's been going on here and just think."

"Aruba?" Jihad inquired. "Yeah, that good; you got this nigga right where I want him."

"Yeah, I jive got his nose wide open. "Roxy admitted. "We plan on being gone for at least two weeks and while Blue is on vacation, Moe is expecting you to find a cure for cancer. You understand what I'm talking about?"

"I got the wolves on that as we speak."

"Do you need me to put one of my girls on that mission?"

"Nah, the stakes is too high right now. I'm going to have to get at this nigga in a way that he don't see coming.

CHAPTER 29

Moe glanced at his watch and noticed that it was a quarter past eleven. Blue's plane had departed from the airport two hours prior and Moe thought that it was a trip well overdue. All the hard work that they've done to get where they were at, his partner deserved to take a break to clear his mind. As he sat at the end of the bar, sipping on his drink he figured he'll go on his own sabbatical upon Blue's return. The El Morocco was filled to the capacity. Moe's eyes gauged the room, watching this new generation wander amongst the crowd aimlessly. They didn't have a clue, traveling through the world without a purpose. He thought back to Zeak and the cohorts of their time. They were much smoother than these kids. They moved with style and had meaning behind their hustle. Unlike this new generation, the women carried themselves with class and respect, holding the man down regardless of the situation. Now a day there's no honor amongst thieves just a bunch of cowboys and Indians in the game with no instructions on how to play; and women without an ounce of loyalty in their blood. Just in and out of bed with any and every hustler who can provide a monetary satisfaction. Things definitely weren't the same. Maybe Blue was right? It may be time to square up and fly straight. There wasn't anything else to prove out here in the streets because they'd done it all. The only thing left is the cemetery or the penitentiary.

Suddenly Moe's thoughts were interrupted by a young man who had slid up beside him.

"What's good Moe? He spoke

Moe was caught off guard but kept his composure.

"What's happening?" He smiled. "Long time no see. How long have you been home?"

YG examined Moe's body language as he reached inside the pocket of his hooded sweatshirt. Never taking his eyes off of the delinquent hands, Moe was relieved when YG pulled out a pack of Newports. He slightly exhaled as he lit up his cigarette.

"Long enough!" He finally answered.

"What's the plan now that you're home?" Moe was trying to fill him out.

"Let's cut the small talk O.G." YG blew out a ring of smoke. "We both know why I'm here."

"Then speak what's on your mind."

From across the room, Roscoe noticed YG and Moe conversing and quickly began to make his way over.

"First of all call off your goon." YG peeped Roscoe through his peripheral. "If I was coming to cause trouble, it would've popped off already. I just want to talk and get some answers."

With that being said, Moe locked eyes with Roscoe and shook his head, indicating for him to fall back.

"Do you see that guy over there, talking to the girl next to the Jukebox?" YG pointed with his eyes.

Moe shifted his attention in that direction as YG continued. "If anything happens to me while we're talking or when I leave, he's been instructed to shoot as many people as his gun will allow him to; and we both know that you don't need that type of heat in your place of business."

"What the fuck do you want?" Moe gritted his teeth.

"I want to know why you killed my brother."

"What makes you think that I killed Gamble."

"C'mon Moe don't play with my intelligence." YG stated. "You probably didn't pull the trigger but you might as well have because I know that the order came from you or Blue. Tell me that Gamble was a Rat or that he was stealing, I can accept that because that's business but don't tell me that you didn't have anything to do with it."

"I loved Gamble." Moe stressed. "He was like family."

"Then why aren't you looking for the niggas that killed him if he was like family?" He barked. "Gamble was loyal to y'all niggas for years and you just throw him to the wolves. That's not love."

There was a brief silence between the two of them as Moe glanced at the bartender and nodded.

"You got a lot of nerve walking in here questioning me about some shit that you really don't want the answer to." Moe became ice cold as he turned his attention back to YG. "You want the truth? Your brother was a damn good hustler, there's no denying that but he wasn't as loyal as you think. And no matter how much love and respect I had for Gamble as a hustler, once the loyalty was gone, there was no longer a place for him in this family."

"So you killed him?" YG looked at Moe with malice.

"As you let that digest, I want you to take a look at my man behind the bar."

YG did as Moe suggested and observed the man aiming a pistol grip pump at him from beneath the bar.

"So listen to me young fella." Moe continued. "Don't be the cause to your own destruction. I know that you want to avenge your brother's death but this is a war that you will not win, so why don't you quit while you're ahead before someone else gets hurt."

A diabolical smirk spread across YG's face as he listened to the old man's speech.

"I'm going to let you have that, O.G." He said. "But you do know that behind every action there is a consequence?"

Yeah, that's a universal law!"

"And you're telling me that I supposed to just accept what happened to my own flesh and blood?"

"No matter if you accept it or clip up and go out guns blazing, the outcome is still going to be the same. Gamble is dead and there's nothing you or me can do to change that. So I advise you to let it go while you still have a chance."

YG shook his head. "I'm not going to be able to do that Moe. You know me better than that!"

"I do; and I know what you're capable of but what happened to Gamble wasn't personal, it was business and someone of your stature should be able to understand that. I'm telling you to let it go!"

"It's too late for all of that." YG said.

"You're going to lose son!"

"I guess that's the chance that I'm going have to take; but until then I'm going to make it real uncomfortable for all of y'all. So watch your back Moe because you or Blue don't know what shadow that I'm going to pop up from."

"That's a threat.' Moe laughed.

"Nah, you can guarantee that!"

"And what makes you think that I'm going to let you walk up out of here."

"You're a businessman and I don't think that you want to jeopardize the lives of all these beautiful people in your establishment."

"Oh yeah?"

"Yeah." YG flashed the desert eagle. "But it's your call; I don't have anything to lose."

"I underestimated you youngin."

"Nah old head, you're losing your edge and getting too comfortable. Ten years ago, a dude like me could never get this close to you. I'm going to let you breathe for now but we'll see each other again. You can bet that!"

Moe just smiled to himself as he watched YG disappear into the crowd and exit the building with his partner close behind. Once they were gone, he signaled Roscoe over to where he was seated.

"That boy is beginning to be a serious problem, get Jihad on the phone."

CHAPTER 30

On the other side of town, Jihad was staring out of the widow of his 2nd floor home, thinking about the recurring events that had taken place over the past few weeks. He was having trouble wrapping his head around the fact that his plan had taken a turn for the worst. People were beginning to get hurt that he hadn't anticipated. For her own protection, he had sent Angela to Virginia to stay with her sister until the heat cooled off. He would never forgive himself if anything were to happen to her. His cell phone rang abruptly, bringing him to the present moment. It was Roscoe calling him for the third time within the last hour. He pressed the end button, sending him to the voicemail. Jihad knew that Roscoe was calling for Moe but he wanted to keep his distance until he could figure things out. After his last conversation with Roxy, he knew that he had to play it smart in order for his strategy to be effective.

Bam... bam... bam... There was a knock at the door.

"Who in the fuck is this knocking at my door like the police?" Jihad mumbled to himself as he walked down the stairs.

He peeped through the blinds and observed Remy standing on his steps.

"You out here knocking like you're the Feds or something." Jihad answered the door.

"My bad Bra." Remy replied. "I didn't want to call you on the phone; I needed to talk to you in person."

"What's up?" Jihad let him in and walked into the living room.

Remy shut the door behind himself and followed him into room.

"I got some information that may be valuable to you." He began.

"What type of information?"

"My man Reef rolled up on me earlier today and told me that some dude name Stacks has been asking some questions about you."

"Stacks?" Jihad questioned. "Who the fuck is Stacks? And why is he asking about me."

"I don't know but Reef said that they offered him some money to find out your whereabouts."

"Hold up!" Jihad looked Remy in the eyes. " . "You said they. It was more than one person asking about me?"

"Yeah, Reef said that it was another nigga there with them but he wasn't talking much." Remy told him. "I think his name was, YB, YC or some shit."

"YG." Jihad confirmed. The nigga name is YG."

"Yeah, that's right. How do you know that?"

"That's the nigga that's been trying to kill me!"

Remy took a seat on the sofa across from Jihad. "So what do you want me to do?"

"Do you trust the boy Reef?" Jihad asked.

"He's cool. We did a bid in Juvi back in the day and homie held me down on more than one occasion."

"But do you trust him?"

"I don't trust no muthafuckin body." Remy expressed. "You taught me that."

"You know what I mean Remy. Can we depend on this nigga?"

"Yeah, he's solid for the most part. He can get a little reckless at times but he's good money."

"Okay." Jihad said. "I want to meet this kid so set something up."

"I can get him on the horn right now."

"Alright, get him the phone and have him meet us downtown at Dinny's."

"That's a bet." Remy got on the phone and dialed Reefs number.

An hour later Jihad and Remy were shooting pool when Reef walked into Dinny's place. He was dressed in a black hooded sweatshirt, jeans and goretex Timberland boots.

"What's good my nigga?" He approached Remy with a pound.

"Maintaining my G?" Remy responded. "I would like for you to meet my peoples Jihad."

They exchange handshakes.

"I was telling Jihad a little bit of what we were discussing earlier today but I didn't get into any details." Remy said. "Go ahead and pull his coat to what's going on."

"Well the other day when I was up in the Jamican spot on Bailey, I was approached by the boy Stacks from Gibson Street." Reef began. "And he was asking me a bunch of weird ass questions about if I knew you and where you be at or if I knew any broads that was in your business."

"And what did you tell him?" Jihad stared the young boy in his eyes.

"I couldn't really tell him shit because I don't know anything about you except that I see you breeze through the hood once in awhile."

"And what about the nigga that was with him?"

"Home boy didn't really have too much to say but he did offer me a couple dollars if I could help them get the drop on you."

"And what did you say?"

"I acted like I was interested if the number was right." Reef admitted. "But I didn't plan on providing them with any information even if I did know something about you."

"Why not?" Jihad questioned. I'm pretty sure that they would've blessed you for that type of info. For all I know they might be outside right now ready to blow my top off."

Reef snickered. "You're right. There's a chance that they might be outside but I don't rock like that."

"You also could've kept it to yourself and left me in the dark. What are you benefitting from telling me this, you don't owe me nothing?"

"First of all, I knew that you were Remy's OG and Bra always spoke highly of you when we were in the bing together and if you are as official as he says you are then it's only right that I attempt to make alliance. Those other niggas is dirt bags and will always be dirt bags and I just choose not to be affiliated with that type of energy. That shit will get you killed."

A gigantic smile spread across Jihad's face as he focused in on Reef.

"I like this little nigga." He turned towards Remy. "He's quick witted and sharp. I might have a job for you if you're willing to play your position."

"I'm listening!" Reef told him.

For the next twenty minutes, Jihad explained to Reef what was expected of him in order for his scheme to be applicable. Reef listened attentively, embracing every word that spilled from the street veterans' mouth. With the cue stick in hand, Remy just stood there nodding, co signing everything that his mentor was saying.

"So if you can handle this for me, I will put you in a position that'll take your game to the next level." Jihad told him.

"Say no more." Reef shook his hand. "I'm on it like a wig on a prostitute."

"Get in touch with Remy if you have any questions or concerns."

"No doubt!"

"If we play it right, they'll never see it coming."

CHAPTER 31

The skies exceeding Aruba were a clear blue. The sun radiated brilliantly from the heavens above, furnishing an angelic ambience to the sandy white coastline below. The humid gleams were shining down on everyone along the shorelines.

"This is gorgeous." Roxy expressed to Blue as she sunbathed on the beach. Everything seems so full of life out here.

Blue looked up from reading the Wall street Journal and took in the atmosphere, feeling a sense of relief. A state of euphoria overtook him as he stared at the clear blue waters and breathed in the clean fresh air. The beach was full of beautiful nude women, walking freely in the sand.

"Yeah, I can get used to this." He told her.

Yeah, I bet you could." Roxy playfully slapped him on the shoulder. "Don't play with me."

"What?" Blue broke out in laughter as he attempted to block the frisky blow.

"These foreign naked hoes, walking around here. That's probably why you wanted to come here. To look at them."

"I got you." Blue was still laughing as he rubbed Roxy's inner thigh.

She blushed. "Mmm hmm, you probably tell all your little girlfriends that."

Blue pulled her over on top of him and stared into her eyes. "I don't need any other girlfriends as long as I got you."

"Blue I am flattered but you don't have to fill my head up with any fantasies." Roxy stared back at him. "I know that a man in your position can have any woman that he desires and I'm okay with that. I just enjoy getting away from the chaos in my life, during the times that I'm with you. When we get back to Buffalo, you'll go back to doing whatever it is that you do and I will do the same. So don't try to make me believe that this is something more than what it is."

"But it doesn't have to be that way." He replied.

"So what are you trying to say?"

"I think I'm saying it." He kissed her on the lips.

Minutes later they were back in their room all over one another. Roxy removed her bikini and pounced on top of Blue like a panther. His strong hands caressed her soft body as she slid down on top of him and began winding in spherical rotation. He kissed her passionately as she took him inside of her.

"Damn this pussy feels good." Blue spoke softly into her ear.

"You like that?" She moaned.

In an instantaneous motion, Blue flipped her on to her back and forced himself deeply inside. Roxy's eyes rolled into the back of her head, enjoying the pleasure mixed with pain. Placing her thigh onto his shoulders, Blue entrenched himself into the pit of her stomach.

"Ohh daddy... get this pussy." She groaned.

Blue increased his speed.

"Whose bitch are you?" He questioned.

"I'm your bitch." She panted.

Delighted in pleasing each other, they lunged into one another for the next fifteen minutes.

"Oh shit, here it comes." Blue groaned.

Feeling him tense up, Roxy pulled him in closer and began to rub her g spot against his shaft to assure that she experienced an orgasm as well.

"Ohh shit... Ohh shit" She yelled repeatedly as she came.

"Aaaahhhh!" Blue grumbled as he released inside of her.

He buckled on top of Roxy, breathing heavily. "Damn, you got that fire."

"That's you with all of that heat." She responded. "Keep fucking me like that, it's going to be a problem."

"What type of problem?"

"A problem that I think you can handle." She smiled as he pulled out of her.

As he attempted to get up, Roxy pushed Blue back on to the bed and began kissing him on the chest. She worked her way down until his penis was staring her in the face. She slowly began licking the discharge off of his semi erection. As Roxy slid her tongue around the head of his dick, she stared him in the face with ecstasy in her eyes. He smoothly palmed the back of her head and ran his fingers through her hair as she went to work. Roxy shoved every inch of him down her throat until his man pole was back at attention.

"What are you trying to do to me?" Blue muttered.

Without saying, he knew what she was attempting to do the way she was gobbling him up. After about seven minutes, Blue felt himself about to explode. When he finally burst into her mouth, Roxy never attempted to slow down; she actually increased her speed until every last drop was dumped into her digestive system.

"You good?" She got up and walked to the bathroom.

Blue didn't respond, he just laid there speechless. By the time he mustered up enough strength to pull himself from the bed and into the bathroom, Roxy was already in the shower. He stepped into the tub, allowing the water to beat down on his sweaty physic. They took turns lathering one another with the soap until they were completely clean. Shortly thereafter, they laid there in silence, sprawled out across the bed intertwined into one another's arms.

"Let me ask you something." Roxy words cut through the stillness of the room.

"Go ahead." Blue replied.

"Do you ever think about getting out of the life?"

"All the time."

"Then why don't you." She questioned. "You have enough money, so why don't you just walk away?"

"First of all you don't know what I got." he told her in a serious tone.

"I'm sorry; I'm not trying to count your pockets." Roxy apologized. "I just don't understand why men in your position don't walk away while they're on top?"

Blue took in a deep breath as he sat up.

"It's not as easy as you think it is to walk away." He stated. There are a lot of people depending on me. I feed a lot of families out there in them streets and if I walk away, those people will starve."

"They'll also starve if you go to prison for the rest of your life too; so why not quit while you're ahead?"

"I would love to square up and ride off into the sunset but the powers that be are not going to permit that right now."

"What do you mean the powers that be? She inquired.

"Like I said before, I've entertained the thought going strictly legit and I've even had discussions with Moe about leaving the game but I don't know anything else but the streets." Blue exclaimed.

"That's not true." Roxy told him. "You're a businessman. You and Moe already have a couple businesses. You have the construction company, the bar and the restaurant that's a good start."

"Those establishments are barely taking care of themselves. We hardly even see a profit so how can I expect that to feed me and my peoples."

That's because your focus is on the wrong thing." She said. "If you were to exert the same energy into your businesses that you apply into hustling, you would be unstoppable."

Blue pulled her in close. "I'm unstoppable now." He began laughing as he kissed her on the neck.

She pulled away and looked him square in the face. "Blue, I'm serious; you need to really consider finding something else to do."

Blue stared off into space and nodded as if to agree with her. It was definitely time to make some changes in his life but where would he begin. He looked back over to Roxy and thought back to the first day that he'd seen her in the El Morocco. Never in a million years could he have imagined that he would fall for this young girl. He eased down into the sheets and cuddled up next to her.

"Only if you do it with me." He smiled.

"That's a no brainer." Roxy kissed him on the lips.

He kissed her back as he mounted her for another round of sex. For the remainder of the afternoon, they continued to enjoy the sexual pleasures of each other until they fell asleep.

CHAPTER 32

It was around three o'clock in the afternoon when Jihad pulled up to the honeycomb hideout on the Westside. Stone, Remy and Lil p were already inside playing the game when he walked into the house.

"What's good?" Jihad took a seat on the couch next to Remy.

"Knocking these niggas off." Stone was the first to speak.

"Quit fronting." Remy said. "You might be that nigga in real life but your call of duty game is suspect my nigga."

Lil P burst out laughing.

"What the fuck is you laughing at." Stone barked. "You need to be quiet before I pop you in ya other shoulder."

Lil P arm was still in a sling from when he got shot.

"Don't get mad at me." He was still laughing. "Remy is the one snipping yo ass from the roof."

"That's some bitch shit." Stone was in his feelings. "Quit hiding and gun it out with me in the streets."

"Nah, that's your game." Remy told him. "I'm going to do what works for me and that's using war tactics."

Jihad just sat there and watched his crew as they argued back and forth over a videogame. He could never understand how an electronical device could have some people under a virtual trance. However, he did find it amusing the way Stone allowed the young boys to get under his skin.

"Is everything good with that situation?" He nudged Remy.

"Yeah everything is Gucci." Remy assured him.

"Good, keep me posted."

"Alright."

Moments later, Stones player blew up after walking into a military mine that Lil p had set up in a doorway.

"That's some bullshit." Stone threw the controller on to the floor. "Y'all little niggas be cheating."

Remy and Lil P both erupted with laughter at their OG, throwing a tantrum.

"Don't get mad, get even." Lil P teased him. "You can't fuck with the kid, this is what I do."

Stone lit up a cigarette and turned to Jihad. "What's good with you, where you coming from?"

"Nowhere in particular, I've been just riding around thinking." He replied.

"You spoke to Moe?"

"Nah, I haven't spoken to him since they put a stop on the package." Jihad told him. "But I'm going to be getting at him real soon!"

"Well we need to hurry up and get a handle on that situation because we on our last leg." Stone sounded concerned

"Word, how much work do we have left?"

"We only got about a half of brick and then another big eight in eight balls."

"Relax bra we'll be alright." Jihad encouraged him. "You know that I always keep an ace in the hole up my sleeve."

"What's up then?" Stone got excited. "Fill me in."

Jihad stood up and walked in the kitchen. "Let me holla at you in here for a minute."

Crushing the end of the New Port into the ashtray, Stone rose from his seat and followed Jihad into the kitchen.

"What's on your mind?" He asked.

Jihad took a moment before he spoke.

"Yo Bra, I think that this is going to be our last run." He finally began.

What do you mean by our last run?" Stone questioned.

I've been thinking about this whole situation with Jamal, Zae and Chris lying up in the hospital fighting for his life. I just think that it's time for us to re-evaluate some things."

"I feel like you're talking to me in code. What are you trying to say?"

Jihad took a deep breath as he looked Stone Square in the face.

"I'm done!" He said

"What do you mean that you're done?" Stone frowned.

"After we finish this last package, I'm done! I can't do this anymore."

"Bra, I know that shit has been kind of crazy lately but don't start bugging out on me."

"I'm serious, Stone! I'm tired of being out here on the hustle, watching over my shoulder. It's time to do something different."

"Like what?" Stone questioned. "We've been out here in these streets hustling since we were eleven years old. What else are we going to do? This is all we know?"

"After we tie up these loose ends, I'm going to go down to VA to start over with Angela and the baby. You should think about coming with me." Jihad declared.

Stone shook his head. "I'm not going anywhere. I'm Buffalo breed and Buffalo bound. This is where I live and this is where I'm going to die."

"You know how crazy you sound?"

"Nah, do you know how crazy you sound?" Stone snapped. "Shit gets a little funky out here in the trenches and now you want to run down south and hide."

"Hide?" Jihad glared at Stone. "Ain't nobody hiding. I'm doing what I need to do to stay alive; to stay free. It doesn't make any sense to get to the money and get killed or catch a life sentence in the process. It's not about being the hardest anymore, it's about who's the smartest."

Stone took a minute to think about what Jihad was saying. He thought about all of the hustlers that had come before them that never had a chance to make it out. Majority of them became victim to the penitentiary, others were slain viciously in the streets and some are even a slave to the same poison that they once distributed. The deeper that he contemplated, the more that he realized that he didn't want to suffer the same fate.

"What would we do down there?" He inquired. "Outside of these streets, we don't have a skill or trade and Burger king doesn't have the best retirement plan."

"I don't know; that's something that we're going to have to figure out." Jihad said. "I was thinking that we could put our money together and start some type of business. We can start a collection agency or get a car lot or something. All I know is that this isn't the way anymore."

"What about Moe? How do you think he's going to take the news about you getting out?"

"Fuck Moe. Him, Blue and YG are all going to get what they got coming to them, it's only a matter of time."

"What about the money that we owe them?"

"We're not giving them nothing." Jihad confirmed. "Roscoe has been blowing my phone up over the last couple of days but I haven't answered. That's going to be some extra paper that we can make something happen with."

"I feel you!" Stone said.

"So are you in or out?"

"I agree with everything that you're saying bra but I'm going to have to sit this one out."

Jihad was astonished by his friend's decision. "What are you going to do; stay here and hold court in the streets? The cards are stacked against us. We're playing a game that we can't win."

"Maybe so Bra but these streets are all that I know. Me and you are different sides of the same coin. You've always had dreams and ideas to get out of the hood and I've always respected that about you. Me on the other hand; I'm a gangster and that's all that I'll ever be so I'm going to take my chance in the town."

"Alright Fam, if that's how you feel." They clapped hands. "But you know that you will always have seat at the table."

"No doubt!" Stone smiled. "And you never know, I might have a change of heart in the near future and come and rock out with you but for now, I think that it's time for me to find my own way."

CHAPTER 33

"What's up with the young boy Reef?" YG questioned Stacks.

"I don't know; I haven't heard anything yet." Stack replied. "Give him a couple more days to come up with something."

Three days had gone by and there still hadn't been any word on Jihad's whereabouts. Reef had assured Stacks and YG that he would provide them with some solid information before the week was out but they hadn't seen or heard from him.

Across from Stacks, YG sat on the edge of the couch in his Living Room, cleaning a pearl handle grip forty five. Every component from the coil spring to the hammer strut was broken down on the coffee table and cleaned with a small nylon brush and lubricant. It was amazing to Stacks how YG could dismember his weapons, cleanse it and then put it back together in a matter of minutes. Once it was reassembled, YG pulled the slide back and placed one in the chamber before setting the gun on the table.

"I'll be right back, I gotta piss." YG stood up and walked to the bathroom.

Once he was out of sight, Stacks picked up the weapon and began inspecting it. After reviewing the firearm, he placed it back in the same position on the table.

"Yo, if your little man doesn't holler at us by the end of the day, we're going to have to pull up on him and see what the business is." YG returned from the bathroom. "We don't have a couple days to wait on this nigga."

"It's whatever you want to do Fam." Stacks replied.

"Whenever ya man can line Jihad up, we're going to make this nigga take us to where it's at before we kill him."

"Yeah, I can definitely use a couple of extra dollars; I'm short as hell right now."

"Don't worry, I know that this nigga got a few of them thangs stashed away somewhere so we should be strait. We just have to do the right thing with it once we get on because hitting licks isn't going to last forever."

"It's definitely time to find another hustle."

The phone vibrating on the table caught both of their attention as Reef name flashed across the screen.

"Hello." Stacks quickly answered.

He exchanged dialog for a brief moment before ending the call.

"Reef said that Jihad is supposed to meet him on the block later on tonight." Stacks turned to YG. "He wants to holler at me in person before we make the play so we know how we're going to snatch him up."

"What are we waiting for?" YG said. "Let go and put this work in."

He stood up and pulled his hooded sweatshirt over his head. On their way out of the door, YG placed a pair of black leather gloves and a mask into his front pocket as he grabbed the 45 heckler and tucked it on to his waist.

Headed down Bailey, both of their minds were racing 100 miles per minute. YG was thinking about all the different ways that he was going to torture Jihad before he took his life. Stacks on the other hand was contemplating something different. He pulled up to where Reef had told him to and parked.

"I'll be right back." He opened the door of the truck.

"Hold up!" YG stopped him. "Where are you going?"

"About to run up in here and tell the little homie that we're outside."

"Why didn't you just call him?"

Stacks paused for a second. "Bra, quit being so paranoid. I'll be right back."

He got out and left the engine running. YG was uneasy as he kept his eyes glued to the side view mirror. As he checked his surroundings, he noticed something strange emerge from the shadows. Quickly removing the heckler from his waistline, YG prepared himself for the worst. As the silhouette got closer, YG raised his weapon and squeezed the trigger... click... click. Nothing happened. He hurried up and cocked the slide back and clutched the trigger again but it was still the same result. At that moment, YG realized that his own partner had lined him up. He accepted his destiny as the hooded figure approached the vehicle with an AR-15 and began letting loose. It sounded like Fourth of July as the shells rang out and ripped through the SUV, shattering the glass. The shots riddled through YG's flesh like a hot knife cutting through butter. After the last shot was emptied, he laid slumped across the dashboard with the jeep still running. The masked character got one last look at YG before vanishing into the shadows of the night.

*****

Meanwhile Jihad was on his way to the El Morocco to meet with Moe to discuss the order of business. He took in a deep and nervous breath before walking into the small establishment located on the corner of Stockbridge Street. Just as he expected, Moe was sitting at the bar by himself watching an armature boxing match on television. When he heard Jihad enter the building, he spun around and told him to have a seat. Jihad did as instructed as he set the duffle bag that he was carrying on to the bar.

"Where have you been?" Moe spoke in a meticulous voice. "Roscoe has been trying to reach you all week."

"I know. I had to go underground for a couple of days to sort some things out." Jihad responded.

"And are they sorted out?"

"Yeah, I'm back on pointe."

"And that situation that we were having a problem with?" Moe inquired, referring to YG.

"That's been taken care of." Jihad established.

"And what do you mean by taken care of?"

"I mean that he's no longer with us." He confirmed

"Good, now we can get back to business." Moe declared. "I'm going to give you ten of them things tonight and another ten first thing in the morning."

Jihad pushed the bag across the bar in his direction. "Here's that paper that I owe you. Sorry it took so long but I had to round up a few dollars from some people that owed me some bread."

"I wasn't worried about that. " He grabbed the bag. "Lock that door and follow me into the back."

Jihad could feel the anxiety building up in his stomach as they entered into the back office. Moe flicked on the lights and walked behind the desk. He opened the safe and pulled out ten kilograms of raw uncut cocaine. As he laid them on the desk, Jihad withdrew his weapon from his hip.

"What the fuck are you doing?" Moe questioned him as he stared down the barrel of Jihad's 357.

"You know what it is." Jihad declared. "Now put the work and whatever money that you have in that safe in the duffle bag."

"Son, what are you thinking? You don't have to do this."

Jihad cocked the hammer back on the revolver. "Nah, what you didn't have to do was murder my father; now put everything inside the bag."

Jihad's words cut through Moe like a ginsu knife as he plopped down into his chair. A feeling of guilt mixed with some relief materialized as he began depositing the drugs into the bag.

"How long have you known?" He questioned.

"The whole time." Jihad confirmed. "But I can't understand why. My father loved you and I thought that you loved him."

"I did love your father."

"Then why did you kill him?"

Moe leaned back in his seat as he took time to gather his thoughts.

"When I was in prison, Zeak was on top of the world." He began. "And being that I was his right hand man everyone knew that I was next in line when I came home; but by the time that I touched down, Zeak had developed a conscious and wanted to get out of the game and go legit. I was young and wild. I couldn't see your father's vision at the time because I was too caught up in the illusion, blinded by the lights."

"So you killed him and took everything."

Trust me Jihad, there isn't a day that goes by that I don't think about what I did to Zeak. What I took from you, your sister and mother. Every time that I look at you, I see that same ambition, that same hunger and I'll be lying to you if I said that I didn't deserve death. To be honest with you, I always knew that this day was coming, I just didn't know when."

"You're still not answering the question." Jihad told him. "Why did you kill the person that you claimed to have loved and take everything from me and my family?"

"I wanted to be the man." Moe shouted. "I wanted to be the number one guy that ran shit in these streets. While I was in prison, Zeak was out here with the town on lock. So when I got out and he was talking about squaring up, I felt that he was trying to rob me of my time to shine."

Jihad looked at Moe with disgust. "Rob you of you time to shine? He would've taken you with him and y'all would've shined bright together. But it's niggas like you that got the game fucked up."

"Nah, it's niggas like you that got the game fucked up." Moe snickered. "It's niggas like you that's too smart for their own good. You got that same naïve spirit that your father had but at the end of the day, no matter how much money you make or how many businesses you own, you're still a street nigga. You can never change that. You can never change where you come from."

"But I can switch directions and choose where I want to go." Jihad fired a shot.

Moe clutched the area where the bullet had punctured into his stomach. He watched as Jihad slowly approached him pointing the smoking pistol at his face.

"I was ten years old when I watched you murder my pops." He spoke in a sinister tone. "I was hiding in the kitchen pantry when you shot my father in the back of the head. You weren't even man enough to look him in the eyes so I want to make sure that I stare into your soul as I take it from you."

"What are you waiting for?" Moe looked him square in the eyes. "Let's get it over with."

Jihad aimed the pistol and pulled the trigger. The impact from the high powered weapon knocked Moe backwards out of his chair and on to the floor. Jihad stood over him and emptied four more shots into the upper body, leaving him motionless. A sense of liberation seized him as he stared at the lifeless piece of flesh lolled out on the floor. Quickly gathering the goods, Jihad wiped down everything that he touched and threw the bag over his shoulder before exiting the office.

CHAPTER 34

The next morning, Blue woke up in the hotel room to Roxy crying on the telephone.

"What's the matter with you?" He inquired with a concerned look on his face.

"It's my aunt Flo!" She replied. "Somebody shot Moe."

"What happened?" He jumped up from the bed. "Is he alright?"

Tears continued to roll down her face as she shook her head. "They found him in the office dead."

A silence fell over the room as Blue declined onto the end of the bed, paralyzed with grief. His thoughts were scattered in a million directions as he tried to piece the puzzle together.

"Who could've had done this?" He contemplated to himself.

Roxy gently walked over and placed her hand on his shoulder.

"Are you okay?" She snapped him from his thoughts.

"Does it look like I'm okay bitch?" Blue pushed her hand away from him. "I'm sitting up here messing with you bullshitting and my man done fucked around and got murdered."

"Excuse me?"

"You heard me." Blue stood up and began walking towards her. "If I wasn't here fucking with you, Moe would probably still be alive because I would've been there to hold him down."

"You're acting like this is my fault." Roxy said.

Blue yoked her up by the neck and pushed her onto the bed.

"Bitch, I will kill you if I find out that you got me down here for a distraction so someone could murder my man." He breathed heavily.

Roxy dropped the phone and clutched on to his hands to avoid from being choked. She panted for air as Blue constrained her against her will.

"You better tell me what the fuck is going on before I choke the life out of you."

"I don't know anything." She gasped. "I swear to you that, I don't know what's going on."

Blue stared her in the eyes as they began to roll into the back of her head. Right before she blacked out, he let her go and started pacing the floor.

"Damn, they knocked my man off." He dropped his head into his hands. "

As she attempted to gather her breath, Roxy rubbed her neck and inched closer to him.

"I'm so sorry for your lost." She struggled to speak.

"You don't understand; they killed my man."

Even though, he had just made an effort to strangle her to death, Roxy's heart was distressed at the sight of a broken Blue. A man who was ordinarily in control at all times with the soul of a lion was now as docile as a lamb.

"It's going to be alright." She tried to console him.

Blue looked up at her and exhaled heavily. "No it's not, but I need to get back to the states so I can find out what's going on."

The flight from Aruba to Buffalo was the longest seven hours of Blues life. The entire time, all he could think about was the last week leading up to his vacation. The murders committed by YG, the discussion that he had with Jihad and his partner Stone to the very last time that he laid eyes on Moe on the rooftop all played back in his mind. As he made his way off of the plane, Blue was approached by a number of agents wearing black FBI and DEA jackets. Immediately, he became alarmed, thinking of all the charges that he could possibly be accused of as they surrounded him and Roxy.

"Mr. Johnson." Agent Wright flashed his badge as he addressed Blue by his last name. "Put your hands behind your back?"

He cuffed him as he read him his rights. The Federal agents secured the airport as they escorted them out of the terminal.

"What's going on?" Roxy asked.

Agent Wright shot her an incredulous look.

"Your friend is going down." He shot back.

"What are the charges?" Blue inquired.

"Three counts of money laundering, conspiring to distribute five thousand grams of powdered cocaine and the murder of Robert Gamble."

They watched as Blues body language changed.

"Murder?" He questioned with a chuckle. "You gotta be kidding me?"

The agents took Blue and Roxy into custody. When they reached the federal headquarters they were separated and placed into different rooms. Staring at him through a two way mirror, the agents watched as Blue sat at a small table, fidgeting with his hands. Agent Wright entered the room and pulled up a seat across from him.

"My name is Agent Wright." He introduced himself.

With no response, Blue examined him with an ice cold stare as he sat down.

"Before we begin, I have to let you know that this conversation is being recorded."

"I don't have nothing to say without my lawyer present." Blue declared. "

"That's your choice Mr. Johnson but let me inform you that there are a number of charges pending against you and I think that it would be in your best interest to help us help you while you still have the opportunity."

Blue snickered. "What type of guy do you think that you are dealing with?"

"I know exactly who I'm dealing with Benny Blue Johnson." Agent Wright stared him in the face. "I've been watching you for a long time and I'm going to enjoy watching you rot in prison."

"Well don't get your hopes up too high." Blue told him.

"Your money won't be able to save you this time."

Blue inclined forward. "Are you done yet?"

"For now!" Agent Wright said.

"Good, now get my lawyer on the phone because this conversation is over." He leaned back in his seat.

Agent Wright stopped the recording and stood up to leave.

"Today hasn't been a good day for you has it Blue?" He stopped short at the door. "First Moe get killed and now this. Can't wait to see what surprises tomorrow bring."

He walked out of the interrogation room, knowing that Blue was boiling inside. Meanwhile Roxy was in the next room being grilled by agent Daniels.

"What is your relationship with Mr. Johnson?" She questioned.

"Who?" Roxy tried to play dumb.

"I'm sorry; you call him Blue."

"What do mean by what is my relationship with him?"

"What is your affiliation or connection with Mr. Benny Blue Johnson ma'am?" Agent Daniels asked again. "I don't have all day to play with you."

"He's just a friend." Roxy stated.

Agent Daniels began notating something onto her legal pad and then pulled out some photos from a brown folder.

"Do you know any of these men in these pictures?" She quizzed.

Roxy recognized Moe and Roscoe but the other photos were unfamiliar to her.

"No, I have never seen any of these people a day in my life." She lied.

"Are you sure?" Agent Daniels pressed. "Take a good look."

Yes, I'm sure!"

"That's strange because the last time we checked; you were employed at the El Morocco, working for this man." She pointed to a picture of Moe.

Roxy started shuffling in her seat. "Am I under arrest because if not, you can let me go?"

"No you're not under arrest but due to federal law, we can hold you up to seventy two hours if we assume that you're involved in any criminal activity."

"What are you talking about criminal activity?" Roxy snapped. "I'm coming back off of vacation with a friend."

"Excuse me ma'am but I think that the terms of your probation clearly states that you are not supposed to leave the state of New York without first notifying your probation officer. Is that correct?"

"Yes."

"And did you do that before you decided to travel outside of the country with Mr. Johnson?"

"No I didn't."

"And how do you think that your probation officer Mr. Hunter would feel if he knew that you traveled outside the country without his permission?"

"Do I need to talk to a lawyer?"

"That won't be necessary if you haven't done anything wrong." Agent Daniels avowed.

In that instant, Agent Wright joined them in the room, drinking a cup of coffee. He examined Roxy as she became more and more uncomfortable.

"What do y'all want from me?"

Agent Daniels removed her glasses before continuing.

"You can begin by telling us the truth." She said. "Now let's try this again. Do you know any of the people in these photographs?"

"Yes." Roxy sighed.

"Who and what is your association with them?" She pointed to the mug shots of Moe and Roscoe.

"My aunt Flo was married to Moe and he allowed me to work at the bar until I got back on my feet. The other guy is just someone that I always see him with on a regular basis, I think his name is Roscoe."

"What can you tell us about their operation?" Agent Daniels stressed.

"Nothing!" Roxy shook her head. "I don't know anything at all. All I did was take a trip with someone that seemed to be alright. I don't know what he's into and I don't want to know what he's into. All I want to do is go home."

Agent Wright released a chuckle as he sipped on his coffee. He hadn't said two words since stepping foot inside the interrogation room.

"So correct me if I'm wrong." He finally broke his silence. "You're trying to convince us that you don't have a clue about what's going on?"

"I don't." She replied.

"Ms. Weber could you please quit wasting our time. I would rather you tell me that you're not going to cooperate than to sit up here and tell me a bunch of lies."

"I'm not lying,"

"Oh yeah?" Agent Daniels pulled out another picture. "What about him? What can you tell us about him?"

At the sight of Jihad's picture, Roxy developed butterflies in the pit of her stomach. Suddenly a Jewish attorney dressed in a regent fit herringbone suit with matching tie and suspenders walked in.

"Good evening, my name is David Cohen." He handed each agent his business card. "I'll be representing Ms. Roxanne Weber so if there's any more questions please feel free to direct them at me because at this point my client has nothing further to say."

Roxy was slightly relieved at the sight of the lawyer and watching as the Federal law enforcement disposition changed. Without another word Agent Daniels along with Agent Wright packed up their belongings and exited the room, heated. Once they had disappeared, Attorney Cohen turned his attention to Roxy.

"You didn't say anything did you?" He asked

"No, I didn't tell them shit." She replied.

"Good! Again, my name is David Cohen and I've been retained by Terrance Smith, I think you know him as Roscoe."

"They were asking questions about him too." Roxy admitted.

"And what did you tell them."

"There wasn't much to tell."

"Okay, I'm going to go out here and talk to the person in charge and I should have you out of here within the next fifteen minutes."

"Thank you so much." She was at ease as Cohen went to get her released.

CHAPTER 35

The very next day, Jihad pulled up to a secluded area on the outskirts of the city and parked. Patiently awaiting his arrival, Stone was already there leaned against the hood of his car.

"What's good Bro?" Jihad got out, holding a Gucci duffle bag. "How long have you been waiting."

Stone gave him a pound. "I've been here for about fifteen minutes. You know that, I always get to a meeting a little bit early. I got that from you."

"And I got that game from an old head. He told me that I should play with a person's money before I play with his time because we can always recoup money but once the time is gone, it's gone."

"That's a fact!"

"And with that being said, it's time to go. We can't keep wasting time in this ratchet ass city; it's time to go explore the world"

Stone looked at his friend for a brief moment and smiled.

"You did it huh?" He said referring to Moe.

"Done!"

"How did it make you feel?"

"To be honest with you, I really don't feel any different, I just knew that it was something that needed to be done, I just hope that my Pops can rest a little bit easier now that it is."

Well as far as that other situation, I did that nigga dishes and I feel great." Stone laughed. "But a small piece of me jive admired ol boy."

"You should always appreciate a worthy opponent because they keep us sharp and on our toes."

"Without a question."

"What about his man Stacks?"

"He was light work." Stone said. "I had the young boys take care of him the same night when he came to pick up his paper for setting YG up."

"Good, we got to make sure that all of the loose ends are tied up because we can't afford for this thing to come back to bite us."

"Believe me, we good."

"I love you bra." Jihad handed Stone the duffle bag.

Stone unzipped it and looked inside.

"What's this?" He asked.

"It's ten keys and a hundred large in there and it's all you." Jihad replied.

"This is all me?

"Yeah, I'm done."

You're not playing; you're dead serious."

"Hell nah, I'm not playing. My bags are packed and ready to hit the highway. Soon as I leave here with you, I'm going to jump right on the I90. You need to really consider making this move with me because it's only a matter of time before Blue pieces this whole thing together and come looking for us,

"Well, I'm not going to be hard to find because I'm going to be right here, doing what I do."

"Bra everybody knows that you're hard as a rock, tough as nails but it's not about who's the hardest anymore, it's about who's the smartest. That's who is going to survive. That's who's going to win."

"That's the thing Jihad; you've always been the smart one. You were always the one with the bright ideas and the dreams of making it out and doing something different. I've thought about the conversation that we had the other day and even if I were to leave and go down south with you, I couldn't see myself living normal."

"Who said anything about living normal? It's plenty of people around the world getting big money legally. We can't limit ourselves to these Buffalo streets. It's a big world out there fam and we deserve a piece of it."

"I hear you but like I told you before, I'm going to take my chances out here."

There was a long pause between the two of them as Jihad stared at his friend with compassion. No matter how much he wanted for Stone to go with him, he understood why he wouldn't. They had always been night and day. Ever since they were kids, they had been in the same race but never the same lane. Maybe it was time for them to depart and travel in separate directions in search of their own individuality. Everything is not for everyone and for a man to truly be a man; he must stand alone and face adversity head on. They have to embrace change with a courageous heart and never allow circumstances to define who they are. Despite their variances, Stone and Jihad were still two peas in the same pot in pursuit of the American dream. They both wanted freedom but in order to obtain it, they had to follow their heart. Jihad wanted to live a more quiet subtle life Where Stone still wanted the fast life of the streets. Jihad reflected back to the exchange of words with Moe right before he killed him and thought about how Moe's bond with his father Zeak was very similar to his and Stones relationship. At that moment, Jihad understood that Stone desired to have his own identity without being in his shadow.

"I understand Bra." Jihad broke the silence. Just know that I'm a phone call away whenever you need me.

"That's without question." Stone declared.

"And make sure that you guide those young boys right. Remy and Lil P have a lot of potential and they will stay loyal to you as long as you play fair with them."

"I'm going to put them in position and give them the game just like it was given to us. I think I'm going to pull the little nigga Reef into circle too; he's a real soldier."

"That's your decision." Jihad said. "Just teach them to never compromise their morals."

"I already know." Stone replied. "Be true to the game and the game will be true to you!"

"That's some bullshit because the game ain't true to nobody, it's all an illusion. That shit is set up for us to fail. The powers that be have the deck stacked up against us and the longer we play, the higher the risk is for us to lose. It's a game and at the end of the day only the house wins."

"I feel what you're saying but it's bread out here in these streets my nigga and as long I have air in my lungs, I'm going to get it."

"No doubt! Be careful out here bra and when you get a chance go and check on my Ma Dukes and make sure that she is alright."

"I got you!" Stone nodded in agreement. "Make sure that you call me to let me know that you touched down in Virginia."

"Will do!"

They embraced one more time before Jihad departed. As he made his way to the car, he glanced back at Stone, hoping that he would reconsider. A variety of emotions swelled up inside him as he started the engine, knowing that he was leaving his friend in the pits of hell to play with the devil.

CHAPTER 36

Roscoe sat in the visitation room at the Federal building, waiting for the guards to bring Blue down from his living quarters. It had been over 20 minutes and there still hadn't been any sign of his boss. Suddenly, Blue appeared from the back room dressed in an orange jumpsuit with a docket number attached to the pocket on his chest. The look on his face spoke volumes as he approached the table and took a seat.

"What the fuck happen?" Blue didn't waste any time getting to the point.

"I don't know Blue, but shit is hot as hell right now." Roscoe said. "I'm taking a risk just coming to see you right now."

"I know but there's some things that we can't discuss over the phone so I had to see you face to face and get some answers."

"Like I said, shit is fucked up right now."

"Any word on what happened to Moe?"

"Nope!" Roscoe shook his head. "

"What about the boy YG?" Blue questioned. "Do you think that he had anything to do with this?"

"YG is dead."

"Dead?"

"Yup!" Roscoe nodded. "Dude was found shot up in a passenger seat of a SUV about an hour before Moe was killed."

"You gotta be kidding me." Blue had an incredulous look on his brow. "I just knew that he was the one behind that shit."

"That's what I thought at first too."

"Then if it wasn't him then who?"

"Your guess is as good as mines."

Blue sat back and allowed his wheels to spin inside of his mind for a moment.

"Did they take anything from the office?" Blue inquired.

"Yeah, whoever did it definitely emptied the safe."

What about Jihad and his crew? Has there been any word on them?"

"I haven't seen or heard from them. The last time I checked, Jihad was supposed to drop off some money that was owed but when I called, he never answered the phone."

"And now Moe is dead."

"Exactly!"

"So do you think that he might've had something to do with it?"?"

"I'm not saying that he did it but I wouldn't put it passed him." Roscoe said. "You know it would've been hard as hell to get the drop on Moe so whoever did it had to know him because there wasn't a forced entry or any signs of a struggle."

Blue took another minute to think.

"That sneaky mutha fucka!" A lightbulb went off inside of his head. "He's been playing us the whole time."

"But why?" Roscoe questioned.

"I don't know but I want you to find him and then you can ask him that question yourself right before you kill him and his man Stone."

"Blue, I don't have a problem with that but it's kind of hard to move right now being that the peoples are watching our every move."

"Then outsource it to our peoples out of Chicago or up in New York City." Blue instructed. "I don't care what you have to do to get it done just get it done."

"I'm on it." Roscoe established.

"Don't drop the ball on this."

"Don't even worry about it Blue, you got too many other things going on right now to be worried about that."

Blue Exhaled deeply. "You're right because these people got me by the balls right now."

"What are they saying?"

"It's a chess game right now but they're trying to sink their teeth into me."

"Do you think that you can beat them?"

"My chances is fifty fifty but as long as I get that body off of me, I'll eat them other charges and be home in a nickel no more than a dime but that body will put my lights out. That's another reason that we have to find this nigga and bury him because he's the only link that can tie me into Gambles murder besides you."

"Say no more."

"Now what's up with Roxy? Blue asked. "Have you spoken to her since she was released?"

"Yeah, she's a little shaken up but she should be alright." Roscoe said. "She asked me to ask you if it was alright to come and visit you."

"Yeah, tell her to come up here Saturday and to bring me something to smoke on and a cell phone."

"A cell phone." Roscoe questioned. "How in the hell are you going to get a cell phone in here?"

"You see that guard over there against the wall."

Without moving his head, Roscoe shifted his eyes towards the person that Blue was talking about.

"Yeah, I see him." He confirmed.

"He's going to call you later on this evening and explain the details on how she's going to drop off the package." Blue told him.

"Damn, you're always bustin some type of move." Roscoe laughed to lighten the mood.

The grind doesn't stop just because I'm locked up." Blue replied. "We still have to keep it moving."

"Okay, is there anything else that you need me to handle?"

"Nah, I need you to lay low until this heat dies down because you're the only lifeline that I can trust right now and I can't afford for you to get jammed up but make sure that you put someone one on Jihad immediately. I want him and his entire crew to suffer."

CHAPTER 37

One year later, Jihad was seated on the fifty yard line of Lane stadium, the home of the Virginia Tech Hokies. Seated next to him on both sides were Angela and his younger sister Kareema, each holding a baby in their arms as they awaited the opening kickoff. Jihad took a look at his family and felt a sense of satisfaction. They had come such a long way in just a short time and life was only getting better. Since moving to Richmond, he had opened a small car lot and was a week away from his barbershops grand opening. Kareema was a full time student at a nearby community college, studying marketing and helping Angela part time at her daycare. Yeah life was good. Jihad was still standing throughout all of the foolishness. The shootouts and robberies, murders and penitentiaries, the early morning hustle and late night shifts, hoping to escape poverty. He believed that he had beaten the odds.

As the game got underway, the crowd went wild. Little Chris caught the kick off deep in the end zone and jetted out, slipping away from a defender in the process. As he slithered up the field, Chris juked another person or two on the opposing team and took off up the sideline.

"HELL YEAH!" Jihad shouted. "That's my little Bro."

The Virginia Tech fans yelled right along with him in unison as Chris crossed the goal line. After he scored, Chris jogged over to the sideline with his teammate, exchanging high fives. When he reached the bench, he turned around and looked up into the stands where Jihad, Angela and Kareema were shouting down to him.

"Yeah boy!... You did that!... That's my bae!..." They all screamed accordingly.

As Chris removed his helmet, he locked eyes with Jihad.

"Thank you!" He mouthed silently.

Reciprocating with his hand over his heart, Jihad understood the young man and sent his love back. It brought tears to his eyes to see Chris starting as a freshman for one of the most prominent football programs in the United States. A little bit over a year ago, he was laid up in the hospital, fighting for his life now here he was in college, doing his thing.

Jihad phone rang. "Hello!"

Angela watched as the excitement on his face disappeared as he spoke to the person on the other end. She knew that something wasn't right from the disturbing look on his brow.

"What's the matter?" She asked as he ended the call.

He gazed up with tears in his eyes.

"We got to go back to Buffalo." He said. "They killed my man."

"Oh my God, who?" She gasps.

"Stone!"

TO BE CONTINUED

Made in the USA
Middletown, DE
21 March 2016